Skin Deep

ALSO AVAILABLE FROM ALYSON

BY NICOLE FOSTER

*Awakening the Virgin: True Tales
of Seduction*

Electric: Best Lesbian Erotic Fiction

Skin Deep

Real-life Lesbian Sex Stories

Edited by
Nicole Foster

alyson books
los angeles | new york

MANUFACTURED IN THE UNITED STATES OF AMERICA.
COVER DESIGN BY B. ZINDA.

THIS TRADE PAPERBACK ORIGINAL IS PUBLISHED BY ALYSON PUBLICATIONS,
P.O. BOX 4371, LOS ANGELES, CALIFORNIA 90078-4371
DISTRIBUTION IN THE UNITED KINGDOM BY
TURNAROUND PUBLISHER SERVICES LTD.,
UNIT 3 OLYMPIA TRADING ESTATE, COBURG ROAD, WOOD GREEN,
LONDON N22 6TZ ENGLAND.

FIRST EDITION: FEBRUARY 2000

00 01 02 03 04　a　10 9 8 7 6 5 4 3 2 1

ISBN 1-55583-538-4

LIBRARY OF CONGRESS CATALOGING-IN-PUBLICATION DATA
APPLICATION IN PROCESS.

CREDITS
•PREVIOUS VERSIONS OF "PLEASE WEAR ROMANTIC ATTIRE" HAVE APPEARED
IN *LEATHER WOMEN II*, EDITED BY LAURA ANTONIOU, ROSEBUD BOOKS, 1994,
AND IN *TANGLED SHEETS*, EDITED BY ROSAMUND ELWIN AND KAREN X.
TULCHINSKY, WOMEN'S PRESS TORONTO, 1995.
•COVER PHOTOGRAPH BY TONY STONE IMAGES.

Contents

Introduction

Almost everyone remembers their first time. But do you remember your second? Your seventh? Your *17th*? When I came up with the idea for this anthology, I couldn't help reflecting on my own sexual conquests: the sassy girl who worked at the college library circulation desk (we sneaked kisses in the fifth-floor stacks, sneaked even more in her dorm room), the soft-butch tour guide on my first trip to the Galapagos (talk about wild animals), the mechanic my friend Melissa (Thank you!) referred me to for my starter problem. If I had a chapter for every wild liaison I've had, I'd have one hell of a book.

That's just what this collection of real-life lesbian erotica is: one hell of a book. After I put out the call for submissions for *Skin Deep,* I was flooded with so many fantastic stories from across the United States, Europe, and Canada, that it physically pained me to say no to the women I didn't have room to include (which is what I probably should have said to the blond cashier with the Doberman and the ultrahyper femme with the black BMW convertible. Oh, but that car, that car!).

The women in this red-hot collection tell erotic stories we know and love (dorm-room bliss, nightclub pickups, coworker "run-ins"), as well as outlandish tales of amorous adventure (sex in a gypsy's van with a Chihuahua audience, a one-night stand with a Lily Tomlin look-alike, lessons in bondage from a very understanding prostitute). Some of these confessions are delightfully brazen, some winsomely sexy, some downright carnal. But what binds them is that they are all true stories, which is perhaps the most intriguing, and tantalizing, aspect of these sultry encounters.

I'd like to thank the women who have courageously shared these personal, intimate stories. Many of us can pick up a hottie, but few have the nerve to pick up a pen! I'd like to thank these women also for celebrating sex for the sake of sex, the exquisiteness of women's bodies, the salvation that only moist lips can bring.

Right now, as I sit in a café penning this introduction, I must close the pages of my notebook (there's a sinisterly sweet babe I must attend to) and invite *you* to open the pages of this truly passionate, and genuine, collection.

Nicole Foster
Los Angeles, January 2000

In Harm's Way

BY ROSALIND CHRISTINE LLOYD

Traveling is one of my passions. Being an airline employee for almost five years permits me to be a low-budget jet-setter. My road partner, Ted, works with me in the international lounge for a major airline at JFK airport in New York City. Ted is a Cartier-obsessed glamour boy, the body-beautiful gentleman's man, soul brother number one. I'm a self-indulging, holistically New Age, semipolitical, Afrocentric, down-by-law, woman-obsessed, androgynous femme, with tastes ranging from the highly delicate, feminine-aggressive personality to the rock-hard, bull-dyke submissive. In other words, I consider myself a well-guided, heat-seeking-missile scorpion. Together, Ted and I scour cities both big and small in search of what we refer to as "stimulating revelations."

This particular trip took us to Amsterdam, the land of coffeehouses, canals, Van Gogh, windmills, tulips, and what I call the big four H's: Heineken, Hashish, the Hague, and legal rights for Homosexuals. I was so excited that after a visit to the sex and tattoo museums, I decided this would be where I would bravely experience my first tattoo.

After exploring a fair share of Amsterdam's shops and open-air markets, Ted and I did some architectural sightseeing. Ted had been to Amsterdam many times and was the perfect guide. Touring the impressive 17th-century mansions and town houses, I could not help marveling at the array of rainbow-colored flags adorning establishments throughout the city. The flags flew over bars, bookstores, cafés, restaurants, and boutiques. Without issue, two women walked by in a loving embrace, strolling the bank of the canal along the cobblestone street. The element was quite free and compelling. I felt right at home.

We came to one gay flag too many not to stop—one waving above a rather inviting bar. Ted suggested we go in. This particular establishment happened to be one of the few lesbian bars in the city, Vive la Reine.

Since it was early afternoon, there was only a small group of women having an animated conversation in their native tongue. Although Amsterdam is a Dutch-speaking city, almost everyone also speaks English. Ted and I sat at the bar and ordered a couple of Heinekens. The bartender was attentive and quite pretty. After telling her we were Americans and that it was my first visit to the Netherlands, I mentioned I was impressed by the displays at the tattoo museum and that I was eager to get my first tattoo while on vacation. I asked her if she knew of a safe and reliable parlor.

"Oh, for sure," she answered in slangy Dutch-accented English, rolling up one of her sleeves to reveal a magnificent tattoo of two mermaids intertwined in an aquatic 69 on her upper right arm.

"It's beautiful," I remarked, amazed at its vibrance against her skin.

"My lover and I have a matching set. We've had them as long as we've been together. Let me tell you where you must go. It is a place called the Psychedelic Scar. It is over on *Reguliersdwarsstr*. Speak to a girl called Pagan. She is bald with a dragon tattooed on her head and a tusk of ivory in her septum. She is clean and by far the most experienced artist there."

Walking from Vive, we decided I would get my tattoo tomorrow night, but on this night we would get dressed up and do some men's clubs so Ted could "get his freak on."

My kinky hair, full of springy spirals, was wild and untamed all over my head. Wearing my hair like this makes me feel recklessly treacherous. My juicy lips were painted a delicious shade of chocolate. I dotted scented oil on my erogenous zones. The outfit I chose made my agenda only that more obvious. A tight black Lycra top with a wide-open neck showed skin and gave my breasts a nice in-your-face presentation. The black suede collar with rhinestones was one of my favorite "fun" pieces I like to call my "pussy collar." My levitating platform boots and black vinyl jeans that remind me of shiny shower curtains finished the look, underneath my overly feminine cropped leather jacket. Meeting in the hotel lobby, Ted looked at me before glancing down at his tight Levi's and white T-shirt and saying, "Is it you or me tricking tonight, Ms. Girl?"

The Inferno is a popular mixed club where anything goes. The line to get in is unforgiving because the place is full of drama-loving drag queens, naked muscle boys, and European trisexual girls, thrown in with a mixture of everything else you can imagine. You are almost guaranteed a mad time.

After a 15-minute wait, we were finally inside, welcomed by a deep house beat that moved Ted.

"Oh, Trina, isn't this place fabulous! Every time I come here I have a good time!" he shouted over the music.

"Honey, I can see why it's crazy in here," I agreed while glancing at a group of gender-confusing people throwing a private party in public. Barring whatever aspects of the performance that did not appeal to you, it was quite daring, a voyeuristic feast for the eyes and imagination, as girls clung to boys that clung to boys that clung to girls that clung to girls dancing together in a (fully clothed) frenzied orgy of affection.

Ted ordered drinks and we made a toast.

"Here's to the Dutch!" Ted's eyes were glazed over; his brown cheeks were beginning to burn.

"The Dutch!" I repeated, clicking his glass and swallowing the contents of mine. That's when I felt it: the unmistakable heat of a stare. The Inferno was very dark, lit only by a carnival of neon, strobe, and laser beams. Through the darkness, her presence, under a solitary spotlight, was undeniable. She had skin the color of gingerbread, and her face had a fine and dignified bone structure. Her eyes, framed with a thick fringe of lashes, were unusually dark, with what seemed an endless depth. Her mouth was the most sensuous I have ever seen, lips longing to be lecherously lingered upon. Standing at the far end of the bar, she posed with one foot poised on a bar stool, adorned in stylishly handsome, handmade black leather boots. The black leather halter top was beguiling, taming two voluminous globes of feminine flesh like sugar cones struggling to contain two scoops of coffee-flavored Häagen-Dazs. Her leather pants seemed designed to caress her every dimension with the high quality of tailored perfection. Her shiny, long black hair was pulled back in a ponytail, falling down her back in dramatic waves—like the waves of the Sargasso Sea at midnight.

While I embraced her vision, her mesmerizing eyes stared back at me with an almost corrupt expression that compelled me to look away.

After Ted finished his drink, a big, beautiful black Dutchman, about 6 feet 5 inches and 250 pounds, approached him, hugging Ted very affectionately. Although it was unclear whether Ted actually knew him, this didn't seem to matter because Ted shouted to me, "See you later, girl," as the man whisked him to the dance floor.

There was a tap on my shoulder. It was the bartender.

"This is compliments of the lady." Before me was a strange-looking cocktail, a double shot of a dark reddish-brown liquor lit by a blue flame. Taking a deep breath, I turned to meet Leather's gaze. She had an identical drink in her hands. When our eyes met she raised her glass in my honor. With one strong puff, she blew out the flame before knocking the contents of her glass to the back of her throat. I looked to the bartender for help.

"It is called a *flamagger*. Here." He placed a straw inside the glass, carefully laying it against the inside edge. "Be careful not to let the straw catch the flame. Just quickly suck on it before it gets too hot," he advised.

Mindfully following his instructions, I did precisely that, treated to a mild blast of the flame at the end of the suck that ignited something within me. I turned around to thank Leather, but she was already heading in my direction. To say she was a sight to behold is an understatement. Her strong, well-sculpted body was decorated in dramatic tribal tattoos that covered her creamy brown skin. A tattoo vine of ivy starting from the nape of her neck wrapped itself around toward the other side of her chest, ending short of her cleavage. An identical bracelet of ivy surrounded her left wrist. An unidentifiable brand mark adorned the inside of her right wrist. A black panther clawed its way down her right arm. Each of her ears was pierced with five tiny gold hoops. As she walked, her breasts seemed heavy, and those long legs in those leather pants were making me crazy. As she grew near, I spotted a moderate-size bulge against her left inner thigh. Exasperated, I started to tremble, trying to suppress my arousal while maintaining my cool. She came right up to me, standing so close I could smell the mixture of leather, perspiration, and body lotion all at once. Her body heat was searing.

"So, you like *flamaggers*?" Her voice was deep and raspy, her Dutch accent heavy.

"Flame—oh, the drink! Yes, yes. It was my first ever. Thank you." I was a nervous wreck just standing near her.

Her beauty was shocking, and her leather was dangerously appealing.

"Let's have another," she said. The bartender had already set up two more. Closing one eye, Leather lit a cigarette, letting it hang from the corner of her lip. "My name is Harmony. But I go by Harm. You must call me Harm."

I shivered when she said it. As she gave some Dutch money to the bartender, her free hand had taken my hand, raising it to her face, gently guiding it to caress her cheek, my hand just inches away from the fiery tip of the cigarette in her mouth.

"I'm Trina—short for Christine," I responded, cringing from the tiny dot of heat from her cigarette.

"Trina." She said it with rolling R's. "I like the way your name feels on my tongue," she added, giving me a modest glimpse of the piercing that adorned her tongue. No surprise there.

"Please, have your shot." She whispered this, moving closer to me, her hands now caressing my hips, the heat of her thigh pressing against me. Gently, she placed the straw between my lips, telling me to suck, and I did without a hint of resistance. After that, Harm lit a blunt joint of hashish with the most bountiful aroma. This signaled the beginning of the end.

I usually resist this type of aggressive female posturing back home. More provocative in my pursuits, I thrill at proposing the most compelling of challenges—in other words, women must earn my submission. But in this exotically foreign country, I found this particular scenario precariously alluring. Besides, I obviously underestimated the power of *flamaggers*. After the third, we were back in a dark corner of the club. I ached as Harm's rock-hard body pressed against me, her breath hot from liquor, cigarette smoke, and God only knows what else, thick in her kiss. Her tongue felt soft and slippery, and she maneuvered her piercing around my mouth and tongue like a divine protrusion. I was melting, my back arched as she went underneath my top, spreading her hands like wings, surrounding the small of my back. I froze at the sensation of her hands against my skin, one in particular now mysteriously sheathed in superthin, well-moisturized black rubber gloves.

As I was too overwhelmed with lust to protest, my arousal amplified when her long, thick fingers found their way to my buttocks. In a few swift maneuvers, she opened my shiny vinyl pants and slid her hands inside. Gently, she rubbed my bottom with an increasing intensity that escalated into aggressive groping. Traveling lower, she concentrated on the rim of my anus with the tip of her rubber-covered finger tracing circles round and round and round. Within my next heartbeat, Harm had rammed her finger into my ass while roughly whispering unintelligible things into my ear, an act that propelled me into a powerful spasm. Covering my mouth with hers, now hot like fire, she seized the opportunity to push her finger even deeper inside me. My ass hungrily swallowing her finger, I knew I was dying from the strength and persistence of my spasms, but the hashish haze carried me to the throes of ecstasy, leaving me desperate for more.

Slowly, she pulled her finger from inside me, removing her glove, turning it inside out, and stuffing it deep inside her back pocket before gently guiding me back to the bar, summoning the bartender for another round. After what had just happened, I knew I would neither be smoking any more hash nor having another shot.

Ted returned to check on me. All he could do was stare—first at me, then at Harm, and back at me again.

"Ted, this is Harmony, and Harmony, this is my best friend, Ted." My voice was reduced to a breathy wilt; neither of them paid it any attention.

"Harm," Leather corrected. "Good to meet you, Ted. I like your friend, Trina. Bartender, give Ted a drink on me, would you, darling?"

"Ooh, Trina, I like her already!" Ted teased, carefully eyeing Harmony's outfit and demeanor. All I could do was stand
there and smile stupidly, still feeling Harmony inside me and
very open for what was to come. The hash had both mellowed me out and opened me up. Ted collected his scotch and
soda and left.

"This toast is to Harm!" she said slickly, raising her glass
in the air, taking the straw from my glass and handing me the
torched beverage.

"I don't think I can handle another."

"Oh, but you must. You must drink. Let me show you all
the good things Amsterdam has to offer, Trina." Harm
pushed the drink toward my lips; we blew simultaneously
and swallowed. My head seemed lighter than a feather, and
my entire body felt the rush of a bushfire. Before I knew it,
Harmony and I were on the massively crowded dance floor.
Holding me so close I could barely breathe, the hard knot
against her thigh inside her leather pants pressed deep into
me until I felt bruised. One of her hands crushed me to her,
while the other manipulated one of my nipples between her
fingers, pinching it so hard I thought I would faint. My inner
core was vibrating to the point where my soul was begging
Harm for it. Placing both of her hands on top of my head,
Harmony pushed me toward the floor until I was in a kneel-
ing position directly opposite her crotch. As she mashed herself into my face, I grabbed her thighs and kissed her cock
with total submission, feeling myself coming again, fast and
hard, succumbing to the burning, tingling sensation in my
bottom. The longer I kissed her, the more my desire increased
for the taste of leather, the taste of her, the arch of her cock
in my mouth, and the filling-up of my ass. She soon took to
banging herself into my face. I fell in love.

I felt an urgent tap on my shoulder, which was difficult to
acknowledge, as Harmony had both of her hands on either
side of my head and was feeding herself to my hungry mouth.

I allowed myself a moment to peek up at Ted, who was flocked by a small adoring audience that had assembled in our honor.

"Ah, Trina, do you have a minute?" he whispered. I looked up at Harm. She had already moved to light a cigarette, dismissing me. I was far too drunk to be embarrassed. Ted helped me up, to a resounding round of applause. All I could do was a curtsy regally as we exited the club.

"Ms. Thing, have you lost your mind?" he hollered humorously. The moon was full, Ted was drunk, and I was totally aroused.

"Ted, I think I did lose my mind, so we better go get that tattoo before I find it."

Humping *a* Hulder *by a* Hytte *High on a* Norwegian Hilltop

It was a classic combination: the American Girl Scout and a Norwegian version of *I Am Curious Yellow* hiking together on a warm sunny day. Me, the perennial Girl Scout, stooping to examine pine needles and flowers along a narrow path winding upward, checking for animal spoor and tracks, while my lover returned to her dense native forest with tall, translucent ferns thick under towering pines, and hatched elemental plots, folklore plots of trolls, *nøkken, nisse,* and alluring, seductive *hulder*.

We climbed higher, breathing crisp fresh air pungent with pine sap and rich soil. Sparkling water in a clear, cold stream beside the trail rushed pell-mell over sticks and stones. An hour into our journey, a small white cabin appeared above us under a canopy of dark evergreens.

"Look! A *hytte!*" my lover exclaimed. "I wonder whose it is." She skipped lightly in blue Norwegian rubber boots along a half-hewn log crossing the stream. "I wonder if anyone's here."

I hurried behind, also curious to check the cabin and the view from its tiny railed porch. Far below steep hillsides of lush forest, a cold and deep blue mountain lake shimmered in the sunlight, home to scary-eyed *nøkken* pointing spindly fingers at passersby—I'd learn later—living among its sunken logs and moss-covered branches.

We peeked in every window of the cottage and saw a tidy, rustic interior with metal cot and mattress, black iron stove, faded green table, four matching chairs, coffee pot, lantern, matches, and split firewood stacked beside the stove.

"No one here," my lover announced. "Not all summer, looks like. Too bad the door's locked. Shall we stop to rest? We could snack too."

We carried with us in knapsacks a thermos of coffee, creamy cheese on fresh bread, and homemade dessert. Norwegians don't bother with American Express cards, I'd discovered already: It's coffee and sweets they never leave home without, unless the host at their destination guarantees to provide them. My lover even packed a red-and-white tablecloth and linen napkins. I was also learning that manners, indoors or out, were nationally important.

We settled on a grassy slope beside the rushing water, watching high puffy clouds drift across a bright azure sky, listening to birds and squirrels rustle leaves and branches nearby, enjoying simple and delicious food, sipping strong, hot, fresh-brewed coffee.

After eating, I continued exploring, ever the Girl Scout seeking new flora and fauna, sighting grazing deer perhaps, or even better, a moose, that electrifying preponderance of Nature, huge and awkward in appearance yet graceful in motion. Happily I wandered, thinking terrariums and leaf patterns, memorizing colors to identify later the tiny, black-and-white bird with rosy chest that followed me into a meadow of wild, knee-high plants with wispy strands of white fiber spun around their crowns.

I gathered a handful of soft silk and stuffed it in my pocket. Laden with the homey treasure, I headed back to show my lover. Approaching the corner of the cabin, I stopped, startled by an unexpected vision: Kristina lying on her clothes on the grass slope; naked body gleaming white in summer sun; enjoying nature Scandinavian-style, knees up; legs spread to reveal a light brown, furry thatch; resting on her elbows; back arched; pushing round tits and long nipples toward the sun. Hearing my approach, she didn't move.

"We Norwegians worship the sun, you know. When it comes in summer, we hardly sleep. We have such long, dark winters to make up for." Head tilting back, she opened large hazel eyes, arched a thin eyebrow, and smiled suggestively. "So what do you think of our Norwegian forest?"

"It's spectacular," I replied, grinning, surprised yet again after years together.

"Do you like what you see?"

"I love what I see."

"Norwegian forests are very special. Too bad you Americans don't have creatures like us in your woods. Trolls. *Nøkken. Hulder,* especially."

"What's a *hulder*?"

"*Hulder* are beautiful women who lure men into the forest. If they follow, they disappear forever. *Hulder* have tails, you see."

"But I'm not a man."

"And I don't have a tail," she flirted, rolling sideways. "See?"

Propping her head on one hand, she slid her other slowly along the long curve of her body to her ass, then continued down her thigh. Scissoring her top leg forward, she stroked back up her leg, trailing fingertips lightly through exposed tufts of pubic fur between her legs and the hot red aureole of her asshole, on over her butt cheek, dipping down her waist, cupping her left breast finally, forefinger and thumb tweaking a hard purple nipple. Eyelids drooping, she slid her tongue slowly over thin pink lips and barely exposed teeth.

"Welcome to Norway, darling."

Welcome to Norway, indeed. The thin pink lips between my

legs pounded so hard I could barely walk...but I managed.

I lay down behind her on my side, enjoying the contrast of clothes against her total nudity, running my hand over satin skin, both tits, the deep dip of a slender waist, to the round hump of a bare ass gyrating a sexy sashay against my jeans zipper. I warmed my hand in her sun-hot muff, caressing her clit with the heel of my hand, pulling her rocking butt closer, joining the rhythm as I nibbled her shoulder and kissed the back of her neck, inhaling the sweet perfume of her hair and skin. I stroked her stomach and played with both breasts, enjoying her gasps of pleasure, trailing lips along her chin and earlobe, feeling the pulse in her neck quicken.

When I touched the opposite side of her face, she turned over to kiss me, pushing me onto my back.

"Give me your tongue," she demanded, tonguing my teeth, tickling my upper palate, unbuttoning my shirt.

I did, holding my breath, willingly.

"Have you ever fucked outside in nature?" she whispered in my ear.

"No," I laughed.

"It's wonderful. You'll love it. I can feel sun hot on my skin and a warm breeze tickling my crotch hair. The sun's energy is pouring through me to you. I'm on fire! I'm alive! Can you feel it?"

She sat back, straddling me to unzip my pants—a potent, sexy, nude woman of 40 with sweet-16 breasts and protruding nipples—she dismissed my clothes, exposing me to sunlight and breezes that felt cold at first on my wet bush and made me gush more inside. Turning sideways, leaning on the ground, pulling up my knee to hold, she pressed her hot crotch against mine and began rocking, spreading her swollen cunt lips with her fingers, then spreading mine, pushing us together, moaning, "Cunt kissing, dear. Can you feel the heat? My heat, your heat pressed together. We've done this before. Isn't it juicy? Isn't it hot? O-o-oh...so hot! So delicious!"

O-o-oh, yeah! Definitely hot!

I pulled up, letting my shirt slide off both shoulders, releasing my bra, enjoying complete exposure, the rush of it: naughty, sensuous, voluptuous, free. Bare skin on skin in a tight embrace, kissing soft lips, and the softest mouth inside. Yeah, we'd done it before. We'd done it a lot since meeting eight years earlier in Lake Placid before the Winter Olympics during a wild party summer of booze, pot, disco dancing, and transitory encounters. Then, surprisingly, we kept on doing it in California, in Houston, and recently in Copenhagen, where I'd landed after a long separation, and now finally here high on a hilltop in Nord Odal where she'd grown up.

We'd keep on doing it, too, despite the separation caused by a custody suit filed by her ex-husband after ten years. Sixteen months earlier, the "unfit" mother with child had secretly fled the United States, a country that can consider convicted murderers better parents than lesbians. I would've done the same to escape the judicial dick-waving. And now it was all worth it.

Welcome to Norway, darling.

Gently, she pushed me back to the ground, silky soft body pressing the length of mine, gliding up and down between my legs. We kissed a long time, slowly at first, tasting each other, connecting, fusing, melting together in the sun. I wrapped my legs around the back of her thighs and pulled her closer, riding the wave of bodies rocking each other. Tiny beads of sweat added salty, humid lubrication to slippery tits and soaked thighs—gliding together faster, more urgent, pressing, humping, undulating. As the rhythm increased, my cunt ached, swollen with need and desire.

"Do you want my fingers, love?"

Oh, yeah.

"Shall I fuck you?"

Please do.

"I love fucking you, you know. Especially outdoors. I

found this place last summer. I thought about bringing you here all this time. I imagined us like this all winter. It got me through so many dark nights alone. Does that surprise you?" she whispered coyly, slipping her hand between my legs.

"Yes...no," I moaned weakly, barely thinking, eyes closed, smiling, arching my pelvis to meet her hand, opening wide to let her inside.

Yes. No. It was the surprises that kept me following her. Across the United States. Across the Atlantic Ocean. Surprises like this. Surprises that either by genetic or cultural naïveté never dawned on me.

She slipped her fingers inside. My cunt muscles spasmed and grabbed. I gasped, missed a breath, heart pounding.

"Do you like feeling my fingers?"

Mmm...yeah! I loved her fingers stroking me inside and out. Like I loved the dirty words spoken in fluent but accented English, a little too formal at times, slightly odd-sounding. Like I loved her physical passion and passion for life: wild, exuberant, theatrical at times, but always genuine and not superficial. Like I loved her regal bearing: the tall, ramrod posture of a Viking queen softened by a woman's hips swaying in long, wrap-around skirts, tight breasts visible in loosely buttoned blouses. Like I loved her costumes: creative, outrageous at times, but always attractive outfits enhanced by large silver jewelry, colorful scarves around a long neck, or waist-cinching belts accentuating a slender waist. Like I loved her raw power and randy, reckless imagination creating real moments like this.

"Do you want to come, my dear? Come with my fingers fucking you?"

Yeah, I wanted to come. I wanted to explode. And I did, ass clenched, toes pointed, nipples protruding hard and puckered in the rich pine air, head back, mouth open, rocking to God Almighty climax—ah, ah, a-a-ah, Je-sus! Yes!

She did me several times before I collapsed on the ground,

sweaty, satisfied, shit-eating grin lighting my flushed face. Her body lying on top felt cool, then hot and silky. I reached into the pocket of my shirt that lay nearby and pulled out the wild fiber I'd picked.

"Look what I found."

I drew it across her back, down one shoulder and arm, back and forth across the crease in her elbow.

"*Myrull*," she said, sounding sexier speaking Norwegian. "Wild wool. They used it in hard times, my ancestors. Made thread and spun cloth. Life wasn't easy here in my country for a long time."

Maybe not, but it was easier now. Easier, safer, tolerant. The "Land of Women," according to political refugees from Muslim countries, who are blown away by so many women in power. A land where the government would've informed my lover if her ex-husband entered the country. A land where Americans don't always win, because Americans aren't always right.

I drew the gossamer thread under her chin, down her long angular face.

She shivered and laughed deep in her throat, "I doubt my ancestors used it for this. But who knows. Maybe *hulder* do. Are you my *hulder*?"

I gave my usual response to questions she asked like that: a broad, goofy grin. I certainly hoped so. I liked the idea: being a *hulder,* her *hulder.* I liked the newness of it and the flattery; it was sexy. The idea of supernatural elements, of enchantment, added potency. It charged the air. I especially liked changing straight myths, replaying them. Same story, different telling; different romance, hotter sex. It was all hot. Naked, naughty, utterly exposed in such a wild, tangled, ancient forest. Very hot!

I rolled her over and felt the sun's heat on my back, a forest breeze tickling my crotch hair. I gazed at her round breasts dominated by impressive nipples, aggressive, insinuating nipples, demanding to be sucked, tongued, tweaked, nipped, pulled, spun, kissed. I leaned over, took a huge mouthful that filled the back of my throat, devouring one then the other until both nipples grew longer, more demanding, hard and hot, so engorged and ready that delicate tongue touches sent groans and exclamations of encouragement rippling through the forest. Arching her back, she pushed her dripping wet pubic tangle against my stomach and grabbed the sides of my face, pressing my head in small massaging circles around each tit.

"Oh, God, that's wonderful. Just like I imagined. Finally. I can't believe you're here! I can't believe we're finally fucking here! Oh, fuck me, please. Will you fuck me, please, darling?"

I slid my fingers between her legs—hot, musty, wet—feeling the sun's heat on my back, its energy pouring through me. Dipping fingers in and out—clit, cunt, clit, cunt—I watched her body arch and convulse, white skin flushed pink with pleasure, wave after spasming wave. *My hulder.* Intoxicating and deeply familiar, yet different in her native land, becoming a whole new mystery to experience and explore. The thought made me tingle and ache all over again.

"Are you sure you don't have a tail?" I teased.

"No. No tail," she laughed. "Just fur."

Sopping wet fur. I felt it on my thigh as it slid gently between her legs. Dewdrops clinging to curly brown pubic hair felt cool against my hot skin as I slid my whole body on top of hers.

"This is a long way from Norman Rockwell, you know," I whispered in her ear.

"Of course. You're in my country now. Our two lands may seem alike but they're not. We have different heritages. I've spent many years in yours. Now you've come to mine. What do you think? Think you'll like living among us northern dwellers with such strange forest creatures?"

"I think I'm going to love living with your strange creatures," I replied, laughing softly, gently trailing my lips along the edge of her jaw to her ear, then down her long neck, thinking how similar yet odd it all was. Even the sun behaved differently, circling the sky all day, barely dipping below the tree line a few hours each night, instead of traversing horizon to horizon. It was definitely worth the wait, enduring the long separation with all its pain and sadness.

I inhaled deeply the smell of her skin—salty, sweet, still damp with sweat. *Hulder* humping certainly beat wool gathering and terrarium construction any day. Nuzzling my face under her chin, I settled into the gorgeous warmth of afterglow, almost as good, as thrilling, as the high-octane, randy charge of the sexy humping and bumping. Almost.

Welcome to Norway, darling…mortal men be damned.

I Swear This Really Happened
(But Nobody Believes Me)

BY ZONNA

Yeah, yeah, yeah...I know it sounds crazy, but what can I say? Stranger than truth and all that, right? I mean, to look at me, you'd never think it possible—not in a million years. You'd sooner believe in the Tooth Fairy. After all, the quarter under your pillow is at least proof of something. Me, I have no proof. But I remember every detail about that night.

It was August 1982 and hotter than hot. Paint wasn't just peeling off the walls of my New York City apartment, it was melting, dripping like gobs of hot white chocolate. Well, maybe that's an exaggeration. It was off-white, OK? The heat and humidity were running a close race, and I was losing. My hair was a mess, limp and stringy. I pulled it back in a blue bandanna just so I could stop thinking about it. It wasn't a fashion statement or anything, believe me. I had just stepped out of my third cold shower of the evening, and I could already feel the sweat beading up on my skin. It was hopeless. My two fans were whining on high, but they were really just blowing the steamy air around so every inch of the room could get its fair share. The window (I only had one that opened) was not helping, either. I stuck my head out, trying to decide if it was cooler outside. The answer was no.

Just as I was about to tuck my neck back into my shoulders, I saw something on the fire escape, kind of gleaming in the street light. It looked like a necklace, but it was probably just a piece of tinfoil or a ribbon or something. I tried to grab it, but it was about six inches out of my reach. Upon closer inspection, I saw it was a piece of jewelry. It looked pretty expensive. Having nothing better to do at the moment than lie in bed tossing and turning in the endless heat, I decided to climb onto the fire escape and retrieve it. I could put a notice up by the mailboxes the next day so whoever had lost it could come give me a big reward.

Did you ever try to climb out a window onto a fire escape? Let me explain something to you: It can't be done without physical injury. I guess whoever builds stuff must figure, *Hey, nobody's gonna be stupid enough to do this unless they're trying to avoid being burned to death in a horrible fire, and at that point, who's gonna care about a couple scratches/bruises/sprained muscles or abrasions?*

So anyway, after bumping my head a few times, smacking my elbow 'til I saw more stars than you can see in the city sky, and twisting myself into positions that aren't even listed in the *Guide to Lesbian Sex,* I tumbled out the window and onto the metal stairs. I stood up. I guess I hadn't realized how far from the ground the third floor really is. I did then. I'm not a height person. I prefer not to venture any farther than the second or third step of a ladder, and the cobwebs on my ceiling will back me up on that. I snatched the necklace and turned around to maneuver back into my private sauna.

Why was the window closed? I hadn't heard a thud—or had I? I must've assumed it was me falling onto the landing. I shoved the treasure into the pocket of my ratty old shorts and tugged on the frame. After about 15 minutes of total physical exertion—including banging, straining, pulling, cursing, swearing, and crying—I realized all I had accomplished was to work up a real good sweat.

I looked down: three flights of rickety, rusty, wrought iron that ended in a six-foot jump into a rat-infested backyard. I looked up: only two flights, with the possibility of gaining access to the roof. Would I find a door up there that led into the building? The way things had been going so far, I seriously doubted it. Still, it seemed the safer bet, unless I missed my footing and plummeted to my untimely death. Up I climbed.

As I reached the fifth floor, I came face to face with a woman sitting by her open window. She looked at me. I looked at her. Something needed to be said.

"Hi. What a scorcher, huh?"

"What are you doing?" she asked.

"Well, I'd tell you, but it's too ridiculous."

She looked skeptical. And cute. Real cute. In one quick swoop, I took in her hazel eyes, long blond hair, and even tan. I didn't recognize her. I mean, I wasn't the welcoming committee or anything, but I had bumped into most of my neighbors over the four years I'd been living there. I definitely would have remembered bumping into this one.

"Um...Do you know if there's a door on the roof that lets into the building?"

"Why?"

I decided I might as well confess before she called the cops or something.

"I locked myself out of my apartment."

"Which one?"

I couldn't see how that mattered, but I wasn't in a position to argue.

"3R."

"O-o-oh, I know you."

"You do?"

"Yeah. You're the one with the dog."

"No, I'm not."

"Oh? Oh! You're the one with the piano."

"Sorry. No dog, no piano."

She seemed confused.

"I swear."

She studied me for a minute, her eyes traveling up and down. A smile cracked the serious expression on her face, shattering it to bits. "That's a real shame, a hottie like you."

Excuse me? A hottie? I was tempted to turn around and look for whoever was standing behind me. On my best day, and this wasn't it, I might be considered—oh, I don't know—maybe something closer to "not bad." I was surprised since I was more used to women doing this little dance first, to find out if I was a lesbian or not, before flirting with me. It had a few definite steps to it, and then lots of little variations. This girl was going right for the dip.

"Um..." I didn't know what to say. My tongue was tied; my brains were fried. I just wanted to get back into my toasty little oven and take another six or seven cold showers.

"You're cute. I have the same shirt."

Now I understood. I was wearing a torn-up pride T-shirt I often slept in. What a break—a sister. Hooray! Maybe she'd let me in, and I wouldn't have to tempt fate any further.

"Thanks. Would it be OK if I climbed in through your window? I really don't feel like dealing with the roof."

"Sure. Come on in."

My entrance was a tad more graceful than my exit had been, but I still wound up in a pile on her wooden floor.

"You're all hot and sweaty."

"Sorry. It's been a bad day." I stared at the multitude of locks and chains securing her door to the wall.

She came up behind me. "How are you going to get back in your apartment?"

I hadn't thought that far ahead. "Um..."

"I know a locksmith you can call."

"OK. Great idea."

"Wanna take a shower to cool off?"

No, I wanted to call that locksmith she'd just mentioned. I

was sure they had 24-hour emergency service or something. They all did. What was she talking about?

Wait a minute. *That's a real shame, a hottie like you...You're cute. I have the same shirt...You're all hot and sweaty...Wanna take a shower to cool off?* You don't have to hit me over the head with a hammer to raise a bump. Was there a possibility of turning this day I wanted to forget into a night to remember? It sure seemed she was making a move.

"Um, a shower? Yeah, that would be great. Sure it's OK?"

"Of course. You can sleep here if you want to, and then we can call the locksmith first thing in the morning. As long as you don't mind—"

Sharing her bed? Sleeping in the raw? Staying up all night working on my good neighbor policy?

"—the couch."

So much for that dream. I tried not to sound too disappointed. "No, the couch is...fine."

She gave me a big fluffy red towel to dry off with and left me alone in her tiny bathroom. I figured I might as well make the best of things. For whatever reason, something had led me here—maybe fate, or maybe stupidity—and now, here I was, in the bathroom of a really cute blond who lived two floors up from me and thought I was a hottie. Maybe there was still some hope. I turned the faucet all the way to the right, trying not to cry out as icy drops pelted my overheated flesh.

I shut the water and stepped out of the tub. I reached for my clothes, but they were gone. Uh-oh. I looked on the floor and behind the toilet—no trace. Shit. She must've snuck in while I was drowning myself. Why would she do that? I wondered if this was a good thing or a bad thing. I had no choice. I couldn't sleep in the tub. She was waiting out there. I wrapped the towel around me as best I could and emerged into the sultry steam of her living room.

She was sitting on the couch, staring right at me. I felt pretty dumb in that towel. Red's not my color. The radio was playing somewhere in the background.

"I couldn't find my clothes."

"I took them."

"Oh?"

"They were all yucky."

"Oh."

"You can borrow something—if you want." I could swear she licked her lips, but maybe it was a mirage.

"Uh, that'd be good." I stood there, not knowing what to do with my hands.

She got up, reluctantly, it seemed, and pulled some shorts and shirts from her dresser. She held a T-shirt up against me. She stood so close, I felt her breath on my face.

"Think this'll fit?"

"Probably. Thanks." I took it.

She chose a pair of shorts. "How about these?"

"Great."

I turned for the bathroom. Then her hand was on my shoulder, spinning me back around.

"I really like you in that towel."

"Oh, yeah?" I felt my tongue sticking to the roof of my mouth.

"Yeah. Do you have a girlfriend?"

Did I? I couldn't remember. I could hardly remember my name, standing so close to heaven. I shook my head.

She came closer. I was sweating again, but this time the heat came from inside.

"Do you think I'm pretty?"

I nodded.

"Do you wanna kiss me?"

I put my arms around her waist and pulled her to me. Our lips collided in a soft crash of thunder. Our tongues twisted together, sending tiny flashes of lightning straight to my toes, among other places. I couldn't believe the change in my luck. I felt her tugging at the terry cloth. The towel fell to the floor.

We moved to the couch. She sat me down with a little shove, then stood before me. She slowly slipped her shorts past her long legs, stepping out of them and kicking them aside. Next, she pulled her shirt off over her head in one smooth motion, revealing herself to me. No tan lines—nice. Then she started dancing, swaying, so slow and sexy. I thought this was my cue to reach for her, but she pushed me away.

"Watch me."

She ran her hands over her breasts, still moving to the music. She spread her legs a little and began touching herself. My eyes were glued open. I didn't want to blink in case I'd miss something. Maybe it was the weather, but she seemed to be moving in slow motion. She stood just out of my reach, teasing and torturing me with a tantalizing display of sweet shamelessness. I was getting wetter by the minute. I held back as long as I could, but that probably wasn't any more than a few minutes. Let's face it, I'm not known for willpower.

I peeled myself from the couch and kissed her. She tasted like peppermint tea. I told her I had to have her, and I took charge, leading her to the bed. She spread herself across it, like an offering, and I lowered myself on top of her. As we moved, I felt the sweat slipping and sliding between us. I slithered downward on my expedition. She opened wider as my tongue explored further. The sounds that escaped her were straight from the jungle.

She rolled me onto my back. She kissed me—my mouth, my neck, my shoulders. She put her lips around my left nipple and softly sucked. I heard myself moaning, almost as if it were coming from the other room. The river was so high already, I was afraid the dam would burst before she opened the floodgates. She put her hand over me—not inside, not touching me, just sort of covering. That took the edge off, and I was able to relax. When I did come, it was like a long, lazy stream flowing through me. We made love for hours and collapsed in a heap of tangled legs and sheets and arms.

When the sun peeked through her curtains the next morning, I awoke and watched her sleep for a while. There was an actual breeze blowing through her window, and it seemed the heat wave had finally broken. It felt good to be able to breathe without scalding my lungs.

We ate breakfast, and I called the locksmith. While we waited, we talked for a while, something we hadn't bothered much with the night before. She'd been subletting the apartment from her brother for two months and would be leaving soon to return to school in California. It was a drag to find out this wasn't going to be any more than it had been. Still, I was kind of glad things had turned out the way they had, my getting stuck outside and all. If I hadn't been such a klutz, I probably never would've met her. For the first time, I was grateful for my lack of agility.

As I gathered my clothes and said good-bye, the necklace fell out of my shorts.

She picked it up. "Hey! That's mine! Where'd you find it?"

"On the fire escape. That's why I was out there in the first place."

"I thought I'd lost it for good. Thanks!"

I smiled. I'd collected my big reward after all.

Maybe One Day

BY CAITLYN MARIE POLAND

I had known Rachel for more than ten years, and I could read her like a book—well, like a comic book, really. Even though I had never been so brave as to analyze a complete collection of written words, I was an expert at perceiving colorful characters. As my chosen career was that of a cartoonist, envisaging Rachel as a flexible character encompassing many idiosyncrasies was far superior to viewing her as a cardboard cutout from a rigid, predictable hardback novel. She epitomized many shades and flavors, and as such I found it inconceivable to describe her via semantics alone.

Of course I have no intention of demeaning any great novel or short story, but I believed could only define Rachel through art, and within my profession I did just that. With Rachel as my cartoon catalyst, I produced a daily four-part comic strip (with obligatory punch lines) for a little known magazine.

My cartoon star, Annabel Furlong, was founded on her, based daily on her, and indirectly fed by her. Through my imagination and via my job, I could mold Rachel and make her my own. Yet fiction was and often is far from reality. And although Rachel was always mine within the confines of the final print, she was never truly mine. Sometimes she felt incredibly close, while other times she felt far away. She was a human paradox: I always knew her every move, even before she made it, yet she never ceased to completely surprise me.

Rachel was an enigma, on a continuum between the overt and covert, and because of all this, and much more, I loved her every waking and sleeping breath. Unfortunately, though, I always knew, deep within my well-concealed treasure trove of emotions, that we would never be together...well, not together on a permanent basis. We had sailed in and out of each other's lives with different agendas, but we had never become more than brief lovers. We had fucked as partners, we had fucked as mistresses, and we had frequently fucked simply to share wet cunts in search of mutual satisfaction. But we had never made any final commitment; we were too emotionally far apart. While Rachel had delusions of grandeur, coupled with career ideals far beyond mine, I craved part-time employment and a child. While she planned to tour the world, contacting her friends only to inform them of her whereabouts, I craved the heavily scented bosom of family. Even though I thought Rachel was never completely satisfied with monogamy, I, unfortunately, could have been.

I would have embraced each and every argument for one-on-one relationships if Rachel had agreed to be monogamous with me—and not just on the occasions I was with her. I admit, there had been times when we both had held to the policy of "love the one you're with," but I only ever truly loved Rachel, and, in all honesty, it was far more than just the physical sense of fucking.

Any such emotions were never given a full airing, and throughout our ten years, Rachel and I drank, fucked, and then drank some more, neither of us really talking to each other or swapping moods. Well, not until September 1998...

Autumn had just commenced its onslaught, and as the temperature slowly dropped, I had begun my usual retreat to hibernation. Rachel and I engaged in the obligatory Friday and

Saturday nights out, either fucking strangers or fucking each other (depending on the circumstances), and she also spent every Tuesday at my side. Beyond that, I lived in my nightgown, duvet, and tartan slippers. So, as my intercom buzzed the announcement of a surprise guest on a Monday night, I was shocked, to say the least. It was around 9:30 P.M., and I was desperately trying to create my next—well, overdue—and now five-part comic strip in which my heroine was purchasing a set of matching luggage. As Rachel had recently acquired a collection of travel bags (for some unknown reason), my cartoon character, Annabel, was doing the same thing. I found it extremely difficult creating a humorous (or even slightly amusing) anecdotal finale about suitcases. I mean, what could possibly stir a strong enough facial movement to resemble a smile when discussing luggage? I was at a loss. But I was saved by the bell, and as the buzzer cried out again I, with no regrets, left Ms. Furlong alone on her shopping expedition. As I pressed the reply button, Rachel's voice greeted me; this time, however, it was louder than I had ever heard it. Her voice took on a pleading tone, which was quite unusual for her.

She never had to plead. In fact, she never had to ask twice—for anything.

"Come on, Lynn. It's cold out here."

I granted Rachel access, and after a few moments she burst into my flat with a lethal combination of enthusiasm, eagerness, and, most of all, alcohol.

"Drink with me?" She lovingly caressed two flute glasses and a bottle of champagne.

This was a very out-of-the-ordinary request for Rachel. Why was she asking permission for something we did all the time? Rachel spoke again.

"You're going to drink with me, aren't you?"

I knew protest would be futile, since Rachel was already struggling to untwist the wire that held the cork tightly on the champagne bottle, and as she succeeded, froth forced its path downward from the summit. In an attempt to control the near-volcanic eruption, Rachel quickly filled the flutes with the sweet Lanson liquid and indicated I take one, which I did.

"Do you like it?"

I did, and it was going straight to my head, but at least it gave me the impetus to ask, "What are you doing here, Rachel? It's Monday."

Perhaps I should not have asked, as she immediately looked upset. It took me more than 15 minutes to convince her I was not disappointed to see her and that I enjoyed her company at any time and in any venue, even as unexpected as tonight's visit was.

To console her, I suggested we might incorporate Monday nights into our routine, or just abolish the routine completely, living spontaneously. In a desperate bid I began to converse inanely, and I rambled on in a very low, monotone voice.

Then, just as I was losing myself uncontrollably in complete crap, Rachel broke the ice.

"I love you, Lynn."

I was well aware she loved me, and I could not help continuing with my verbal diarrhea.

"No, Lynn. I really love you."

"I love you too," I answered again.

"Look, dimshit, are you getting the fucking point here or what? I'm in love with you."

This time Rachel did more than break the ice; she melted the polar ice caps, and as my mind ran over her last statement, for what must have been a million times in a matter of seconds, she moved toward me.

"In love," she reiterated.

I had registered her words, but for the first time in my life I was speechless.

"In love."

Silence. I was still speechless.

"In love."

Silence.

"For fuck's sake, Lynn. *In* love…kiss me."

She didn't need to ask again, and as we moved closer together, I welcomed the familiar warm, wet softness of her lips. Her sensuality, as usual, was overwhelming, and as she encouraged me to move my mouth further, she repeated that she loved me, only stopping when my tongue demanded hers, halting her speech.

I immediately began to suck Rachel's tongue and gently bite her bottom lip. It had always turned her on, and if she meant what she had said, I had every intention of making this the last, but most definitely best, fuck of our single status. Rachel did grant me her tongue, but it was short-lived, as she quickly moved it to my ear and then slowly licked her way down my neck. She knew every time her tongue stroked my skin, she stirred inexplicable tingling sensations in my throat and made my cunt become wetter and wetter.

While every lick prepared me further for whatever she was going to force into me, her every move only left me further in anticipation. But anticipation was nothing new; although I knew her well, she had never been predictable, especially in bed. Even though we had fucked many times, I never truly knew just how she was going to make me come, or when or where.

"Turn around, Lynn."

Rachel again broke the ice, and I felt I should respond to her request.

I wanted to face her, watch her put her fingers inside me, wait for the expression on her face when she felt how wet my inner thighs and cunt were, observe her blend of pleasure and pride when she realized she had created what she was feeling.

"Please, Lynn. Turn around."

I did so, knowing whatever she was going to do, I would enjoy. I turned, and as I moved 150 degrees, she slid her arms under mine, whereupon they met at my front to untie my nightgown. The gown fell quickly from me, and my bare flesh leaned against her fully clothed body. Rachel sighed deeply, and I felt completely content in her obvious appreciation. I had always had a heavier build than she, about which, with other people, I had felt uncomfortable at times. With Rachel I had never felt that way. She knew every line of my body, and she had intimate knowledge of every crevice. I always felt completely sexual and confident in our encounters, and this time was no different.

I relaxed, and as I felt her belt buckle meet the base of my spine, I molded on her figure. Rachel caressed my back, kissed the nape of my neck, and smoothed my outline, from my shoulders, past my hips, and finishing at the back of my knees (a sensation that always headed straight to my cunt with excessive speed). Then, suddenly Rachel grasped my wrists, and with one quick movement she drew them backward. I felt a cold surface and heard a loud locking sound. I was cuffed.

"Bend over."

I didn't hesitate, and as I leaned forward, she turned me slightly, this time only 90 degrees. I was now resting on the back of my sofa. For a moment she moved away, and in seconds dozens of thoughts crammed my mind. Then I recognized the distinct sound of a zipper being undone. But once more there was silence, and as I tried to turn to see my immediate future, Rachel's hands brought me to a halt. Without warning, she forced her way inside me, but not with her fingers or a hand-held vibrator or even the end of a nearby hairbrush (which had often been my savior). Rachel entered me with a strap-on vibrator. It had been one of those things we had always talked about but had never quite gotten around to. I suppose our shagging had always been far too spontaneous to plan for the provision of toys, and we had often simply used whatever was at hand, so to speak. This time Rachel had planned every move, and I was not about to complain. I was not in a position to do so, anyway, since she was now leaning over to place her chest on my back, and she began to move rhythmically in and out of my cunt, responding to my groans. The sensation of her being in me, out of me, in me, then out of me again, coupled with the movements of her breasts upon my back, brought me close to orgasm much faster than ever before. I heard Rachel, reacting to me, begin to reach her own climax. As my cries grew louder, so did hers. As I slowed down, her gyrations did too, and when I finally came, she did too, forcing the vibrator as far and as ferociously as she could inside my cunt, refusing to stop, with the last final thrusts causing my clit to throb violently.

As Rachel withdrew, it was almost as if her toy were uttering a clear sound of reluctance. It probably did, together with my cunt. After we both recovered, we fucked for several more hours. I sat over her while she sat and licked my clit, masturbating until my juices dripped from my own cunt onto hers. While Rachel fucked my face, I fucked hers. While clawing my back, she experienced the strong force of the strap-on toy, until we both finally gave way to sleep.

When I awoke, I was alone, and contrary to my initial hypothesis, Rachel had not taken up residence in my lounge, the kitchen, or even the shower.

She had left. *Why? Fucking why?*

Then I realized...while Rachel had spent most of the night confirming she was "in love" with me, I had not returned the favor. All Rachel knew was that I loved her, as I always had, as a friend. I had neglected to confirm my truth.

To date, in my hallway there are still three empty suitcases—three of the six Rachel had purchased earlier that week. She must have put them there the night before she left. Three suitcases and one note:

Without your being IN love with me, I just couldn't stay. Maybe one day...

My cartoon character, Ms. Annabel Furlong, also left that

day, her unpredictable love affair eventually coming to an end after neglecting to ascertain her partner's true feelings. Instead, she walked out before any compromise could be reached. I can wholeheartedly say I hope someday Annabel, with Rachel, will return.

Maybe one day.

Stone Femme

BY REGAN MCCLURE

Stone. A stone butch is a woman who doesn't allow herself to be fucked.

It was a setup from the very beginning. My matchmaking friend put femme and butch together and produced a cocktail party. There are only five of us here. It's an intimate party, and the theme is gin drinks: martinis, gimlets, gin and tonics. I mix them up in the kitchen, and we knock them back together.

There's this femme here, one of those loud women. She's trading opinions with someone else, and it isn't exactly difficult to overhear their conversation.

"Most of the come-ons I get from butches are just so pathetic, you know, I can't be bothered. What's the point of going to a bar when that's what you have to look forward to?"

I mix myself another martini in the kitchen.

I'm a quiet one. I don't make much of an effort to flirt, especially with someone who seems more than likely to take me down a peg or two. But as her limbs brush against me, over the course of the evening, I don't try to move my leg away from her either. When it brushes against me and stays, I don't dare move at all. Fortunately for quiet butches like me, she's neither quiet nor shy, and when we go to a bar that evening, she pulls me against her as we dance. Our bodies bump in happy collision, and we slip along each other's legs. She takes my shoulders and turns me around so my back is against her. Pushing her hand against the back of my neck, she bends me over and grinds her pelvis against my ass. I hang there, bent over, with my ass in the air, thinking, *If I take this woman home, she's going to want to fuck me.* I let my head drop down and listen to the roar of blood rushing to my face.

"Got any plans for the evening?" she asks when I've regained my posture. My face is still red from being bent over.

"Funny, I was just thinking about that." I smile.

She continues, "Would you like to get busy tonight?"

"Yes," I say, trying in a single word to strike a balance between pleased and panting.

Stone. A femme woman who doesn't allow herself to be fucked with.

Stone femmes do it differently than stone butches, of course. A femme will always win, as long as she remembers to ignore the rules. She's quick to test the limits of my personal space by sliding her leg along my innocent thigh. As I slide my hand along her waist, I know it doesn't touch the same places inside her. Stone, in a femme, is camouflaged behind an open cunt, warm hands, a distracting mouth, so smoothly covered you can rest on top of it and never know.

Stone. Stone can be found in butches and femmes, and when they're flirting you can almost hear them clack together like cloth bags filled with marbles.

We roll on the bed, wrestling to take off each other's clothes. We tumble together like a rockslide as we wrestle to get on top, then wrestle to get on bottom. She tugs at my flesh with her hands, kneading me like warm clay. She pushes and pulls me around the bed, and I let myself be moved.

"What can I do for you tonight?" she leans back to ask. Even in candlelight, she remembers to make eye contact.

That's supposed to be my line. I don't know what to say.

Stone. The relocation of sexual response away from one part of our body to another.

"How can I touch you?" she asks again.

I roll over to have my back stroked. This always feels safe to me. My neck and back are some of the most receptive and sensitive parts of my body, except perhaps the fingertips of my right hand. And, I discover as she licks the back of my knees...*there, ah yes, there.*

"Well, I got you to say something at last," she teases. "You better be careful, you might lose your composure."

I didn't even know I'd been talking out loud.

Stone. Stone melts in intense heat.

I stretch out next to her solid, strong body, and I feel the late August heat rise from her, as if this femme laid out next to me is a banked, underground fire.

She turns me over.

"Please, let me touch you."

Please. I don't think anyone has ever said please to me before. Suddenly I realize this is a need for her, a desire to give pleasure to a woman as deeply as she is allowed. If she hadn't said please, I wouldn't have spread my legs. If more women said please, perhaps I would spread them more often.

Stone. A stone femme will invite you to dive into her warm mouth. You might as well dive into a volcano.

Her hands caress me deep enough to touch me two inches underneath my skin. Her hands bring my knees up to my ears. Her tongue brings me closer to my gods.

My turn. Time to see what I can do. I start with her feet because I love feet, and most women have pain in their feet that moans for massage: *Warm mouth, oh, yeah, suck my toes.* But she's different. She becomes...still. So I move on to something else. I don't take her like a firestorm. I am patient and thorough, the way the ocean erodes a rock, turning it over and over to make it smooth and polished and wet. I slide up to her cunt and give her my best: my mouth, my hands, then both at the same time. I wish I had more hands.

Stone. The ability to hide much of yourself from view.

She talks about many things. I have learned that my skin is soft, solid colors would look good on my bedroom walls, I have a nice ass, she has an erotic interest in blood, and roses are an excellent addition to any garden. She says my name at the end of every third sentence. She reveals everything and nothing, and I'm not sure if I'm hearing more or less than what she's telling me.

We lie tangled together in a lube-sticky mess. She's getting up after three hours of sleep because she's got somewhere to go. She looks fresh and sated, while I feel the rumples in my skin and stains on my character. Her hair is still pinned tightly to her head; there are just a few curls artistically out of place. My low-maintenance crew cut is ruffled from rubbing against the sheets, and a ridiculous fan of hair sticks up on the crown of my head. She's slept with her rings on. I can't even find my glasses. The gin and smoke have left my mouth feeling furry, and as we kiss I realize she's already brushed her teeth.

Stone. The place on our bodies where even pleasure is an invasion. The place where we hide a little piece of ourselves for safekeeping.

She eats the meager breakfast I provide. I have not cooked, but foraged in my kitchen. As she sits cross-legged on the bed, I catch a glimpse of her feet. Her toes look torn and neglected, and as she catches me looking she hides them with a self-conscious flick of the blankets.

I realize I've found some part of her stone. I'd passed through this territory earlier in the night when I caressed her feet. This is her reserve. Her cunt is open city, but here I can't touch. I smile to myself at the irony of her low-cut leather fancies, femme armor daring the world with her strutting sexuality, and all the while her boots have been laced up knee-high.

I didn't touch any place she didn't want me to. She didn't

let me touch her stone or her sadness, and it didn't seem right
to push it. There's no point trying push a stone; that's something I should know. I think, *Now is not the time*. I'm still
learning the art of the one-night stand, and I forget that there
is no later time, only the moment that has come and been lost.
I don't ask for her phone number; she doesn't ask for mine.

Sometimes, scratching the surface of a personality is like
scratching an itch. I wish I had told her more about the
smooth feel of her skin. How her energy felt in her body and
how I could feel it in mine. How blue, wet flames licked off
her fingertips inside me and set off a supernova in my belly.
As she leaves, she almost forgets her underwear, half-hidden
under the bed, but she spots it and stuffs it into her pocket. I
wish she had forgotten it. I would have wrapped it up and
sent it with a bouquet of blood-red roses and a note telling
her how much I wanted to melt her stone.

Notes on Becoming a Babe

BY TASHA PERNA

When she told me her last girlfriend, even though she was a vegetarian, got so that she would cook a steak for her, I promised right and left that I would too, that I'd love to, that I'd do it in a minute. "I mean, not right now, of course," I told her. I won't even let anyone cook meat in my house, or in my pans, and it is much less likely I'd do it for someone else, but there I was, lying and believing it. She wasn't fooled.

Shane has short blond hair, narrow hips, and freckles. She's 5 foot 4, thin, strong, and tan, and she looks like a 16-year-old boy. She's a recovered alcoholic...mostly recovered. She no longer drinks, but she still only sleeps about five hours a night. She can never sleep past 4 in the morning, no matter when she goes to sleep. When she wakes up, she has coffee and sits down to write poetry, and around 6 A.M. she cares for her horses as well as her fields of vegetables and strawberries. These tasks, along with her landscaping jobs, keep her occupied every day in the summer. But at least she's self-employed.

The first time I met her, I was visiting my parents, who have retired in western North Carolina. I went to one of those places that seem more like a stage set than a bar, with women shooting pool and smoking cigarettes in the center of a dimly lit, smoke-hazy hall. I watched from a distance as they chalked up cues and talked loudly, one or two resting a cowboy boot on a chair. They were full of bravado and beyond the reach of a shy girl like myself. No one seemed to notice me. I felt invisible. Here I was, my first time in a lesbian bar, and no one said a word to me, except for one drunken woman, held up by her friend or lover, who winked at me in the ladies' room and offered a slurred, barely comprehensible greeting, "Well, hi there, honey!"

After wandering downstairs, where the stage was set and ready for the evening's musical performers, I got a drink at the back counter. I got it because the bartender was sleeveless and muscular, not because I was thirsty. When she asked me, "What will it be, babe?" I started in surprise because I didn't realize I fell into that category. Maybe New Yorkers like myself are a bit more reserved, or maybe it's because I'm too serious and wear glasses, but no one, man or woman, had ever addressed me that way before, and I was 30 years old. Could have been my long blond hair or the tan I had picked up on the beach before coming to my parents' house, but I wasn't wearing makeup—just jeans and a sleeveless T-shirt. I don't see myself as a babe, but I admit I liked trying on the identity.

The crowd gathered. The music began. I leaned against the wall and put my earplugs in because I have never appreciated deafening noise; I prefer music. I know, I'm hopelessly granola-nerdy. I even wear Birkenstocks. To me, noise is another wall, and I was interested in communicating. Inundated by impenetrable volume, I now felt unheard—as well as unseen—in the crowd.

As I scanned the room, the feeling that I no longer existed allowed me the freedom to fantasize without fear of repercussions. I tried to decide if there was anyone I felt attracted to and who seemed approachable. It was easy to think that way because I had no plan to act. I was too nervous and too inexperienced to actually flirt with a woman, and anyway, everyone seemed to be there with someone. Groups of women huddled together, laughing and talking.

No one stood out in my mind—except, who was that? Look at her! Just seeing her felt like rocking in the shock waves of an earthquake. From the moment I first saw her saunter across the smoke-clouded dance floor, I felt drawn to her. She looked like someone who lived in the woods, tan and sinewy. One hand held a Coke, and the other hung casually in the pocket of her well-worn jeans. She looked alive and real and unpretentious. She was handsome and obviously proud of that. I stared at her and followed her with my eyes as she greeted and hugged several women. She was alone, however, and kept moving from reception to reception.

I don't know what moved her, or if maybe one of her companions noticed my fixed gaze and told her, but she moved gradually through the crowd until she stood by my side. My heart was beating hard, and I rested my elbows as casually as possible on the narrow ledge along the wall behind me. Both of us stared straight ahead at the stage, and she made no acknowledgment of my presence. I had to say something. "Nice music!" I shouted over the din, wondering if she could hear me.

She shrugged as she turned to gaze at me, and then answered, her mouth about an inch from my ear, "I couldn't care less about the music. I come here to meet women."

I nodded and looked back at the stage, dumbfounded. I couldn't think anymore. I was starting to sweat. She moved an inch or so until her elbow pressed down on my arm, as if holding me in place. I felt like a frightened squirrel treed by a hungry dog. For a minute or so we stood together in this unacknowledged intimacy, the bare skin of her forearm generating heat against mine. I listened fixedly to music I couldn't hear anymore, and then, abruptly, she turned to face me and said dismissively, without explanation, "Well, so long," and walked away.

With a sinking sense of desperation, I watched her rapidly

disappear across the room. Nothing seemed appealing about this bar anymore. What had I done wrong? Was there a lesbian language I didn't understand? I thought of leaving but lingered instead, barely admitting that it was in hopes of bumping into her again. I had another drink, orange juice as always, got called "babe" again by the bartender, absentmindedly admired her arms, and returned to my place by the wall.

And then the woodswoman appeared again. "Well, I'm leaving," she said, placing her hand high on the back of my thigh. Once again I was thrown off balance and didn't know how to react. I had been yearning to be touched by her, and she had been so indifferent, and now she was touching me and was about to disappear out the door. At that moment I couldn't imagine a world without her touch.

"I'll walk you to your car." Had I said that? Unbelievable. She nodded and led the way, even held the door open for me, which made me hesitate and lose my bearings. I paused for a moment as if waiting for her to slip through in front of me. She put her hand on my lower back and pushed. "Go ahead." I did.

She drove a pickup truck, a full-size Ford that had seen better days. We stood beside it talking in a friendly way about this and that until she claimed to be cold, although I found it to be a balmy summer night. She suggested we sit in her truck. We climbed inside, and she revved the motor and turned on the heat. I find it extremely uncomfortable sitting in an idling car, thinking of exhaust fumes destroying the environment, but she was in the driver's seat, so I held these thoughts to myself.

"You're not exactly shy, are you?" she ventured.

I turned toward her, meeting her eyes. "Well, actually I am."

She laughed then and rested her hand on my thigh. "So what's your name?"

"Tasha, and yours?"

"Shane. You live here?"

"No, New York," I answered. "I mean a little town in up-state New York that actually reminds me a lot of this one."

"Oh." She sounded a little disappointed. "You'd never catch me living up there. I like it here in the South. It's too cold up there. What brings you here, anyway?"

"My parents retired here. They like the mountain air."

"Yeah, the mountain air is refreshing, but the trees at the highest elevations are dying off from acid rain. Sad, isn't it?"

"Yeah." I didn't know what to say. We were quiet for a while. Then I told her I was a graduate student and asked her what she did.

"You mean besides two-stepping and softball?" she joked. "I'm a farmer and landscaper on the side."

Then Shane told me a story to me about how earlier that morning she had taken off her shirt while cutting a vast field with a tractor mower, and how some girls had waved to her from the road, thinking she was a boy. She waved back, she told me, obviously pleased with herself. She also told me she had been repairing her truck the week before and had gone to an auto parts store. She had grease on her face and hands, and wore a baggy shirt over her skinny frame. The man behind the counter had called her "sir," as he did every time she came by.

"He's never figured it out."

"Amazing," I answered, studying her profile, "because I would never mistake you for a man. I mean you're masculine, and I find that attractive..." I wasn't sure where I was going with that.

I think Shane blushed when I said this. Women are never as tough as they seem; there's always a hint of vulnerability, and I think it is this slippage, a once-removed male-female gender leaking out through the seams, that I have since grown to love about butch women. It's an identity that can't be contained. The toughness is always there, but without the edge of superiority and distance, without the separation I've learned to feel from the male domain.

The weird part is that even so, the more male a woman is, the sexier I find her. There was an unmistakable masculinity to Shane's young-boy face and angular body, and even to the manner in which she stood or crossed her arms. Something in the way she moved seemed cocky and assertive. But I also noticed a shade of prettiness in her profile, an edge that made her tough-looking for a woman but somehow slightly too soft for a man. I found that exciting.

Shane shifted in her seat, studying my face, and then casually encircled my own rather broad shoulders with her lean arms. She kissed me lightly on the lips and said she had to say good night for now because it was late, and she worked seven days a week. She gave me her address and phone number and invited me out for the next evening. She looked tired, and I knew I should let her go, but instead I asked if I could kiss her again. She exhaled a slow and deep barely audible "yes" and sat perfectly still as I leaned forward again, careful not to touch any part of her. I brushed my lips against hers, barely moving, just kissing lightly. Slowly Shane began to knead my lips with her own, pushing more and more forcefully. I held my body inches from hers. I felt her every motion and responded, yielding and accepting. Then she broke through the portal between us, and I tasted her tongue, moving wildly and demanding space. I wanted to touch her, but I didn't because I wanted to her to touch me more.

Shane pulled away then, breathing hard, and said we had to stop now if she was going to be able to stop at all. I was disappointed, but acquiesced. My pussy was tingling. I watched her drive away as I walked slowly across the parking lot to my car. My underwear was drenched. She might have gone to sleep that night, but I didn't.

Shane lived alone except for her dog, a German shepherd who was a little big for his britches, in a small, one-story house on the end of a dirt road. She answered the door the following evening in tight jeans and cowboy boots, and showed me around: her waterbed in the bedroom, her closet-size study, and her living room with an old couch and battered coffee table. Everything looked neat and comfortable. Her hair was damp from a recent shower, and she said she was starving. She told me about a gay restaurant in town and asked if I wanted a burger. I mentioned I was a vegetarian. She said there'd be something there for me. I shrugged. "Let's go." I was too nervous to eat anyway.

The restaurant/bar was brightly colored and fast-paced, with music a little too loud. Everyone seemed to know Shane. A pretty waitress greeted her and teased her about me, even pulled her aside to ask a few quick questions. After she returned and we sat down, a tall, youngish man came and took our orders. Shane ordered a rare burger, fries, and a Coke while she lit a cigarette and asked loudly in mock annoyance where the hell the ashtrays were. The waiter grabbed one from another table and turned to me, "What will it be, babe?" Again this babe thing. Maybe having long blond hair in the South means something more than it does in upstate New York. I'm not a little lady. I'm 5 foot 9, I run, I lift weights. I hardly ever wear makeup and rarely wear a dress. I'm a feminist, and if a man called me babe, I mean a man who wasn't an overly familiar gay waiter, I'd probably spit at him. For that matter, I wouldn't go out for a burger with a man either. I'd make him compromise on Chinese food.

I ordered fries and an orange juice. Shane ate and more than once mentioned how busy she was all the time and how she sure wished she had someone to clean her house, wash her clothes, and maybe cook her a meal or two. I ran this information through my reasoning banks, but its impact didn't seem to register. As if reading my part in a script, I assured her I was the kind of woman who would do that for her.

Shane winked at me and said, "Yeah, that's what I like about you, you're the *kind* of woman who would do that," as if she knew I probably wouldn't, at least not too well and not forever. And she was right. I was lying through my teeth. I couldn't help myself. On the drive home she mentioned how sore her back was from working all day, how she'd have to make an appointment with a masseuse, and I immediately felt jealous of whomever this woman might be, because she would certainly be feminine and good-looking, and Shane would surely flirt with her and sigh as she felt the woman's tender hands knead her tired muscles. "I'll massage your back. I'm great at giving massages," I responded, following her cue without pausing to think what I was saying. But this time I wanted to follow her suggestion. This time I meant it. She smiled teasingly and said it was nice of me to offer.

I followed Shane up the steps into her living room, carrying with me a small backpack. I felt suddenly awkward in the bright light from the lamp on the coffee table. Waiting, even from the night before, was wearing on my nerves. I wanted her to touch me, to kiss me. Instead, she offered me a drink—all she had was water and some obscure brand of neon orange soda. I took the water. We stood about two feet apart. I leaned against the counter, looking shyly in different directions, uncomfortably aware of her intense, penetrating gaze. The more nervous I felt, the more calm and confident Shane seemed to become. As she reached out to brush my hair back from my forehead with one hand, she told me she had been thinking about me all day.

She moved a step closer and whispered into my ear that I was a beautiful woman, and then pressed her lips against mine to silence my polite denial. We embraced, her body hard and strong against my own, her hands moving in restless patterns across my back and down my sides. And then she slowly unbuttoned my faded green flannel shirt and began to massage my breasts, teasing each nipple with gentle, undulating movements. My body was exploding with pleasure. I felt giddy. My crotch was buzzing, asking to be touched. On their

own, my hips began sliding against her, a rhythm I gave myself over to. She licked my nipples and touched and prodded
my belly and the waistline of my jeans.

I held her shoulders for balance. I was now looking down
on the top of her head. Shane paused, holding onto the still-
zippered waist of my jeans, and looked up. "I'd like to make
love to you." She voiced the words softly in an even tone. I
thought about telling her that *two* people make love to each
other, but instead I kissed her lightly on the lips, and followed
her into the bedroom, clutching my backpack in one hand,
and not even knowing when or how my shirt had disappeared.

"Take these off," Shane said, reaching for my jeans. She
was still fully dressed. I obeyed.

"What do you like?" she asked.

"I don't know."

"I bet you know," she said, playfully pushing me onto the
bed. She was now standing over me. She pulled her T-shirt
over her head. She stared down at me with desire in her eyes.
I stared silently back, taking in the lines of her powerful pecs,
her rock-hard biceps, and the thickness of her forearms. Her
handsome face was lit in shadows by rays of light pouring in
from the living room. We stayed like this a moment, not
speaking or touching, just breathing each other in. Then she
told me to wait a minute. She'd be right back. I heard her
head for the bathroom.

Gathering my courage, I took advantage of her absence to
follow through with my fantasy. I opened my bag and pulled
out the maroon satin nightgown I had purchased that afternoon with shaking hands. It was nothing special, almost
plain, with just a little lace around the edges and two thin
straps. It fell just barely over my hips. The last touch, some
rouge lipstick (I had to ask the woman at the counter to help
me pick the shade). The last time I'd worn lipstick was for a
job interview a year before, and it had left me feeling self-conscious and inadequate. After all, pretty women wear makeup,

and on me it could only look out of place. But meeting Shane made me feel I might be wrong in my negative self-estimation, that just maybe I was more than adequate, that I had nothing to hide anymore.

Shane returned wearing men's white underwear bulging with a hard-on. I was a bit surprised but pleased. When she saw me she gasped audibly in astonishment. She then joined me on the bed, and without saying a word she pulled me back so I was lying next to her, or maybe it was him now. Kissing me gently, he whispered again that I was beautiful. Trying to catch hold of my cascading emotions, I held his body against mine. Despite my attempts to regain composure, tears fell from my eyes as past memories of pain and awkwardness bubbled to my surface. I felt my vulnerability keenly. I could only hope I wasn't making a fool of myself. My arms encircling his ribs were in turn encircled by his own, and I buried my head in his chest. Stroking my hair softly, he raised my face to his and kissed my lips again and again with soft, gentle caressing pressure. The tears gradually faded, and my desire for him spread like an electric current through my body.

His back was broad and strong. I stroked his shoulders, his ribs, and his soft, yet muscular, belly (which I noticed had a few soft black hairs trailing a line to his groin). In response, he cupped and squeezed my breasts and kissed my nipples through the shiny fabric. Then he reached down to remove my lace panties. I wish I could better recount the events that followed, for what I remember most are sensations rather than photo images. I remember the way he twirled his tongue inside the lips of my vagina, sliding in and out, penetrating and possessing me. Then he flicked his tongue rapidly against my pulsing clit, and then sucking, held my life between his lips. Just as the intensity became overwhelming, he shifted back to soothing strokes against my labia. I felt wave after wave of ecstasy as our bodies offered up oceans of scent and sweat to each other. I felt like a fountain quenching his thirst.

Again and again I was at the brink of coming, and as he held my thrusting hips with his strong hands, I was open and wet and swimming in desire. Squeezing my eyes shut, I let him guide and carry me to the edge beyond myself.

With each brush and prod of his/her fingers I was awakened with liquid light. When she touched my slippery wetness a tingling circle moved through my abdomen and circled out through my body. We rocked together on the waves of the bed, and she coaxed me with her own sighs, "Come on, come on. That's right. Come on, come on." Her fingers unwound a slippery part of me, and I flowed in waves and waves around her. Crying out, my voice mingled with hers, and I clung to her with a tight grip, gasping and panting wildly until my breathing slowed.

And then gently he turned me so he was behind me and we were both on our knees. He slipped the already disheveled satin gown over my head and brushed his hands downward along my naked body. Then he guided me forward onto my hands and knees. The waves of the waterbed slurped and sloshed to accommodate our movements. He was on his knees behind me, making soft noises between breaths. His hands on my hips pulled me back so that my ass felt the warm flesh of his thighs and stomach. As he rocked us softly, the lukewarm coolness of his hard dick bumped against the cheeks of my ass provocatively.

He paused to remove a condom from the nightstand. "You know, safe sex," he said in a honey-soft woman's voice. I looked back over my shoulder for a moment at the curve of her breasts dangling as she reached for lube which she generously smeared over her cock. And then her voice drifted in from behind me. "I want to hear you say you want me, that you need me."

Without hesitation, I answered, "I do." I felt a thrill of embarrassment and excitement mingling with the eagerness of my cunt, waiting to be touched, to be filled. He touched me lightly with his finger, then pressed his thumb slowly inside me. I pushed back, taking it in, aching and taking.

"I want you to make love to me," I added, my voice cracking, nearly failing me. Suddenly, I felt tense and afraid, but his strong hands gradually massaged away my fear.

"I mean, I want you to fuck me," I told him, my voice trailing off to a barely audible sound. Then I could feel the rubber tip of his dick pushing in against my labia.

"I want to fuck you, baby. I want to take you. I want to make you come. I want you. I want you. I want you." He pulled me back against him, and with each thrust, my fleshy butt slapped pleasantly against his thighs and abdomen. The waterbed was sloshing as though a hurricane had hit. I wanted more and more. Each thrust was the movement between the thirst of wanting and release. I felt myself lost in the churning, in the sound of lapping waves causing the soft impact of our flesh. His belly and hands were my psychic home; otherwise, I was gone from this Earth. And then the wave, a rhythmic pulsing, struck, and I collapsed as he held on. The buzz of life, the melting ache, flowed through my groin and thighs in exuberant pleasure. Exquisite peace flowed through my veins.

Shane and I lay down, our heads side by side on the pillow. Our hands traced one another's outlines, and gradually the ceaseless caresses across our skin became quieter. Eyelids began to flicker lazily. In those last moments before sleep, I held dear the memory of her/his voice coaxing me to voice my need. There was a sweetness to knowing Shane that I will always carry with me. I carry also a sense of wonderment at her masculine beauty. And no, I never cooked her a steak. I never even did her laundry. I thought about it, but instead I left for my home in New York, where, she assured me, I would break some hearts.

Reprise

BY LINDSAY TAYLOR

"No, baby, we can't! We're going to be late!" I exclaimed as I reluctantly pushed Patricia away and fumbled for the black high heels underneath the nightstand. "The parade starts at 11 o'clock sharp. I'd love to, but you know they won't wait for us and our Harley!" I proclaimed, groping for the second shoe.

It was the morning of the annual pride parade in San Francisco: the day when 400,000 people line Market Street, three and four people deep, just to watch this five-hour spectacle and that institution known as Dykes on Bikes leading it off. For many, including Patricia and me, Dykes on Bikes *is* the parade. All else that follows is merely traffic, San Francisco style.

Lacy femmes to the left. Handsome butches to the right. There's so much to take in that I can barely remember to keep my arms wrapped around Patricia's waist as she jockeys for a position among the hundreds of bikes. My heels cling to the newly shined chrome running along the length of her Harley-Davidson. If I do say so myself, I look fab-u-lous: My black fishnet stockings find their way up to black lace underwear that snaps at the crotch, a studded black leather jacket, and matching garter belt. Patricia's shiny black cowboy boots, jutting out from underneath her tight blue jeans, make a definitive *clunk* as they hit the pavement. Topping it off, Patricia's snug black bodysuit accentuates her luscious round nipples.

I've redone my lipstick nine times since we arrived. It's one minute before 11 o'clock. My labia flutter from the vibration of the bike. Patricia eases the engine into a steady, even rhythm. At this point, I could benefit from similar handling.

*   *   *

Patricia and I became lovers two years ago. She was 42 at the time and in her seventh year of private practice as a civil rights attorney. I was a junior arts administrator in San Francisco and in the throes of trying to turn 30. On first impression, Patricia was reluctant to get involved with a baby dyke whose main focus seemed to be "the scene." I had reservations about getting involved with a 40-something dyke from the burbs, a.k.a. Berkeley, who seemed too staid. For Patricia, I was too "out there." For me, Patricia was not "out there" enough. But after our first night together, our concerns were more than quelled, which culminated in Patricia's feeling she had finally found someone who could keep up with her in bed (I have humbly concluded) and my nearly wanting to have Patricia's baby after I sat on the beautiful Harley-Davidson she showed me in the morning. When we rode together in Dykes on Bikes later that year, I finished the ride knowing I could now die a fulfilled woman.

*   *   *

A large, leather-clad butch dyke raises her right hand, as if she is about to take an oath, and uses her left hand as a makeshift megaphone. She bellows the command, "Ladies, start your engines!" but her words are barely audible over the roar of the bikes already in gear. She signals "go" by blowing hard on her whistle, saliva shooting out as she exhales. The piercing sound of the whistle slices through the din. Patricia and I lurch forward and veer down Market Street. For the next 30 minutes, this famed urban thoroughfare, connecting the San Francisco Bay to Castro Street U.S.A., belongs to 300 strong, proud women.

I grow hoarse as we make our way down Market Street but continue to yell and wave to the appreciative throng on either side of us. Tall buildings hover above the crowd, casting long shadows over the thousands of people clapping and whistling. A bare-chested woman on a nearby motorcycle blows kisses to her newly found adoring fans. At the corner of Market and Powell Streets, site of the famed cable car turnaround, a quintessential band of tourists stands frozen in its tracks. Before long, the aptly named Ferry Building, located at the end of Market Street, draws nearer, signaling that this extended quasi-orgasm, mixed with leather, adrenaline, and sweat, will soon end.

* * *

In the "these are a few of my favorite things" category, Patricia enjoyed skiing and backpacking. I enjoyed writing and reapplying lipstick. In the beginning this partnership saw its share of culture clashes. But after ten months of dating and shuttling back and forth over the Bay Bridge to see one another, and in the process growing more appreciative of each other's differences, Patricia and I decided to move in together. After much debate, I moved out of the city and into Patricia's home in the East Bay. In doing so, I became the very thing I bemoaned Patricia for being: a suburban dyke. As I tried to reconcile this fact, I came upon the realization that by moving to the East Bay, I would finally have a parking space to call my own. Given the slower pace there, maybe I would even get to that novel I had been talking about writing for the past ten years.

* * *

As Patricia glides past the base of the Ferry Building, the walls of my vagina throb. She pulls into a vacant spot in a long row of bikes. She shifts the engine into neutral and reaches for the kickstand with her left boot. In unspoken sync, we rock the bike into a parked position, steadying it between our thighs as we move. "My God, another year, and it's already over," I protest.

I want more.

I wrap my arms around Patricia's waist as she moves to get off the bike. "Finish what you started this morning, baby," I challenge. "Fuck me," I whisper, squeezing her from behind.

Without uttering a word, Patricia hurls the engine into first. I'm already in third. The sound of the ensuing parade fades, as she makes her way down Folsom Street, running red lights when the coast is clear.

Patricia pulls into the famed Dore Alley, located off Folsom Street near the equally famed Powerhouse leather bar. "Get on your back, baby," she instructs, hopping off the bike and positioning herself next to me.

I turn myself around on the warm, sweaty seat and slowly, teasingly slide onto my back. In return, Patricia slowly, teasingly spreads my legs along each side of the bike. "I want you to fuck me so badly," I whimper, as she unsnaps my fishnets and peels each of them down to my ankles. I raise my buttocks off the seat just long enough for her to unsnap the crotch of my lace underwear. With one quick snap, Patricia unleashes the black leather belt from her jeans, yanking it through all her belt loops in one fell swoop. With it, she secures my wrists to the handlebars. "Fuck me, baby...I can't wait another second," I groan.

Patricia rips the top half of her bodysuit down the middle. Her breasts pop out and spring toward me. She spreads my thighs and runs her nipples along the insides of my labia. The strain from my hands being tied makes me want to burst. I dig my heels into the chrome. "God, baby, just go inside...*please*," I beg.

Patricia knows I'm desperate...and completely given over to her. Just the way we like it.

She enters me and moves forcefully inside. "Hard and deep...ride me...fuck me as hard as you can," I call out, as those familiar vibrations begin to swell. I've surrendered to her and am loving every single second of it. The ripples keep coming as she moves steadily inside me.

As the ripples subside, I draw my knees together, signaling Patricia to stop. She edges toward my face, kissing me softly on my lips and forehead. Her breath lingers outside my ear, sending ripples back down my legs. "Fuck me again, baby, and give me *all* you've got," I command, spreading my legs.

Now Patricia is mine. All mine. Just the way we like it.

* * *

Bruno the cat rustles in the kitchen, breaking the Sunday morning silence. I turn to read the clock: 10:15. Patricia stirs beside me. "Oh, my God, baby, we've gotta hurry! The parade starts in less than an hour!" I exclaim as I reach for the black high heels hastily cast under the nightstand the night before.

* * *

As Patricia and I zoom off to the parade, I have a good feeling about what lies ahead.

Close Encounters

BY LOU HILL

It was summer 1977. I was in the military, stationed in San Antonio, Tex. I could tell it was going to be a strange weekend. I was oddly at loose ends. Nowhere to go and no one to play with. Betsy was visiting her folks in New Orleans, and Rose had gone camping with her lover, Ann.

Betsy was my live-in lover. Rose was my lover on the side. Maybe on the sly would better describe it. I considered calling Cathy, then decided against it. No need to complicate our little afternoon delight arrangement.

I know, I know. My love life sounds complicated, but it was really quite simple. I lived with Betsy, and Rose lived with Ann. Rose and I got together every chance we could. Sometimes I'd stop by her place early in the morning after Ann left for school. We made love in the bed they shared each night. They still cared about each other but were sexually incompatible. Actually, Rose was crazy about Ann, but Ann's energy was consumed by school. Betsy and I were still playing at being a couple, but the relationship was slowly unraveling. Betsy's sexual hang-ups consumed her, and it was beginning to wear thin.

Cathy was a good-looking young woman who strongly resembled a young Gloria Steinem, with long golden-brown hair and large round glasses. We got together a couple of times a week to share our lunch hour. Sex was sexy, and we had a great time together. But ours was strictly a sexual thing. I'd never spent much time talking to her.

So, what to do? I didn't usually like to hit the bars alone, but I decided to go out. I needed the noise of other people.

The bar was busy. I sat alone the first part of the evening, just watching the women on the dance floor, listening to the music, studying the crowd. There weren't many familiar faces. A new class of students at Fort Sam Houston partied noisily, admiring each other's new tattoos. I missed Rose. I wondered what Betsy was doing in New Orleans. For one fleeting moment I thought I should have gone with her.

A woman approached my table and asked me to dance. We sat talking together. I don't remember her name or what she looked like. She was only a small piece of the bigger picture. She told me about a concert the next evening.

"If you're not busy, perhaps you'd like to go." I thought about it and decided what the heck. I wasn't busy, so I agreed. She said she would pick me up.

Saturday evening arrived. I began to think I should have canceled, but I didn't know her number. So I dressed. And I waited. I was not attracted to this woman. The evening was merely a diversion, a way to kill time.

The doorbell rang. I opened the door, greeted her, followed her out to the parking lot, and climbed into the back seat of a waiting car. She introduced me to her friends, Carol and Jen. I paid little attention to the couple in the front seat. They seemed indifferent and hardly noticed one another.

The concert filled some time. Afterward, we decided to go to a bar on the other side of town. It was a different crowd. I was curious. We found a booth and slid into the seats. I watched the dance floor and wondered if I would see anyone I knew.

Then it happened. One of the women—I thought her name was Carol—asked me to dance. I agreed. I slid from the booth and moved to the dance floor. Carol followed me. I turned and allowed her to envelop me in her arms. She pulled me closer to her. A sudden electric rush ran through me. The hair on the back of my neck stood up.

I leaned back and stared at this woman, this stranger who had elicited such a reaction. Our eyes met, and I could tell she knew. I saw in her liquid brown eyes that she had felt it too. We didn't speak. I leaned against her and felt the tingle pass back and forth. Her hands slid down my back, and her touch was strong. Her breath warmed my neck. I heard the little catch in her breathing, and I knew she was wet. She wanted me. And I wanted her.

But there was still the problem of her lover. The dance ended. We moved reluctantly away from one another. I was afraid to look at her, afraid her lover would see something in my gaze, something that would give away the desire I felt.

The evening came to a close. They dropped me outside the apartment and waited until I had opened the front door. Then they drove away, and I was alone.

Sunday morning. I was sitting alone in the living room, drinking coffee and reading the newspaper. The doorbell rang. I opened the door.

Carol stood on the front step. She extended a single red rose. She moved toward me, wrapped her arms around me, and pulled me to her. I closed the door behind her. Our lips met, and I felt certain I would melt into the carpet. She exuded sunlight, and its warmth coursed through me.

I stepped back and studied her. Dark brown hair framed her face. Her nose was thin and straight. A deep cleft divided her chin. Her lips were full, sensual. She was a handsome woman.

Bashfully, she handed me the rose. I brushed the rose against my cheek. Her smile revealed perfect teeth.

"I wasn't sure you would come," I said.

"I couldn't stay away," she answered.

I took Carol by the hand and led her up the stairs. We undressed each other slowly, without words. She was taller than me. Her breasts were small and firm, her bush a thick, dark forest. Her skin was pale beneath her clothes, contrasting with the dark tan of her face, neck, and arms.

We moved to my unmade bed, the bed I shared with Betsy. Sunlight streamed through the slats in the blinds. Carol covered me with kisses. There seemed to be all the time in the world. Her kisses grew deeper and harder as her desire grew.

Carol's mouth found my erect nipple. She sucked hungrily. My body responded without question.

I explored her body. I ran my hands over her back. She was muscular and lean. I squeezed her ass, and she moaned, grinding her pelvis against me. She quivered in anticipation. I didn't want her to come, not yet, not like that.

I pushed hard against her, and she rolled onto her back. I knelt by her side. Carol looked at me expectantly. Her right hand moved to my waist and squeezed. I leaned down. My lips met hers. I explored her mouth with my tongue.

I pressed my body against hers. The electricity was strong. Carol arched her shoulders, as if to come even closer. I held her down. I knew she was stronger, but she didn't fight.

She spread her legs, opening herself to me. I moved down her body like Hansel and Gretel in the forest, leaving a trail with my lips and tongue. A tiny moan escaped her throat.

I lay between Carol's legs near the bottom of the bed. Her eyes were closed, her head against the pillow. I pushed the palm of my hand against her, massaging her mons. She pushed against my hand. I slid my hand downward and ran my fingers along the glistening wetness of her desire.

My fingers parted her labia. Her swollen clit was exposed for my inspection. I pushed my crotch against the bed. I buried my face in her crotch, my tongue in her slit. Carol moaned louder this time. My stomach rose and fell. Now the moan was mine.

She pushed against my face. I licked her clit, tickling it with the tip of my tongue. I ran my tongue across her asshole. I felt her muscles tighten, so I moved away. She relaxed as I lapped the juices of her cunt.

I was like an addict. Deeply, I inhaled her scent; I drank her taste. I reveled in the velvet feel of her passion. I pressed my flattened tongue against her, as I moved against the knotted covers beneath me, my own passion growing more urgent.

I filled Carol's emptiness with two, then three fingers. She swallowed them greedily. She moved with me, her breathing growing louder, more erratic. Sexy little noises filled the air. Slowly, rhythmically, I circled, caressed, and nibbled her pulsing clit.

Carol was coming closer and closer. I slipped my fingers from her vagina and pressed one to the pucker of her ass. My tongue moved more quickly over her clit. I pushed my thumb deep into her vagina. This time she didn't protest, and my finger pushed past her defenses.

I squeezed my finger and thumb together, marveling at how close they were to each other, one in her ass, the other in her vagina. She exploded. Her clitoris heralded the arrival of her orgasm like a tiny trumpet. Her muscles clamped down, convulsing against my finger and thumb.

"O-o-oh," she cried.

I was so close, so close. I slipped my fingers from her and moved to the head of the bed. I straddled her face and spread my lips for her. Carol pushed her hands against my ass and licked me furiously. It was over in seconds, and I leaned against the wall, feeling the convulsions of my own orgasm.

Afterward, we lay in bed, not talking, barely breathing. Only after we had showered and dressed did we engage in the small talk normally associated with a first date. She was in the Air National Guard. She told me she and Jen were having problems. "I met someone while I was on a temporary duty assignment in Georgia. We had an affair. No big deal, but she followed me home. I don't really love either of them right now."

I smiled. Life was just too complicated sometimes.

"Can I see you again?" she asked.

"I don't think so," I answered. "It just wouldn't be a good idea. I've got too many people in my life already. And so do you." She nodded. She said it didn't matter. She would accept whatever time we could find. I kissed her and told her I would think about it.

Carol and I saw each other just once after that. We met at a football field on the base where we both worked. I sat waiting in the bleachers. I recognized her car when she pulled into the parking lot. She climbed out and strode toward me. She was wearing fatigues.

Oh, God, I thought. *She looks so sexy.* I'm a sucker for a woman in fatigues.

She told me she was transferring to Houston. She needed to get away from the women who were driving her crazy. We shook hands, and then she drove away.

I've thought about Carol once in a while over the years. And I wonder if she remembers that one Sunday afternoon we shared when we were both so young and wild.

Song of the Siren

BY BRENDA HANSON

What you are about to read is true. The names and a few subtle details have been changed to preserve my dignity.

Karaoke has never led to anything good for me. I should avoid it altogether, but something in me can't resist the possibility of the perfect performance. I know what you're thinking, but I never actually get on stage. I go to watch and listen. There thrives in me an irrepressible admiration for anyone with the nerve to submit their vocal cords to the scrutiny of a drunken crowd of armchair opera stars. No matter how bad, how dissonant or sloppy, I am charmed. The problem, however, is not my affection for the audio underdog. The problem is my susceptibility to sirens, my lust for the fierce, intoxicating notes. My ears are sluts.

I found Heather at the Ridge, a frat-boy–infested bar and grill in the university district. I was 18, and wasn't supposed to be able to access the karaoke—something about "live entertainment" and the magic number 21. But the karaoke made its home in the front portion of the restaurant, well outside the walls of the bar, and 15 or more of us, all graduates or graduates-to-be of a nearby high school, made our home in the front of the Ridge every Saturday night. With the exception of me, everyone in our group got up to sing, usually the same few songs every week. Fortunately, most of them could more or less carry a tune. I enjoyed watching them—their fascination with songs that should have died with the rest of the '80s, their endless seductions of one another over the microphone. I especially appreciated their lack of attention to my social voyeurism.

One week someone from our group brought friends from another nearby town to join our karaoke clan. Among those who came that night, I remember only Heather. I watched as she joined the table next to mine and began flipping through the songbook. Every couple of pages, her head tilted and her lips parted and seemed to twitch. Maybe she was trying to hear how a particular selection would go over. I don't really know and at the time didn't care. I was much more concerned with looking her over as inconspicuously as I could.

Heather had long nails, full breasts, and the sexiest mouth I had ever seen. Everything she did with that mouth dripped with sensuality—the way she smoked, the way she ate, the way she spoke, smiled, laughed, and breathed. It made me want to put my tongue or finger in there and just let it roll around in the sex of it all. I lusted after her mouth from the start. Then she got up to sing.

I may never understand what about me Heather first found intriguing, but I've no doubt what it was that drew me to her. She had one of those voices nature seems to endow a few folks with on some ecstatic whim, one that no amount of training can match, and she delivered the words to every song with a tone so sultry she could make the national anthem sound like a come-on. That night she had chosen "I Wanna Dance With Somebody (Who Loves Me)," and as I watched her hips shift and her arms open, I could tell she meant it. The good thing about karaoke is that you have permission to stare at anyone on stage. The great thing about Heather and karaoke was that she closed her eyes for considerable periods of time while she sang.

I watched Heather intently, studying her gestures. She gently pressed her fisted fingers just under her diaphragm when she held a long note. When she broke the note, her hand swept to her side as if clearing the way for the next breath. Her hips swayed not in response to, but in anticipation of, the rhythm. She smiled a lot when she sang. It could have been a nervous response to performing, but I preferred to think the music truly delighted her. Heather didn't simply sing along to the music; it was as though she became the music. And watching her was like hearing it through my eyes.

Heather became a regular at the Ridge. I became a puppy. I still went to karaoke to watch and to listen, but my focus had narrowed considerably. I strategically sat so no one watching the stage could see me watching Heather. Sometimes she sat at the same table I did, but mostly she didn't sit at all. Along with four or five other girls from our clan, Heather danced near the brass railing separating the part of the restaurant we were in from the passageway to the door. I've always been fascinated by the way straight girls dance together, seemingly oblivious to the touches that pass between them. I watched Heather press her palm flat against the small of the back of the girl facing her, her body full of mock passion, her mouth laughing. Even in the dim light of the Ridge, the stone on her left hand flashed and bounced with the rest of her, announcing on the half-beat, "straight, taken, straight, taken." Heather, I soon learned, was engaged to a military boy stationed in Hawaii.

One night I overheard a conversation between Heather and the friend she was with: Her friend wanted to leave, but Heather wasn't ready. Despite my studied shyness, I interrupted.

"Heather," I said, privately savoring this first passage of the name past my lips, "I can take you home later if you want."

She regarded me for a moment, seeming to take me in for the first time. We had shared a few casual exchanges, and I knew from friends that she had inquired into my quiet,

stand-offish ways. She also had been told I was a dyke.
Would she be willing to be seen leaving alone with me, to get
in a car with me, to let me take her home? Of course, she had
the magic ring on her finger to protect her.

"OK," Heather said. "Thanks."

It was a just-add-water kind of friendship; one day we
were strangers, the next inseparable. I think my mother
(whose house I still lived in on the nights I actually came
home) worried for me. I had been out to my mom for almost
a year. Although I had mentioned Heather was straight, I'm
sure she saw the change in my eyes when Saturday came
around and I knew I'd be staying at Heather's place post-
karaoke. Nothing compares to watching the object of one's
desire in a shimmering public display for hours before lying
quietly beside her and facing the other way. I acquired an intimate knowledge of Heather's eastern bedroom wall over
those many weeks.

I wrote her poems—some in my head, some on paper, all
of them bad. I shared them with her anyway, and she fussed
over them. None of them mentioned my desire for her. I told
myself I wasn't willing to jeopardize our friendship, but
telling her would simply have been redundant: One look at
my face when I set eyes on her was statement enough for anyone. Everyone knew I wanted her. Heather knew it, and she
encouraged it. It's flattering to be desired; who could blame
her for delighting in it? She gobbled up every morsel of my
doting and licked her lips for more. I delivered.

"Do you ever wonder what it would be like?" Heather
asked. She was sitting on the edge of her bed, eyeing me as I
crouched on the other side of the room stuffing the clothes I
had just changed out of into my backpack. That night at
karaoke, she had dedicated "That's What Friends Are For" to
me, and I had been distracted with overanalyzing its signifi-
cance. I wanted simply to accept it as a sweet gesture, but
wondered if Heather was underscoring the fact that what we

shared was only a friendship. Was she reacting to the predictable rumors circulating about us? Although I was quite aware of the difference between lust and love, I did care about Heather and wondered if maybe it wouldn't be better if we separated for a while, since clearly I couldn't disguise my feelings.

"What what would be like?" I asked over the zippering of my pack.

"Us," she said. "If we, you know, if something happened..." her voice trailed off.

Answering honestly did not seem advisable, even if she had brought it up. I resisted opening my mouth for fear of pouring out the lurid details of my explicit imaginings. I played dumb and stared at her, expressionless. Was this the beginning of the conversation I thought it was?

She held my gaze for a moment before dropping her eyes and saying, as if to the fidgeting fingers she held in her lap, "It's just that I've been thinking lately, you know, about us, about how we are together." She glanced up at me briefly, undoubtedly hoping for a little help. I felt for her, and I could see she was nervous as hell, but I didn't have it in me to go out on a limb for her. I'd been bitten by too many squirrels already. Besides, how did I know she wasn't just fishing for the thrill of hearing me say, "Heather, I really, really want you"? Maybe she was an attention addict. Maybe my adoring gaze alone had ceased to produce a high. She took a tight breath and said, "I've never, you know, been with a woman, so how do I know it's not something I want?"

I refrained from telling her I hadn't either, but I knew what I wanted. I certainly didn't want to talk her out of anything. I had to say something. "What do you think you want?" was the best I could do.

"I want to find out."

I could've sworn in that moment I saw something small and hairy scurry from under the bed and make a break for the door. I thought it looked like a guinea pig. I stared at the floor until I had finished an internal debate on my willingness to walk out onto a rodent-infested stage.

"Are you saying you want to sleep with me?" It seemed like a safe enough question—no commitment from me, and a clean opportunity for her to give me precise insight into what I desperately wanted her to be saying. I still wasn't prepared for her answer.

"Yes."

Neither of us moved. I didn't need to express my willingness. Despite her nervousness, I doubt if Heather ever questioned it. The question was how it was going to come about. It has never been easy for anyone to convince me that I am desired, but the women who want to be *seduced* by me face the greatest challenge.

"So," she said after several minutes, "what do we do now?"

"I don't know." I honestly didn't. I had come out at 17 without knowing a single other queer. I had read every book on the subject I could get my hands on. I had pointedly marked myself as a dyke at school and had pushed every person I encountered to open their mind to make room for me. Although I was by no means the first to journey out, I had blazed every trail on my own, and I had really hoped that when this moment finally came, someone else would lead the way.

"Maybe we should get in the bed…" she said. Heather clearly didn't want to be in charge, and it was more of a question than anything, but it was a directive enough for me.

"OK," I said, and gratefully made my way over, flipping the light switch en route as she scooted toward the pillows.

We got into the bed, sliding beneath the covers as we had so many times before. Exactly as we had before. We lay on our backs, arms at our sides, a good two feet between us. I was paralyzed. I was so accustomed to containing my desire that I was unsure how to express it. It made no difference that I had imagined this moment a thousand times—once in it, I was at a loss for inspiration. Finally, whether out of courage or impatience, Heather rolled over and curled into me. I pulled my left arm from between us and wrapped it around her, drawing her in. Her left leg slipped between my thighs and settled somewhere between my knees and my crotch. I was sure if she moved it any higher, my heat would burn her. I drew the deep breath of an involuntary sigh, bringing the head that was resting on my chest close to my face. She smelled of soap and cigarettes, with a hint of the perfume she had put on that morning. From its resting place on the arm she had wrapped around me, I brought my right hand up to her head and touched her hair. To my surprise, it was soft (Heather had the kind of hairstyle that keeps Aqua Net in business). I stroked her hair, occasionally letting a finger or two explore the line of her cheek. How daring.

After a couple of minutes, Heather said, "That feels nice, but it's putting me to sleep." It was already almost dawn, and letting her sleep didn't sound like a bad idea. I couldn't, in that moment, actually imagine anything more lovely. I could, however, imagine her waking up the next morning having changed her mind. I don't think it occurred to me that this might be a "onetime thing, no matter what." I could only think of experiencing firsthand how good my imagination had assured me this was going to feel.

Somewhere in my belly, desire joined forces with courage. I rolled Heather onto her back and brought my face to hers, pausing only to glance at the slightly parted lips of the mouth that had first brought the taste of desire into my own throat. The tip of my tongue found the swell of her lower lip and made its way slowly to each corner before flicking lightly over the cleft at the center of her upper one. Heather lay perfectly still, hands quiet at the small of my back, only her quickening breath on my chin offering any encouragement. I was beginning to have doubts, but when I pushed my mouth fully over hers, her jaw loosened and invited me deeper. I don't know how long I was lost in the wet heat of that mouth before I remembered my hands.

Simply because she was wearing a flannel top with buttons, I felt the need to undo them rather than slip the shirt off over her head. I've never worked so hard at anything in my life. I shook and fumbled, eventually employing both hands, all the while determined to maintain our kiss. Heather dragged her fingernails back and forth from my waist to what would be my hips (if I had any) as I finally freed the last button from its hole and spread the shirt to her sides. I gave up the kiss to pull back and have a look at her.

I was the only woman with whom I'd ever truly been intimate. Heather's body could not have been more different from my own. Where I was small and tight, Heather was full and soft. I was fascinated by the texture of the breasts that spread over her torso. Mine were barely distinguishable even as I arched over her. Her hands slid under my T-shirt and managed to find them anyway. I clamped my mouth over her nipple to conceal my gasp. Now, I've never had my own nipple in my mouth, but I'm certain that if I could get it in there I wouldn't find it to have the same slippery quality as Heather's. I kissed my way down to the softness of her belly while my own jumped and tightened as her nails skidded over it and under the waistband of my leggings.

With her hand cupped over my cunt, she drew me back up for a kiss. If nothing else, I would have complied out of fear of those nails. I was embarrassingly wet and decided it was probably a good thing Heather's hand was pinned against me by the tightness of my leggings since their elasticity seemed to be the only thing helping her keep a grip on my slickness. Her palm and the lengths of several fingers pressed and rubbed against me, seeming less than sure of how to handle me. The clumsiness made no difference; I'd never been so aroused in my life. Desire won out over shyness, and I came out to play.

My mouth locked on hers. My hips driving eagerly forward to meet her hand, I inched Heather's boxers down over her broad hips and pressed my palm slowly into her hair. It was thin and soft—a surprising contrast to the coarseness of my own. Somewhere in my head, a little voice struck up a chant about snips and snails and puppy dog tails, and Heather suddenly seemed all sugar and spice and very, very nice. I slipped one finger down the center of her and began a slow series of strokes from the opening of her vagina to the top of her clit and back again, distributing her wetness as I went. I left her mouth and let my tongue, lips, and teeth explore the length of her throat, the round of her shoulder, the crook of her elbow. I slid the palm of my left hand to the back of her ribs and allowed the toes of my right foot to get acquainted with the arch of her left. I was lost in her and loving it. That's probably why it took me several minutes to recognize that Heather had stopped moving altogether.

I brought my face back into alignment with hers and moved my hand from between her legs to her waist. Heather removed her hands from me entirely and folded them on her belly. She didn't meet my eyes.

"Are you all right?" I asked despite the obvious fact that somehow she wasn't.

"Mmm-hmm."

"Do you want me to keep going?"

"I don't know."

I knew this was a lie, that certainly she didn't want any more of this, and I felt somewhat relieved since I really wasn't sure what I would have done next if she had wanted me to continue. Still, it did seem sort of awkward just to stop. I didn't know who I would be if we sat up and tried to resume being *that which friends are for.*

I moved off her and lay propped on my elbow, watching her rebutton her shirt. She made it look so easy. Both of us were silent as she enclosed herself back into her boxers and disappeared out the door into the kitchen. I stayed in bed for a few minutes, staring at the western wall for a change. It was early morning and light outside again. Everything I had previously felt willing to brave seemed suddenly more naked than we ever had gotten, more vulnerable, more pathetic.

I found Heather sitting at the kitchen table staring in alternation at the clock and out the window. I sat in the chair next to her and waited, choosing the center of the table as my fixation point. As long as I maintained my focus on that spot I was sure I could keep all this from spinning out of control. Heather turned her face to me and distracted my gaze.

"I'm supposed to be at church right now."

I had never known Heather to go to church on any other Sunday morning, but I knew perfectly well that wasn't her point. Heather had already turned her face away from me again, and I was staring at the profile of her beloved mouth, trying to understand how it had changed with its most recent words, when she gave a little laugh and added, "You know, Greg always talks about his fantasies of me with another woman. At least when I call him at the base and confess this, I can tell him I granted his wish even if he wasn't here to see it."

I returned my gaze to the tabletop, trying and failing to find its center, and reviewed the facts: I had been seduced by a high-femme, long-nailed straight girl while she was supposed to be at church, who now intended to titillate her fiancé with the details of her experimental sexual encounter with me. My sex life, not even properly begun, was already a lesbian cliché.

I stood up and went into the bedroom. The sheets lay twisted and tangled on the bed. I didn't bother to change; I just pulled my jeans on over my leggings and put on my coat, slinging my backpack over my shoulder.

"Well, see you later," I mumbled as I passed her on my way to the door.

"Yeah," she said to the clock. "See you."

Days passed. I felt like an ass. It's funny how granted wishes can take the form of nightmares. I had wanted to be with a woman, and Heather had become that woman. I had touched her, tasted her, breathed her in. I had done most of everything I had wanted. Technically speaking, my desire had been fulfilled; in reality, I only felt empty.

The next time we saw one another, it was in the safety of about six million of our closest friends. We heard all the same old songs, watched the same old moves, gave the same old performances for one another. Nothing was the same. I hardly looked at Heather that night, and she never came over to my table. I peered at every piece of the Ridge I could see, trying to understand how a place could be so unchanged and feel so different, how Heather could be just feet away and seem so inaccessible, how I could be there of my own free will and still feel trapped. I finally got her alone by giving her a ride home. She sat in the passenger seat staring straight ahead. It wasn't until I pulled into her drive that she finally spoke.

"I'm sorry," she whispered.

I wondered which of the million things I felt miserable about might be the one she meant.

"I used you," she said, "like a lab rat." *Guinea pig,* I thought. "I don't think of you as one, but I used you like one."

"It's OK," I said before she got out of the car. What I didn't say was, "I used you too."

A Lesson in Manners and Locution Well-taken

I worked as a secretary at a large law firm in New York City. Naturally, I would wear the attire I was expected to, but I would add my own twist, so to speak. I'd wear one of those butterfly vibrators strapped inside my panties, which would get me really hot during the day. Then I'd take a lengthy bathroom break to take matters into my own hands.

A client was coming into the office, and she arrived sooner than scheduled—that is, before I had a chance to indulge myself in the bathroom. She was an older woman, and despite the suit, I could tell she was a dyke—a butch to be sure. She was very businesslike, which made my perverse, transgressive nature come to the fore. I leaned forward just enough for my silk blouse to reveal two very firm breasts. I made sure she got a great view of my tight ass. There was an instant chemistry between us, and although I was my usual efficient, professional self, I felt jarred inwardly. I was extremely attracted to this woman. Toward the end of the day, she asked if I knew a good place to have dinner near her hotel. She invited me to join her, and while the conversation remained superficial, images of what it might be like to submit to this very handsome butch danced right behind my eyes.

It turned out she had left some documents in the conference room at the office and had to go back. She needed me to
accompany her since I had the key to get in. We reached the
conference room, and I was aware of an urgent, pulsating
throb in my groin. I stood facing the window against the corner of the conference room table. I felt her behind me, and I
could smell her cologne. I leaned forward just a little so she
would be rubbing up against my ass. She was slightly taller
than me, and as she reached around to caress my thighs, I felt
something hard in the small of my back. She reached up to
touch my breasts, and I began to get nervous.

"I don't think we should be doing this. There are still people in the office," I said.

Her voice was low and self-assured. "Listen, you bitch, I've
been smelling the musky scent of your cunt ever since I
walked in here, and I want some," she said determinedly.

I tried to move away, and then she ripped open my silk
blouse. She wedged her foot between my feet and pushed them
apart. I was completely off balance, and she pushed me forward. I felt like an animal submitting myself for approval. She
lifted my skirt to mid thigh, and I heard something click *snap*.
She had taken out a small switchblade. I was both terrified and
excited, and felt my cunt juice getting caught up in my panty
hose. She was biting my neck and spread my legs even farther
apart. She took the switchblade and ripped through my panty
hose. I am meticulous about shaving around my cunt, leaving
only a tiny triangle of pubic hair. Thus, my sweet, throbbing
cunt—pink, slick, and very vulnerable—was completely exposed. There was nothing between it and her hard fuck pole.
She placed her hands on my hips and pulled me toward her. I
whimpered, begging her not to hurt me. She told me she was
packing and had ten inches of raw, hard dick—which was at
least two inches wide—strapped to her waist.

"I've never had anything that big inside me before," I
whispered.

"I'm honored to be the first."

She mounted me and began to tease the edges of my cunt with her prick, moving her hips in a circular motion to stimulate all my sensitive spots. I needed her badly but wasn't sure I could take all that inside me. I moved forward just a little, and suddenly she thrust herself deep inside. I yelped; the pain was intense and exquisite, and she started to ride me, thrusting in and out. She told me I felt like a bitch in heat, and she wanted all of me. I wanted to be possessed by this woman. She was thrusting hard, and she was in so deep I could feel the front of her thighs, hard, muscular, and sweating against the backs of mine. Her hands controlled the movement of my hips, and as she thrust in forcefully, she pulled my hips toward her. I felt as if I were being ripped apart, but I was also aware of the pressure building up like a tidal wave deep inside my cunt. My muscles were starting to contract around her prick. Suddenly she started to pull out of me.

"Since you've teased my cock all day, I thought I'd reciprocate the favor," she said, as she slowly started to withdraw, inch by inch, enjoying how slick her cock was with my juice.

"Don't go, come back inside," I begged, as I rotated my hips and ass, as if that would magically beckon her back.

"Come back inside where?" she imitated my plaintive tone. "I don't know why you femmes have such a hard time saying 'pussy.' I want to teach you how to say it—slowly and with a purr. It's such a shame someone with a pussy as sweet and fine as yours can't say it."

Haltingly, I obeyed and whispered, "Come back inside my pussy."

"My, my. Now that we've learned a new word, have we forgotten our manners, or did we not have any to begin with? I want you to say 'please' as you beg for my cock, and I want you to tell me just how badly your sweet pussy wants it," she demanded.

"Please come back inside my pussy and fuck me hard. I

need your cock. Please give it to me. I need you," I moaned.

Slowly she obliged—it was excruciatingly slow. She could feel my pussy pulling at her cock, milking and wrapping tightly around it, afraid to let it go. She was groaning, telling me she wanted to explode deep inside me, fill me with her love juice, that she wanted to impregnate me, but that she also had never allowed herself to come while she was inside a woman. "It's about control," she said.

Gaining a sense of what might turn her on, I urged her not to come inside me. "I'm not using anything, and I'm in heat. Please don't come inside me."

"No self-respecting butch would pull out of a sweet, tight pussy and waste her seed on the floor," she hissed. Her thrusting became more urgent as she yelled, "Goddamn you! Shit!" I felt the front of her thighs tensing against the back of mine, and she lost her control, pulling at me, and biting hard on the back of my neck as she came. The idea of being possessed by her like that drove me over the edge, and my cunt started to contract. I was shaking, convulsing, unable to stop. As I started to come down from this wave, she took her thumb, reached around, and moistened it with the cream that was streaming down my legs. She moved her thumb to my asshole and started making circular movements. I told her no and started to bite her arm, which was pulling my shoulder back. She insisted we weren't done yet. With her prick still inside my cunt, she forced her thumb into my ass. It burned and hurt, and my head jerked back from the pain, but strangely, being so filled made my cunt begin to throb again.

After fucking me several more times, she withdrew from my ass and cunt. I could barely walk. She got on her knees and licked the juices dripping down my legs, and kissed my clit gently. She told me I should go home and get some sleep and that tomorrow was going to be a busy day at the office.

Lipstick Boy

BY KRISTEN E. PORTER

Provincetown. My birthday. Friends. What could be better?

We are at the club—the only lesbian club in the area, which is strange for such a gay town. I dance a bit by myself and am furious to find out that during my jaunt to the dance floor my friends decided to go back to the hotel. I sit myself down, waiting for the clock to strike midnight and have my 28th year finally be over. Tick. Tock. Twelve. I'm overwhelmed that here I am, it's my birthday, and no one is here to celebrate with me.

I begin to think about my ex-lover who was supposed to be here. We just broke up a few days ago, and I told her not to come. It isn't unusual for me to be alone. Nor is it unusual for me to be forgotten about. My thoughts ride quickly down, spiraling into a sea of self-defeating feelings. 12:10 A.M....still my birthday...still sitting at the club. Tears roll down my face.

Maybe people will think they are just drops of sweat from dancing, or maybe no one will notice in this dimly lit bar. Jesus, I told myself this year would be better. Saturn is supposedly outta my damn sign. I can't believe they left. Before midnight, even! This sucks. What am I supposed to do? I've gotta just let go and move on. I can still have fun by myself.

With that thought, I glance over to the bar and spot a delicious woman walking by. Our eyes meet. She smiles, and perhaps with one too many cosmopolitans, I blurt out, "It's my birthday!" She saunters over, wearing a burgundy lace slip and leopard-print jacket. She is an exotic beauty, a goddess appearing from nowhere. Her skin is a translucent olive color, and right between her eyebrows sparkles a deep red jewel of some sort. Not a real one, but one of those trendy stick-on jewels.

With a sexy smoker's voice, she says, "How 'bout a birthday kiss?" Her eyes are like a Persian cat's and burn right through me. She leans over and puts her lips against mine. Soft and strong. Her tongue darts for mine.

We kiss deeply for what feels like a few minutes. The space between my legs throbs, and my hunger for her melts into a wetness I haven't felt during a kiss in a long time. With my arm around her waist, I feel the strings of her thong, the curve of her hips.

Is this really happening? Is it really happening to me? Shit, I wish I could stop thinking and just kiss her. Just enjoy her.

The club lights turn up, and in their fluorescent horror her crimson stain appears all over my face. She grabs some bar napkins and wipes my face.

Leave your stain on me so I'll have a memory of your gift. I don't care if your lipstick stays on my face forever. I am in awe of you, the situation. I am immersed in a fantasy I can't even imagine, let alone believe, is happening right here, right now, to me.

"Do you want to get a slice of pizza?" she asks.

"Yeah, sure," I answer, thinking I never want tonight to end.

We sit on the sidewalk eating our slices, watching the people pass by, chatting. Silly talk. Friend talk. Sex talk. Drunk talk.

"What's your name?" I wonder if this will ruin the mystery and magic.

"Asia," she replies.

Like the continent, I assume, although I'm not sure I heard
her correctly. "I've traveled all over Europe, the U.S., and
Asia, and picked that up as my name. I think I'm off next to
the Islands. I want to open up a bed-and-breakfast there."

"Wow. That's adventurous. How do you support yourself
along the way?"

"I go to a place, stay for a while, strip until I save up
enough money, and move on. I live in my van with my dog."

This all sounds too bizarre. Maybe she's a struggling ac-
tress and is trying out a new role on me? Maybe she's a
pathological liar? A scam artist? Maybe she is a stripper
named Asia who lives in a van and travels around the world
with her dog. I can hear my friend Michael's voice: *Leave it
to you to pick up the homeless for your birthday!*

I chuckle to myself.

"What are you laughing about?" she asks.

"Oh, just how strange this all is."

"Let's go back to my van. I have to let the dog out."

Well, here we are. The van does exist. It's probably a 1990
model. The burgundy paint clashes with the orange rust
spots. The windows are covered with material so I can't see
in from the outside. She opens the door, and the inside drips
with silks and velvets. Purples, blacks, crimsons, and forest
greens fill my vision. Rich, deep colors. The kind of colors
you would see in a Victorian tapestry. The backseats of the
van are folded down, and a futon mattress lies on them, covered with a patchwork quilt. Seeing me look at it, she says, "I
made that from old skirts and dresses."

Seems like Stevie Nicks should be singing "Gypsy" in the
background.

Out pops the dog, a Chihuahua named Lipstick Boy. I climb
in and try to make myself comfortable while she walks him.

A dog. Cute. Not really. I don't like dogs. But I'd better pre-
tend to. Dykes and their dogs, you know. Hope he doesn't
jump all over me. I hope I don't have to let him lick my face.

When she returns to the van, she falls into my arms on the mattress. Her full lips are on mine with a fierceness that instantly makes me hot. Our tongues dance so well together, no awkward steps, no tripping over each other's feet. Her body melts into mine. Her softness eases the rigidness in my body. My hipbones get lost in her roundness.

I can't wait to get this slip thing off her. Up over the head, that's it. Her breasts are toppling out of her black lace bra like gourds in a cornucopia. Oh, they feel so good as she rubs them lightly across my own. Is this a front or back closure? Back, good. Off with the bra. She must have already taken off her G-string. The pressure of her tits against mine makes my nipples feel as if they could explode through my tank top. Please touch them. Bite them. Something. A pinch, even.

Right to business for Asia. She climbs off me and kneels on the floor of the van. "Do you mind if I fuck you with my strap-on?"

"Uh, sure, as long as you have a condom for it."

God, sometimes I sound so stupid. Why couldn't I have come up with something cute and witty like, "Sure, slip into something more erect"? She's so forward...perhaps she's the town slut and this is a nightly routine for her. And for me it's just another birthday.

She pulls from under her bed a leather harness and marbleized dildo. She suits up.

Oh, jeez, she's opening the condom package with her teeth. Staring at me with those kohl-smudged almond eyes. Tiger eyes.

She rolls the rubber down her erection. I turn over on my stomach, my ass in the air, as she comes from behind and teases my cunt with her silicone. I slide myself back onto her cock, my hands reaching behind to her thighs, and pull her close to me. She begins to fuck me with the rhythm of an African drummer.

I'm so glad I don't need any lube. I'm wet. Dripping wet. One thing I don't need to be embarrassed about. Thank God I have no zits on my ass.

I lean onto my elbows and move my hand to my already swollen clit. I step up the tempo of my vibrating fingers.

Oh, yeah, this feels too good. I wonder what it looks like from her view. My alabaster ass in the air. Her dildo fucking deep within me. I want to feel her. Does this turn her on? Are juices dripping from her velvety lips?

I take my hand and reach for her, but she grabs my arm and stops me. "No, you can't do that. You were just touching yourself. It's not safe."

God, she's right. I feel stupid for being scolded. I should've thought about that. It's been so long since I've been with someone other than my ex-lover. I feel naive again.

I go back to playing with myself. The tension starts to build. Our angles are perfect. I can feel her rubbing against my sweet spot.

God, let me come. Please. I know I had a lot to drink tonight. If you let me come, I'll never drink this much again. Promise. This night is too perfect to fake it. Shit. OK, relax. Stop praying and enjoy. It's starting to build.

My hand is getting tired, so I switch from circles to side to side. Close. Very close. She reaches her hands around and grabs hold of my tits. She squeezes my nipples hard in her fingers, and before I even know what is happening, my back is arching uncontrollably, and a wave of pleasure comes over me. She's still fucking me, and I ride the waves.

Was that scream from me? Was it out loud?

I collapse onto the bed, her on top of me. I lie there, still, silent, catching, until it is my turn to ask, "What do you like?"

"I want you inside me." She removes the harness. She reaches under the bed again and pulls out a glove. She's on the bed now, face up. I put the glove on my right hand and begin to rub her clit slowly, softly. Sweat sweetly glistens on

her body. I notice her triangle-style clitoral piercing—a silver
ring, hanging—and I feel myself getting wet again. As my
hand works her, I move my mouth to her neck. Biting. She
likes it. Her moans tell me to bite harder. And I do. Her tits
hang slightly to the sides of her body. Large, full, round. Nipples erect, waiting for my mouth.

Oh, yummy. The salty sweaty taste of skin.

"More, put in more," she moans. "Yeah, fuck me harder.
Yeah, like that."

I hope I'm not hurting her. Only two fingers left outside
her swallowing cunt. Now just the thumb.

"Ooh, yeah, like that."

My whole fist is up there. And I fuck. I fuck like my hand
could come, like if I fuck hard and deep enough, my hand will
ejaculate. Faster. Her insides open up to me like a succulent
lily. It's so warm in here. So squishy. So sexy.

Her breath quickens, and I can feel her lower back tight-
en. Harder. Faster. She lets it out. A moan saved up just for
me. Her nails digging into my thighs. Her body goes limp.
It's over.

I awaken the next morning and look around at my surroundings: Lipstick Boy jumping on velvet bedclothes.

Wow, it's still my birthday. She is more gorgeous than I
remember.

Small talk. And it's time for me to go. I've got my legs
hanging out the side van door. As I'm putting my boots on, I
notice something all over the right thigh of my jeans. "What
is that?" I wonder out loud.

She puts a hand down to her cunt and removes it, saying,
"Oh, I guess that's me—I'm bleeding."

Oh, my God, bleeding! My only pair of pants for the weekend, and I've got some chick's menstrual blood all over
them...and she lives in a van.

I collect myself, half laughing, half wanting to scream, as
we say good-bye. I wish her well on her journeys. She wishes

me a happy birthday. And just like it started, it ends. With a kiss. And her crimson stain on me. A birthday present for my memory.

And I go my way.

Virgin Once Removed

BY RAVEN SPRING

I was outta there. It was the day after Christmas, 1990, and I had thrown the last tent stake into the back of my car. Ready to get out of town. It was cold, and the roads were still wet with last night's snow. As I pulled out of my gravel drive, I said a little prayer to my god of the day and stepped on the gas. I was living in Santa Fe, N.M., and had decided through my vacation interviewing process that I did every year, that Padre Island, Tex., was a nice place to spend the week between Christmas and New Year's Eve. The road to Texas was long and icy. It took 15 grueling hours to get there, and when I finally arrived, instead of the expected sunshine and balmy breezes, it was raining so hard I could barely breathe without inhaling water. This put a slight damper on my camping plans. Instead, I put myself up in a cute, nonpretentious, noninvasive, nonstick motel named something like "The Clamshell" and settled down to have a good time.

Interlude

While I'm unpacking, a little background on myself. I was 34 years old at the time and had a dreadful track record with relationships. All my best friends were women, but I kept sleeping with men. I would inevitably end up in a clutch of lesbians wherever I went, but men were always the catch of the day (or night). I would even joke about how I was a lesbian in disguise wandering amid the unsuspecting straight world. A wolf in sheep's clothing, so to speak.

Interlude over

As I finally put the room in order, I started looking around for things to do in beautiful Rockport, Tex. You can imagine, small town, Texas, woman all alone, ack! But I, being the tenacious woman I am, felt I had to stay and make the best of it. So I did a lot of walking, some swimming, and somewhere during that time, I ran across a boat trip on which one could see the famous migrating whooping cranes, a local yearly event in which people load onto a small boat for the day and motor to the outer island fringes to catch a glimpse of the ever-elusive nesting cranes before they leave. Why not? How could bird watching be dangerous?

It was a rare sunny day as I boarded the boat and plopped down on the first wooden bench available. I sat there looking out to sea, feeling a sharp breeze on my face and the pale sun on my back. We neared an island, and I walked to the railing and looked out at the nearby beach and reeds for signs of the great white birds. I stood and listened to the reeds rustling in the wind. Suddenly, I realized I was also listening to a group of women standing next to me, near the full-service bar on board. Half in daydream from the sound of the motor and the rocking motion of the boat, I heard one woman say to another, "What do you see over there?"

"Give me those binoculars. I think I see something. No, it's only a rock."

"Ha, you're always seeing rock birds, Nor."

"Very funny. Hey, hand me my beer, would you?"

"Would you like one?" a voice said to me. I started as I realized a plastic cup of beer had been shoved into my open hand.

"Oh, thanks," I blushed.

"Hi, my name's Christine," she said, sticking out the hand without the beer.

She was a tall woman with a stocky build. She had a fierceness about her that one couldn't argue with.

I introduced myself, squirming and blushing again.

Christine then introduced me to her friends, Mary and Noreen. Mary was a slight, mousy gray-blond who seemed to have little to say. Noreen, on the other hand, had a lot to say. Not so much in words, but in the language of the eye. She was shorter than I, with cropped blond hair, a round and full-breasted body, and plump but graceful fingers she held out for self-inspection from time to time. But it was her lips that held my eyes. They were thin and when parted had the effect of a veil being torn away to reveal the bright sun.

"So, what are you doing in these parts?" inquired Christine, breaking my lip reverie.

"I'm from Santa Fe, on vacation. Trying to find some sun, actually." I replied, taking a quick sideways glance at Noreen.

"Welcome to Texas," said Noreen, her voice soft and drawly like syrup.

I pried my eyes from her lips to smile a noncommittal thanks.

Suddenly a flock of huge white birds the size of small planes flew up, interrupting our awkward introductions. For the next half hour we were involved in searching out and gawking at the splendid white-feathered creatures. Finally the sun began its homeward march, and we were about to follow suit when Christine turned to me and said, "Hey, we're going over to the Crab Pot for dinner. Wanna come?"

"Sure," I said, swallowing the last of my beer and wondering what the Crab Pot was.

"Let me get the last round." Noreen walked over to the

bar. She returned loaded down with foamy beers. She saved
the last one to hand to me with a little smile, her lips pressed
tightly together as though they might grow beyond her control if she let them stand on their own.

When we got back to land, we all piled into our cars, and
I followed the gang to dinner. The Crab Pot turned out to be
a restaurant of local legend where one wears a huge plastic
bib—more like a tablecloth—plucks various crustaceans
from a large pot, and cracks them open with a wooden mal-
let that looks like it came from a child's tool set. Once we
slaughtered a half dozen crabs and many beers, conversation
resumed.

"What do you do for a living?" asked Christine.

"Oh, I clean houses," I mumbled, "but I'm looking for
more worthy work."

"Wish you'd come clean my house."

I swear I saw Noreen wink at me.

"Hey, how's about we have a nightcap over at your place,
Nor?" Christine piped in.

"Sure," she drawled.

We all piled back into our respective cars and drove a short
distance over to Noreen's condo. We chatted noncommittal-
ly for some time until one by one the others said their good
nights. Then it was just Noreen and me.

"Nice view," I said, wandering over to the window. I saw
her reflection in the glass; she was just standing there watching me. I was fuzzy from all the beer and knew I wanted
something. I wanted sex. I felt sex in the air, like the pushing
pressure before a storm, palpable, still, hot, sticky. Tension
gripped my head and loins. But I couldn't understand. The
only other person in the room was a woman. Where was this
pressure, this brooding sensual radio wave coming from?
And why was I receiving it so intensely? I went and sat back
down next to Noreen. Then I watched myself as though I
were watching a late-night movie. My fingers reached for the

top button on her shirt. She pushed my hand away and buttoned it back up. Her lips parted in a small smile.

"I want to kiss you," I said.

She said nothing, a smile dancing on her lips.

"I want to kiss you," I said again.

She still said nothing. Her lips pressed together. I leaned toward her and touched them with mine. Silence. I kissed her again, my lips pressing into hers, my heart beating hard.

"I've never done this before," I said. "Kiss a woman, I mean."

Her eyes widened. "You're kidding," she breathed in her Texan drawl.

I put my hand up to her blouse again and unbuttoned the first button. This time she hesitated, then unbuttoned the next and the next and next. Suddenly I was scared, but a heat was growing in my chest. She looked hard into my eyes.

"Take off your shirt," she said, suddenly the demanding one.

I drew my shirt over my head, arms shaking the tangled sleeves. I felt her hands warm on my back unclasping my bra hooks. As I pulled my shirt free, I felt my breasts loosen from my bra and then Noreen's mouth hot and wet sucking my nipples, one, then the other, back and forth. The heat in my chest spread to my belly. She pressed me down to the rug, sucking, licking my nipples hard, then as softly as a feather brushing across the sand. Slowly, she sat up and unclasped her bra, her breasts falling to her chest, two white melons perfect and succulent. The heat in my belly sank between my legs, and I felt my wetness flow as she undid my pants. Unzipping her pants, she lay on top of me, our bare breasts pressed to each other, nipples rubbing against each other.

"I want you," she whispered. "I've wanted you all day."

I felt the urgency in her voice and tried to understand what was happening. Quickly she slid her hands down my belly and pulled my panties off, her fingers brushing across my bush. The whisper of expectant joy cried out. She slipped her panties off, and I looked up at her. What was I supposed to do now? She took my hand and slipped it between her legs. And there, I felt myself, and yet not myself. There was wet, hot sex under my hand, but it was she who sucked in a gasp of air as my finger found her tiny button which grew hard as I rubbed my fingertips back and forth, over and over. She slid down next to me and thrust her hand roughly between my legs. Suddenly I forgot her wetness, her sameness. I was overwhelmed with the need to thrust myself toward her pleasuring fingers. Her wetness grew under my hand as I moaned in desire and confusion.

I closed my eyes and felt my pleasure grow, mounting, mounting as I rubbed her thrusting sex, and she fucked me with her fingers. Then suddenly her hand wasn't there. I was caught in mid thrust. My eyes flew open as I watched her slowly turn, her eyes on me. She turned her face toward my throbbing cunt, and I felt her great wetness descend on my mouth. Her pussy, all salty and hot and sticky, lay in my mouth like a huge oyster ready to suck down. I began to tongue her wetness, her knot growing harder. She pulled my legs apart and immediately found my hard clit and started sucking. Again I closed my eyes and surrendered to the pleasure. I saw a field of flowers. As I drew closer, the flowers, all wet and cool, grew hot under the noon sun and began to open. I began to open. I felt Noreen's mouth searching, sucking, felt her hot cunt pressed into my mouth again and again. I felt her need as I opened and opened. She thrust five fingers into my huge wet vagina, and I moaned and bucked into her sucking mouth. Her tongue, finding my hard clit again, licked faster, faster. I saw the orange-red flower in the noon sun open full of gladness, black in the center, as I suddenly held her head still and climaxed into her waiting mouth again and again. I came harder and harder, feeling my appetite as I fucked her mouth and pressed her head between my legs, crying out, then moaning as she let loose her coming cunt into my mouth and groaned. She thrust and thrust and then lay still against me, breathing long and hard, then more softly.

Exhausted, excited, and amazed, we stumbled upstairs to bed.

This is how I lost my virginity to a woman.

Shake Your Moneymaker

BY ANGELA HARVEY

The first time I saw her she was peering over the top of a racing form, shooting me a glance every few minutes. I sat at a table a few feet away from her at an outdoor Santa Monica café, alternating my right hand between an iced hazelnut latte and the task of balancing my checkbook: It looked grim. I had just $43 and was a week away from payday. After two years of writing freelance articles for local L.A. rags and walking dogs three times a week for ten bucks a pop, I was still eating macaroni almost nightly, and my '89 Tercel wasn't getting any younger.

I sighed.

She smiled.

Her dark hair fell in slinky curls to her shoulders, framing a pale, nearly wan face. She appeared almost as if she were not well, a little blue around the gills, as if she might faint at any moment. There's some part of me that relishes this: the look of a fragile soul, the look of *please*. An atrociously sexy sadness around the eyes. Greta Garbo as Camille. Greta Garbo as anyone.

Her lips were outlined in red and had the smoothness of apple.

I'm a terrible flirt, and when I say terrible, I mean terribly bad, so when she flashed me a little teeth, I quickly picked up the *L.A. Weekly* that lay in piles on the chair next to mine and buried my nose in its folds. A Freudian slip of the fingers landed me inside the depths of the personals. I sighed again. I wasn't just broke—I was horny too.

I went back to my checkbook. I could barely even afford new batteries for my '89 vibrator. Out of the corner of my eye, I saw her circling horses with a red Sharpie. She tucked an errant lock behind her ear, then glanced up. I sighed louder.

"That's the third sigh inside of five minutes." She grinned again and scooted her chair next to mine. "What's wrong, baby?"

Baby? I can't imagine being that ballsy.

"I'm broke."

"I'm Alex."

And so the story truly begins. During the next two hours I would learn many things: She was 33, grew up in Philly, waitressed her way through three years of New York University, dropped out to play poker professionally (That didn't work out: "A flat-nosed loan shark named Costello..." Was she for real?). She hightailed it out West ten years ago. Here's the kicker: She played the ponies—and she was damn good, so good she had just picked up a three-bedroom Craftsman five blocks from the beach. Her system was flawless.

It was decided I would give Alex 40 bucks (Did she say clams? smackers? big ones?) to place on a shoo-in at Hollywood Park. She dragged me, motherly, by the arm to the nearest ATM. I punched in 5812, then hit FAST CASH, sighed a cyclone-size sigh, and forked over the dough. I wrote her number in my checkbook next to the freshly penned entry that read, "8/7/97, Mistake of the Century, $40.00." She handed me a yellow matchbook from a place called the Cat's Meow (it had a jocular black kitty head on it), and I scribbled my name and number on it and slipped it into her palm. She might have said something about Mr. Chester in the fifth, ten to one, but to tell you the truth, I was too preoccupied with the delicate skin of her slender neck to pay her words serious attention.

"I'll call you after the race. Then we'll celebrate," she cooed, as if she always won, as if she were a winner. She placed a wet kiss by my ear, then shot me a wink with one inky fat-cat eye. As she strutted away, I swear I saw emerald dollar signs float around her head, then descend almost religiously to the sidewalk.

Later that night, before digging into a meal of mashed potatoes and French toast (I'm the worst kind of vegetarian), I said a prayer to St. Jude. "Come to my assistance in this great need," I concluded, "that I may receive the consolations and succor of heaven, in all my necessities, tribulations, and sufferings, particularly that I may win big at the track and get laid afterward!" Sacrilege? Not when you're dirt poor and haven't had a woman in eight months.

As I lay in my bed (mattress on the floor) that night, I closed my eyes and summoned Alex. Wholesome hips curvier than the 110 freeway. The tortuous bump in her nose. Her ah-ahh pouty mouth. The spot between her neck and collarbone where I could have lived a leisurely lifetime. The sadness of her face that contrasted sharply with her bold demeanor, her halo of luck. Money in the bank. I slid my hand beneath my panties and went for it.

Around 6 the next evening the phone rang. I made a beeline.

"Hello?"

"Four hundred clams, baby!"

I did a little dance, almost spiked the cordless onto the floor, as if I had just won the Super Bowl and were shimmying for a TV audience of millions.

"Hello? Hello, are you there?"

I gave Alex my address. She lived just ten minutes away. She'd be over in 45.

After hastily scanning my closet, I decided on a short black skirt, low-cut navy poly-blend blouse, silver necklace with tiny red beads, and sling-back heels. A touch of gel on my tousled pageboy and a smattering of Rueful Red across my lips completed my broodingly sexy look.

Too soon the doorbell rang. When I peeked out the window, I thought I would pass out. A 1970 olive green Catalina convertible was parked outside, its curves and lines as fluid as the body of the woman now at my door.

Holly Golightly sunglasses. Hair pulled back and piled thoughtlessly atop her head. Black vinyl pants. Creamy silk shirt freckled with tiger lilies. Kick-ass motorcycle boots. Five feet nine inches of Hellrific woman. Need I say more? As soon as I opened the door, she produced a stack of bills bound in a silver money clip, reached into my blouse, and tucked it carefully inside my lacy black bra, her thumb grazing the oh-so-sensitive skin of my left breast. Oh, heaven! Oh, Gods! Oh, baby!

"Tonight's on me," Alex said, real gooey, honey dripping from her chin and down her smooth-as-a-dollar neck.

She led me to her car—or should I say sex machine?—and we climbed inside. As I buckled up, I scanned her body, bent at the hips and seated. Emboldened by the spirit of cash, I traced my finger from her shoulder, down her arm, to her long fingers, then clutched them. "Thanks, sweetie," I offered. She leaned over, slid her hand behind my neck, and pulled me in, placing her lips urgently on mine, like a kid on a sucker. Our tongues did a little jig, then she turned back and started the ignition real matter-of-factly, as if she'd just won, of course, again. My crotch kicked into fifth gear.

As we barreled along to a Cajun dive a few miles east, I complimented her on her shirt and proceeded to tell my tiger lily story, which always makes me feel ethereal but real: that the flower is my favorite, that my grandmother had given my mother two tiger lily plants, that the lilies still grew against the brick face of my mother's house years after my grandmother had died, that they roared into the sun, a testament to life itself. As I spoke, the tiny orange petals on her shirt bloomed into love, and though I had met this woman just a day before, somehow I knew the sexy hand of fate had pulled us together, had patted me on the back and said, "Good job."

Once we were seated at the restaurant, Alex ordered us a bucket of oysters on ice, a basket of French bread, and a couple of dark amber beers. I love letting women order for me, savor playing girl to another girl. She reeled off stories for the next three hours, occasionally grabbing my knee for emphasis: Her father had left her and her two sisters when she was four; one of her girlfriends had had a coke habit and robbed her of $1,300, then was found dead three weeks later; she loved green olives, chocolate doughnuts, and bridge (for fun, not cash).

"I've got an idea," Alex said, real businesslike, then dragged me out by the arm.

We wound up at a sports bar a mile from my apartment, where she won me another 75 bucks on video keno. Pure gravy. Mother always said I should find me a good provider.

It was pushing midnight, and I had two beagles to walk at 7 o'clock the next morning, so despite the tingling between my legs and in my heart, I asked her if we could call it a night.

"OK, baby, I'll take ya home," Alex said. Somehow I knew it wouldn't be that easy.

We made our way to the Catalina that was parked at the far end of the dark lot. At the passenger side door, she said, "Hold it," then pressed me against the warm metal of the car and slid her hand up under my short skirt, over my panties, and held it there for what seemed an eternity. With her other hand, she pulled my head to hers, then swept my bottom lip with her tongue.

"You have the most spectacular lips," she breathed.

"Every woman I've ever been with has said that." I knew I wasn't making her feel unique, but it was true, and every time a woman complimented my lips, I felt compelled to make that remark, as if I were bringing each former lover to my side to ooh and aah. Oh, to be adored. Oh, to be won.

After making out for five or ten minutes, we hopped into her car and she drove me home. Outside my apartment, with the car's engine still rumbling, I pulled her into me, moved my tongue from her mouth, down her chin and neck, and across her elegant breastbones. "How 'bout one more drink?" I smiled. The dogs would have to make other plans. I needed her bad.

Inside my apartment, I whipped up a couple frosty Manhattans, and we lounged on my sofa, Pink Floyd's "Money" piping through the room.

"I could make you rich," Alex said, real serious.

"I could make you a sandwich," I fired back, all goofy-eyed.

She laughed so hard, she—accidentally?—splashed her cocktail onto my chest. I started to get up for a paper towel.

"Hey, wait, stop," she said, and pulled me down by the arm. Alex leaned in and licked the vermouth off my neck, then lingered just above my right breast. The combination of the cold liquor and her warm tongue sent shivers straight to my crotch. Slowly she unbuttoned my top and pulled it open, pausing briefly to unhook my bra at the front. Her tongue flickered across one full, white breast and landed on a rosy nipple. As she gently nipped and sucked, it hardened under her teasing, each nibble shooting tiny bolts of electricity through my body. She eased down my stomach, licking up the stream of vermouth that had found its way to my belly button, which was adorned with a silver ring and tiny bead. "Gracious, I thought you were a good girl," she whispered, then tugged at the ring with her tongue and teeth. Still circling my navel with her silky tongue, she pulled my skirt down my hips and removed it. I was still wearing my shirt and opened bra, while she remained fully clothed. *Hot.*

Alex climbed on top of me, her black vinyl pants rubbing against the bare skin of my thighs, sticky and warm. As she urged her body into mine, a wadded $20 bill slipped out of her pocket. "My moneymaker's still churning out," I chuckled. I palmed the loot and placed it between my teeth. She grabbed it from my mouth with her pearly (but slightly crooked) whites, like a dog on a bone, then took it in her hand and slid it under my panties. Bill in hand, she started on my clit. "I bet you like the feel of money, baby. I bet it's making you wet," she said as if she were parlaying her entire day's winnings toward a much more substantial windfall. She rubbed the twenty ferociously into my folds, from my hard clit to my vagina and back again. My snatch gushed as I bucked into the cash and her skilled fingers. They always say you never know where money's been. Now I know why. Dollar signs, snowy and translucent, swam around her head again. Maybe it was the Manhattan. Maybe it was love.

Alex withdrew the bill from my panties (Was Andrew Jackson smiling?) and inserted two fingers into my drenched hole, the smell of cold hard cash and come rising from between my legs. As she expertly fucked me, easing in and out of my body like a favorite dream, my entire cunt became engorged, filling with adoration and pleasure, the intense of high of lovemaking, as if I had stomached her whole. I always come quickly, so it didn't take much to push me over the edge. I like it like that. There's so much to look forward to: Round One, Round Two, Round Three…

"Jesus Christ!" I screamed, and I swear to God the entire Last Supper flashed before me, each apostle rolling his eyes in smirking approval. I was panting hard, my breathing as ragged as the crumpled twenty now on my pillow, tears streaming from the corners of my eyes. She descended on my face, kissed the tears away just as she had the whiskey.

"That was fast," Alex said. "I'll have to go slower next time."

"Next time?" I asked, attempting to bust her overwhelming self-confidence.

"Yeah, in Vegas, baby, Vegas!"

Three months later we were hitched in Nevada.

That night I won $800 on slots. I spent 20 of it on a jar of garlic-stuffed olives, a box of chocolate crullers, and a deck of cards.

Transplants

BY AMY WANDERS

A land flowing with milk and honey is the best way to describe this perfectly imperfect woman. Trace (Tracy) and I
have been friends since we were teenagers, about ten years
now. We met in high school, two East Coast transplants out
of our element. It wasn't long before we lost our accents and
acclimated to the Northwest with the best of them, reminiscing in the rain that each city had a smell, trying to remember
what home smelled like 3,000 miles and three time zones
away. It's funny, the things you miss and the clarity of what
you remember.

As teenagers, we experienced many firsts together: first
drink, first cigarette, date, dream, job, all the things that seem
so important to teenagers and cement relationships by their
very content or lack thereof. As we grew older we drifted into
different interests. For me it was swimming and academics.
Trace had a steady boyfriend by the time she was 15 and
most of the time was devoted to him. By 20 I had more
boyfriends than I could count on all my fingers and toes and
had somehow avoided STDs, pregnancy, the bad things that
can happen to the young and sexually active. Over coffee I recounted my rendezvous in detail to Trace, the two of us
laughing at my outlandish behavior—Trace wanting to do

the same but afraid of losing her boyfriend, choosing instead to experience vicariously the real-life dramas I recounted, and sometimes wiping my tears when lust went awry.

It was comfortable, the way two people are when they know each other well. We were and are the kind of unconditional friends who look the other way when one of us has transgressed, but not beyond forgiveness. I remember first thinking she was beautiful one night when she looked at me, brown eyes grayed behind the smoke of her cigarette. Hadn't I looked at her a thousand times? With her short, curly black hair and made-up face, Trace looked a decade older than her 23 years, but soft, the way women are when they are at peace with themselves, and hard, the way women are when they have lived. This night was typical. One of us called the other to meet for drinks, somewhere, anywhere, downtown Portland. Saying no to that sort of invitation was rare, and this night was not supposed to be full of exceptions.

Conversation was lively, as usual, each of us expounding on the weekly drama of our lives. Her loyal boyfriend of eight years bored her, what else was new? My boyfriend of six months could have started a support group with Tracy's guy; I couldn't remember the last time I wanted him to stay for anything more than sex. The last month together I don't even think we saw each other nude. Just basic sex, Bruce on his back, lying there with eyes closed, smirk on his face as I came; we had it down to under five minutes. What was the difference between this and masturbation? Several hours and drinks later, Trace decided there was little difference and that we should both just masturbate.

Soon we were verbalizing our fantasies, our alcohol-induced confessions leading to uncharted territory: *Had I ever tasted myself? What did I think? What was the most arousing thing I had experienced lately?* This was amazing, I thought, tasting myself in the bathroom at the office had distracted me all day, had made me want to do it again, with someone else. My head was spinning. Why hadn't I thought about this before? Surely it was always there, whatever "it" was: the lifeguards on the high school swim team, smelling like an intoxicating mixture of sweat and chlorine, their small breasts half white, half brown, flirting with the swimsuit fabric, the way my stepmother's hair smelled, Tracy's breath, men's shaving cream on a woman's body, the taste of myself in my boyfriend's mouth, my fondness for lesbian erotica, stolen kisses with strange women in funky clubs, all the little things I observed and encountered out of context all came into place. Did she want to come over?

In retrospect, neither of us remembers the ride, only that it was raining, it was dark out, and Tracy Chapman was crooning through the speakers. Trace drove, the windows were down a crack, the air was damp, her hand brushed my cheek. I remember the feel of the conversation but not the words. I loved this woman, I knew her better than anyone—and she me—and we were going home. I felt both frightened and excited. I didn't want to mess up. Would we still be friends?

My apartment was a mess, smelling of half-burned candles and half-dead flowers limping in their vases. The main hallway was strewn with shoes, books, reports to be edited. A messy house for a messy life. But no one was passing judgment; the place was comfortable and safe, lived in.

It was surprisingly unawkward, letting her touch me, touching her. Hesitant, clumsy kisses grew more deliberate, then passionate, her tongue tracing my teeth.

I couldn't get enough of Trace, her small dark nipples on her tiny breasts, replying by contracting as I sucked them. My bra was pushed up in a hurried manner, nipples turning to rocks as she bit them, then softening under her tongue. It was the first time, and it was as if we had done this before. In her mouth I was alive, her tongue soft and patient. It was the ultimate, like a choir in unison, synchronized. I wondered what she was thinking as I grazed her olive skin with my tongue.

She convulsed as I lightly scratched her, my nails leaving their mark. My thighs turned to steel, nipples solidified, as I gripped the sheets and uttered something inaudible. Coming is not violent but nevertheless intent, full of clarity. The choir reached a crescendo. *Coming. It's sincere. I'm here. Absolute release of self, energy, of distilled emotion.*

Trace tasted like me, salty and real, like skin and sweat, like tears and rain and wine. I was surprised at how soft she was, just like me, but I never noticed. Her clitoris grew hard under my tongue as I licked lightly, her hands grabbing my hair as if she were in pain. I cupped my mouth around her clitoris and sucked while licking softly. She came quietly but with conviction. Her hands running through my hair, I fell asleep, exhausted.

I woke up thinking I must have dreamed, but Trace lay there soundly asleep. The mirror in the bathroom reflected the inevitable, wine had stained my lips a maroon color, and there were bruises on my neck and breasts. I smelled her on my face, on the sheets. I stroked her face. I took in her beauty: voluptuous with small breasts and beefy thighs, short black hair framing a round face, looking as if she took a time machine from the '20s and landed in my bed. My breasts are large, my body is slightly plump; she calls it Rubenesque. My hair is a mass of short brown curls that look like they could belong to an unkempt three-year-old.

When I woke up Trace was smoking and watching me sleep, her free hand tracing my breasts. This time, we made love sober, more slowly, more carefully, but nonetheless passionate. She lay on top of me, her thigh between my legs, parts of bodies touching in the semi-darkness of dawn. *I don't want this to end,* I thought. Covered in sweat, I came with her hands grabbing into me as she sucked on my neck, my clitoris at the mercy of her heavy thigh, unable to move. Rubbing the sweat into my belly, Trace penetrated me with her fingers. Still sensitive from coming, I shuddered as she pushed two fingers inside me to feel the throbbing. I came in her hand as if it were mine. Her wetness was on my face as she pushed her crotch into me. I pulled her closer as she un-dulated over my mouth. I savored the way she felt in my mouth, the taste, the texture of skin as I explored a body that was so like mine. She placed her hands against the wall as I pulled her closer into me. Instinctively, I knew her body like I knew my own; it was like fucking myself. Sighing, she col-lapsed on top of me.

After a little while, I mumbled something about coffee and went to the kitchen. A few minutes later I came back with freshly brewed coffee, with extra cream and sugar, the way we both take it. As we sipped our too-sweet concoction, I looked at Trace and smiled. Soon we were laughing at the absurdity of the scene: two good friends having coffee in bed, post sex. Trace smiled, "We'll have to get together more often."

Next

BY ISABELLE LAZAR

It was in Arizona. Such a lonely time. I don't know how many nights I spent alone on my couch, falling asleep in my clothes, waking up the next morning only to change, shower alone, and start anew. The only loving I'd known was intermittent flings with men...boys from my school. I knew I wanted women. But didn't know where to find them. I was terrified. What if they—*she*—rejected me? Guys were easy. I did the rejecting there. Everything on my terms—and those were my terms. Whenever and wherever I wanted, as much as I wanted and also as little. I chose whether they would come or not and had them trained that way. I guess I was luckier than most, though I didn't feel that way. All my female friends only talked about trying to snare one. I smirked silently, longing for them instead. I still wasn't prepared to face reality. It stands to reason then that when this happened, I paid it no mind, not consciously, until years later, until I could retrace my steps and know, absolutely, unequivocally, that I am a lesbian and loving it. But then? What did I know then? Less than nothing. But so like an animal, my instincts were unmistakable. Why didn't I listen to them?

It was all so ethereal. Like a distant dream...and not my choice of locale: a women's clinic. A female, middle-aged doctor. Well, I thought her middle-aged then. I was a punk myself. She couldn't have been more than 32–35 at the oldest. I lay down on the cold, steel table, slid my heels into the stirrups, and assumed the position.

Who says out-of-body experiences aren't possible? I have them every time I see a gynecologist.

My body is not my own. They're not doing this to me. I don't feel this discomfort, this humiliation.

She inserts the fucker, gently. She is very kind. I shouldn't be here, but I am. I think of her and start to get wet. *This won't do,* I think. *She'll see!* But I console myself; the liquid will ease the insertion and withdrawal of the speculum.

She's talking. Blah, blah. I can't hear. I only feel her. I think of her in a way I shouldn't be thinking of her. Is she getting hot? Not at all. Just as monotone as the rest.

"You need to be careful with unprotected...blah, blah."

"Yes," I say mechanically. She takes out the metal dildo and replaces it with her hand. I get wetter. She goes deeper, all the way up, to feel my ovaries, presumably. Does she feel me?

"You're a smart woman, aren't you?" she says. What's that in reference to? Oh, yeah, safe sex. I nod.

"Huh?" she whispers. *She whispers.*

"You are a smart woman, aren't you?"

I look at her.

"Aren't you?"

I fix my gaze. I am in my body. I shouldn't be here, but I am. Her fingers are so deep, a moan escapes my lips. Oops.

"I thought so," she says. What...what the hell just happened? She's pulling her gloves off, antiseptically writing me a prescription for birth control pills. She leaves it on the counter and allows me to get dressed in dignity. What? No good-bye kiss? At least a hug? OK, how about a cigarette?

As I leave the clinic's back offices, she doesn't even look at me. I reach the door and turn wistfully, a bit dumbfounded. Her look? I can't describe it. There are no words. Reproachful, dispirited...pick an adjective. Perhaps she knows something I don't. I should have asked her. I should have asked her where the lesbians go. I think she would have known.

The Way to Succeed

BY SANDRA LUNDY

I caught the crosstown bus at 72nd Street and headed for Peeches. I figured it was the best place to get lucky. And I really needed to get lucky. Here I was, 29 years old, a cute, muscular butch. And still a lesbian virgin.

It was almost a year to the day since my lesbian epiphany, almost two years since my divorce. I'd been sitting on the sofa bed in my tiny west side apartment, staring out my dirty window and brooding about an awful blind date the night before. *What's wrong with me?* I asked myself. *Why am I having such a hard time meeting decent men?* Then wham! A part of myself I had never heard before bellowed back, *Because you don't like men, stupid! You like women.* Just like that, out of the blue. A lifetime of denial wiped out with one insight.

I couldn't wait to share this earth-shattering discovery with my friends (all straight), who yawned and wondered what took me so long. Then, model graduate student that I was, I put aside my dissertation on narrative deception in the late novels of Charlotte Brontë and began researching a far more interesting topic: my identity. I read every book about lesbians I could get my hands on, from dime-store paperbacks with covers that made me wet to medical treatises with

illustrations that made me nauseous. I spent hours in thera-
py discussing the who-what-where-why-and-when of my
nascent lesbianism. I listened to Adrienne Rich at Woman-
Books and became a devotee of the music of Alix Dobkin
(hey, it was 1981). I attended lectures by Mary Daly and re-
galed my friends with the finer points of lesbian feminist eth-
ical theory—until finally one of them said, "You know,
Sandy, being a lesbian in theory is fine, but it's kind of like
the sound of one hand clapping."

She had a point. All my life I'd been much better at fantasy than reality, which had made it easy to obsessively fantasize about women without disturbing my sleepwalk through
heterosexual life. It was crunch time. I had embraced every
facet of lesbian culture, but the thought of embracing a real
woman was terrifying. What if, despite having memorized all
the illustrations in *The Joy of Lesbian Sex,* I did something
really moronic in bed? What if I couldn't please her? What if
I were really straight and that lesbian epiphany was just a
cruel celestial hoax? (My friends assured me it wasn't.) The
fear of doing it wrong haunted me. That says a lot about who
I was in those days. But that's another story.

So here I was at Peeches at 9 o'clock on a strangely mild
February night, all decked out in my purple tie, black shirt,
and khakis, trying to look so cool and, well, experienced. The
place was pretty empty. I took a seat in the middle of the long
mahogany bar and ordered a Glenlivet, straight.

I'd been to a couple of dyke bars before, where I usually
sat by myself all night and absorbed the atmosphere like a
thirsty paper towel. Unlike the hardscrabble bars in the Village, Peeches was quiet and softly sexy. Warm light played
over the highly polished wood of the bar and off the cream-
colored walls. The volume of the music surrounding the tiny
dance floor in the back was always low, even for disco music.
But what I liked most were the tree branches hung parallel to
the ceiling behind the bar. They were painted white and

strung with tiny yellow lights, an understated Christmas. I didn't feel intimidated here. I could handle this.

I was, as I said, a graduate student, and scotch was expensive. I drank slowly. From my perch at the bar, I checked out the dance floor, where a couple slow danced, melting into each other like lit candles. I'd never been much for dancing. I was envious.

I only stopped ogling when I felt—rather than saw—someone sit next to me. She could've sat anywhere.

"I'm Cathy."

Cathy was a pretty, buxom woman with strikingly round, blue eyes and full, dusky lips. She wore a low-cut, rose-colored dress she'd obviously chosen to perfectly compliment her curly, light brown hair, but somehow it didn't. Cathy held out her hand and flashed a broad, uncomplicated smile. Even in the dim light, I could see she was blushing, as if she'd just surprised herself.

"You must not be from the city," I said, returning Cathy's handshake. Her hand was warm and slightly moist, and I was getting a bit moist myself.

"I'm not," said Cathy. "I'm from Utica. Here on business. My company sent me down here for a meeting. Travelers Insurance."

"Well, Cathy, I'm glad you traveled here. Can I buy you a drink?"

I ordered a kir for Cathy and imagined myself on the phone with my best friend, Louise, the morning after. But Cathy was speaking to me, lightly resting her fingertips on my biceps, and I willed myself quickly back to Peeches. Putting my hand over her fingertips, I said, "Yeah, I know what you mean," figuring that response would cover just about anything.

"It's so nice to get away, even for a night," she continued. "Utica's like a fishbowl. I was only with Jeannie four months before she dumped me. And now everywhere I go I run into

Jeannie and her lover, or Jeannie and her friends. New York is so huge. I bet you don't run into your ex-girlfriends everywhere you turn."

"You're right," I replied.

"Are you single now?"

"For the time being, yeah. I like your dress," I added. "You look sexy."

"You've got a great smile."

The place was getting crowded now. We pulled our bar stools closer together.

We talked about our work, who we were out to and who we weren't, and only a little bit, thank goddess, about our families. As we talked, something weird happened to me: Internal gremlins worked overtime. Some primitive genetic imprinting roared in my DNA, and I found myself becoming charming. Little did I know, but I'd been thrust into the time-honored synergy of butch and femme, where the mere hint of encouragement from a pretty woman incites an avalanche of effort.

I was getting more than a hint of encouragement. Cathy's blush was gone. Her huge eyes coursed over my body in a private conversation all their own. I usually hate it when people touch me to make a point. But not with Cathy. As the night wore on, Cathy's touch got firmer, and she leaned in close. Pretty confident for Utica, I thought.

It was pushing 11 o'clock when, in a spasm of daring, I leaned toward Cathy and kissed her, lightly at first, then long and deep, feeling her tongue tease and coax my own. As we pulled away, Cathy nibbled my lower lip.

"We could have another drink here," I said. "But the drinks at my apartment are free."

"I'd love to."

My briefs were soaked. My thighs were like snare drums. Cathy paid for the last round, and we walked outside.

The air was colder now. It woke me up. *What the hell am*

I doing? I thought. I had to think fast.

"I live right across Central Park, in the West 70s," I said. "We could take a cab or go by bus. But why don't we just walk across Central Park?"

"Great idea," said Cathy. "I love parks, and I haven't seen Central Park yet."

"I'm not sure you'll see a lot of it tonight," I said. "But let's go." We headed toward Fifth Avenue.

Is she nuts? I thought to myself, as Cathy marveled aloud at the elegant storefronts and the tall buildings. *Doesn't she read the papers?* Apparently she hadn't read *The New York Times,* where accounts of muggings and murders in the Park were a staple. Or maybe Cathy just assumed I knew what I was doing.

We entered Central Park at 79th Street and Fifth Avenue. Almost as soon as we stepped inside, I saw the shadows of a couple of men looming a few yards ahead of us, to the left. The bushes on either side of us rustled. My impulse for annihilation struggled with a desperate urge to survive. I tasted my heart.

We walked closer to the shadows. Then over to them. Then past them.

Cathy was admiring the trees.

I tried to quicken our pace, figuring the shadow guys would jump us from behind. But my legs were like California redwoods. We moved slowly along the drive. The slivers of lamplight were no match for the surrounding, wooded darkness. For minutes at a time we were completely enveloped by night.

"It's such a nice night for walking," said Cathy, snuggling closer. At one point, she turned to kiss me, but I pretended not to notice.

Then from the bushes, a shout. Grizzled, thick. I grabbed Cathy tight. We froze.

"Ooh, ooh, ooh!" A guy was coming.

"Ooh, Christ!" Another guy.

Cathy giggled into her hand. I tried not to faint. We'd already walked two thirds of the way through Central Park, each step bringing us closer to my apartment. *Where were the goddamn muggers?*

Most likely right there in the bushes, watching our every move, figuring that the only two broads stupid enough to walk through Central Park at midnight were probably cops.

And so, after 45 minutes that seemed like a light-year, Cathy and I emerged intact at the West 72nd Street entrance and headed for my place. I was sweating like a polar bear in Arizona. I was chilled.

Cathy said, "That was really beautiful."

I pulled her closer to me, arm in arm. That was a dangerous thing to do in public back then, but after what we'd just gone through, I couldn't care less. In a few minutes we were at my door.

When it comes to erotic moments, I'll take a walk-up apartment over an elevator building anytime. What could be hotter than slowly climbing the stairs together, the person behind watching, the person in front so aware of being watched. As Cathy walked in front of me, coat off, her firm hips swaying lightly as she mounted the steps, I almost felt myself on top of her. The tide had turned again, and I was bold and ready.

We kissed as soon as I bolted the door. Passionate, searching. This was fire. I could have stayed like that forever, embracing this unknown woman who was at once so light and so full. But Cathy pulled away and fixed me with those cornflower eyes. "Don't you want to fuck me?"

"Do trees grow in Central Park?" I replied, hastily unfolding my couch into a bed. *OK*, I thought, heart racing. *This is it. Remember the illustrations.*

We sat on the edge of the bed and undressed each other. All the lights were on. I placed my hands on Cathy's full, high breasts. She moaned. Her nipples were round and dusty-red like the last nub on a raspberry. They tasted just as sweet. I laid her down and arched over her, never moving my mouth from her breast.

My body rocked on top of her, my wetness sliding into hers. And I was incredibly, incandescently happy. Being with another woman was as intimate and true as knowing my own name. I had come home.

I was aware, though, that at the same time I was having a transformative spiritual experience, Cathy and I were having awkward sex. Yes, Cathy moaned and squirmed and bucked underneath, spreading her legs wide and digging her fingernails into my ass. But no matter what I did, the sounds never varied. She never opened her eyes, like she was directing a movie in her head and I was the key grip or something.

Maybe if I go down on her, I thought. I'd dreamed about going down on a woman for months. Yet I have to admit that when I finally got there, I got lost in the geography. Frantically, I pulled an index card from the file box in my head. *Remember, do to her what you'd like her to do to you. That's the way to succeed.* But wait! How was that going to help me out if I never... Before panic turned to flight, the thick salty moisture of Cathy's cunt, the movement of her wide hips, gave me all the direction I needed. My tongue danced on the viscous surface of hair, skin, and bone, while three supple fingers massaged her tight, warm cave. Apparently, it worked. Cathy pulled my hair, pounded my shoulders with her fists, screamed louder than the guys in Central Park, locked and unlocked her legs around my back.

Then, with a few sharp gasps and a loud wail, Cathy came (I think). She pulled me up to her and hugged me tight, my face on her sweating breast. *Was it OK? Did I do it right?* I was desperate to know. But of course I'd led Cathy to believe that I was Miss Lesbian Experience 1981, so this conversation was pretty much out of the question. Maybe when it was my turn, I'd be able to figure it out.

We lay in each other's arms for a good ten minutes, maybe

more, not saying much. Cathy stroked my hair, and I let my hand play over her body. I was so ready. I needed her to fuck me. Then Cathy whispered in my ear, "That was wonderful," got up, and started to dress.

"Hey!" I said, bolting upright. "What about me?"

"Sorry?" said Cathy.

"Aren't you—I mean, isn't this a two-way street?"

"I thought you wanted to fuck me," she said, flustered. "I—I didn't think you wanted me to fuck you too."

Cathy was genuinely distressed. She sat down on the bed and reached for my hand. I drew it away. "I mean, I told you I just broke up with someone," she said mildly, as if she were explaining simple math to a slow child. "I told you that at the bar."

"Maybe you should leave," was all I could think of to say without crying.

Cathy got up, went to my desk, wrote down her name and number. "I'm sorry if you misunderstood. But I had a really nice time. I'd like to get together again. Looks like Travelers will be sending me to the city a lot. Call me."

After she left, I lay back in my bed and stared at the cracked ceiling as my jumpy, open body cooled down. Every negative emotion I'd ever had—anger, resentment, frustration, humiliation, embarrassment, the works—swirled around in the bed with me. Then, right before I fell asleep, I burst out laughing.

Cathy moved to New York City about a year later. The first time I ran into her, at the Duchess in the Village, I didn't remember who she was. We went out once or twice after that, coffee, nothing more. Then she found a girlfriend, I found a girlfriend, and we fell out of touch. I never told her she was my first.

That was 18 years ago. Peeches is long gone. They've cleaned up Central Park. I moved to Boston. Still, every so often, usually around February, usually if the weather is mild, I find myself wondering, *Hey, Cathy, was it OK? Did I do it right?*

Brvncrzy

by Cathleen Busha

When I heard the knock, I sprang from my sofa, seized a bottomless breath, and unlocked the front door. In the porch light, she didn't look anything like I'd imagined, and that was not a bad thing—I'm really not sure what I'd expected. She had described her features perfectly: short brown hair, blue eyes, bright smile, and an adorable dimple on her right cheek. Of course, as I studied her, her eyes inspected me too; she seemed pleased.

"Cathy?" she asked.

"Yes," I acknowledged, with a purposely coy smile, "Gretchen?"

She nodded as I invited her in.

I ambushed her with a lingering hug; I wanted her to smell my beer breath and vanilla-lotioned skin. I wrapped my tan arms around her strong torso. She felt as stiff and unresponsive as a lifeless computer. Later, sometime during the weeks to follow, she would tell me my embrace had taken her by surprise. She assumed I would have been more withdrawn and nervous, considering it would be my first time with a woman.

Not to say I had agreed to have sex that night; but, after a month of flirting with each other online and over the phone, I had expectations of my fantasy incarnate.

We had met over the Internet, in an online chat room. I used her screen name, "brvncrzy," as a starting point for conversation.

"So," I typed, "are you just a Melissa Etheridge fan, or is there more to your screen name that you want to tell me?"

I hit RETURN and waited, smiling, while my words transformed themselves into currents, slithered over the miles of wires from Lancaster, Pa., to Manassas, Va., and metamorphosed into words again on her screen.

On the Internet, I had found an outlet for my lesbian curiosities. From the safety of my bedroom, I typed messages and questions to women who identified themselves as queers, dykes, bisexuals, soft butches, and lipstick femmes. No worries of the local schoolteacher being discovered in some back-alley dive or pornographic bookstore where "those people" shop.

After a few seconds, her reply appeared: "How are you tonight, Cathy?" Since I had not given her my name, I knew she must have checked out my profile. "Yes, I am...a Melissa fan," she continued, "but I'm also brave and crazy. Believe me?"

I grinned. An online flirt. Always an exciting find.

"Prove it to me. Tell me the bravest and craziest thing you've done," I typed.

While I waited for her response, I glanced over her online profile again. It was purposely vague, not giving her real name, a birth date, or location. All the missing data didn't frustrate me, however; it just increased the intrigue and mystery of this woman connected to me by only words, wires, and wonder.

After a short time, a reply filled my screen: "Hmm...well, once I drove all the way from Virginia to Washington State just to meet a woman I had met online. I drove 12 hours a day. I stopped only to catch a nap in my car, get gas, or go to the bathroom. I even ate from drive-throughs just to save time. By the time I finally got to Washington, I could only spend a day with her before I had to turn around and drive back home—but it was worth it! Does that qualify as brave and crazy, Miss Teacher?"

As I read and reread her message, my emotions wavered between admiration and terror. Even if she was lying, I valued her creative and romantic tale. I was fearful, though, that she was telling the truth and would ask me what brave and crazy things I had done. My life had been 23 years of careful planning and smothering inhibitions. I had no such romantic conquests to share. The only response I could muster was, "Wow. Yes...that was really crazy. Hey, since you know my real name, may I ask you yours, brvncrzy?"

"Gretchen" came over my screen, followed by "It's nice to meet you, Cathy. I see we share the same birth date, May 23. Except I'm a little older than you. I was born in 1967."

Thus began our online exploits. For the next few weeks, I'd hurry home from my teaching job to read her E-mails and find out when she would be online that night. Religiously, I'd sign on at the appointed hour, and we'd type away the words of our days, our dreams, our fantasies, and our increasingly personal questions about each other. Constantly, I slipped into fantasies about the faceless, bodiless Gretchen, imagining what her voice might sound like, her eyes might look like, and her soft tongue and rough, electrician hands might feel like all over my athletic body.

Then one night, as we were clicking away on our keyboards and sharing our ideal romantic vacations, the message "What's your phone number?" appeared on my screen.

I froze.

"Why?" I responded.

"Because I must hear your voice," she urgently typed. "I'll bet you have a very hot, sexy voice."

I froze.

"But what about your phone bill?" I argued weakly. "It's long distance."

"I'd pay any price to hear your voice right now."

I froze.

I knew she wanted to cross over from the comfort of the computer screen to the vulnerability of voice. *What will I say to her? If she calls tonight, will she still E-mail me tomorrow?* Fears, questions, and insecurities immobilized me.

As if reading my mind, she typed: "Cath, are you OK?"

Careful not to mistype any digits, I entered my phone number, hit RETURN, and waited...and waited...clutching the mouse...staring at the screen.

"Thank you" popped up on my screen, followed by "Hang up, and I'll call you in a few minutes."

My palms were clammy hot, and my stomach was spinning like a CD-ROM.

"OK," I typed and signed off.

I sprinted to the bathroom and combed my hair. Before I could brush my teeth, I laughed nervously as I realized my foolishness.

Then I heard the phone ring.

"Hello?" I hesitantly answered.

"Hello, Cathy."

If voices could be scents, Gretchen's would be patchouli.

"Hi, Gretchen," I murmured, amazed that a real woman was behind the words of my old Mac Classic monitor.

Oddly, we talked as old friends, while carefully walking the tightrope of flirtation, breathy pauses, and steamy unspoken desires. At times I felt like an eavesdropper listening in on a conversation between someone similar to myself and this butch vixen on the other end.

"I'm glad I've finally gotten to hear your voice, Cathy. It will make you even more real in my fantasies. All that's left now is to meet you."

I froze.

She could read my mind.

"Not tonight, silly," she playfully chided me.

"When?"

Suddenly her tone was serious. "Soon, very soon, my love."

* * *

And now here she was—tangible, tantalizing—seemingly beamed into my living room.

Only three hours before, we had been talking on the phone like any other night, discussing our days and the possibility of meeting each other in person—the ever-elusive someday.

Interrupting her own sentence, Gretchen suddenly blurted out, "Cath, I wanna come see you tonight."

I froze.

She continued, "If I leave now, I can be there by 10. Would you like to see me tonight?"

Hesitantly, I managed to whisper an exposed "Yes." Not a deep, throaty passionate whisper, but a scared, anxious realization.

"OK, then it's done. I'll be there in three hours. May I spend the night...you know, on the couch or something?"

I froze.

"Of course," I eventually replied.

"E-mail me directions, and I'll see you soon, hon."

"OK...drive carefully."

"I will. See you soon, Cath."

"See you soon."

"Bye, sweetie."

"Bye."

In three hours I would meet the voice. In three hours I would kiss the voice.

I froze.

A silent stream of questions flooded my brain: *What if she doesn't like me? What if I don't match up to all the women she's been with before? What if I don't like her? What if she wants more than I can give? What if I get scared? What if I'm gay? What if I'm not gay? What if I lose my teaching job? What if my family finds out?*

Then I realized what an opportunity this was—to finally be with a woman and have the home-court advantage. *No matter what,* I thought, *I'm at least going to kiss her.*

I vaulted into the shower. As warm jets flooded my body, I closed my eyes and imagined Gretchen massaging my clit with what I expected to be formidable hands. Instantaneously my fears were washed away and replaced with longing and desire.

I dried off and coated my body in vanilla lotion. After wriggling in and out of four different outfits, I settled on the relaxed, I'm-not-really-trying-to-look-good look: a white T-shirt (to contrast with my tan) and a pair of cutoff Levi's.

I skipped downstairs and filled my stereo with Melissa Etheridge CDs. Then, like a spider weaving her web, I scurried from room to room, dimming lamps and lighting candles everywhere. The house was set aglow like a fine, blazing-warm trap. Waiting, I pounded a few beers and swished the suds through my teeth like mouthwash. Over and over, I stared at the TV, the clock, the door, and then the TV again. Finally, I heard the knock.

And now she was here, in my living room and in my arms. As I released her from my gripping hug, I saw her eyes dart from candle to candle—she heard Melissa Etheridge pleading, "Come to my Window." The seducer knew she was being seduced.

I offered her a beer, took her hand, and led her to the living room. After plopping down on the couch, we talked about random, nervous topics—from my multitude of houseplants to her drive up I-95—anything but what it felt like to finally meet, to finally connect.

As I thanked her for venturing so far to see me, I slipped my hand on her knee. She looked more tense than I felt. She took a sip of her beer. I leaned over and kissed her cheek. As if reading my mind again, she placed one of her immense hands behind my head and pulled me in closer.

Her lips hovered over mine like a snake about to strike a mouse. I gasped for breath and leaned closer to her. We kissed passionately—surges, sensations I was not used to. I swung my leg around and straddled her lap.

We kissed again, and her fingers wandered over my neck to my shoulders and then brushed over my breasts. Powerful and weak, nervous and confident, I smiled, then moaned, then giggled. As we kissed, she whispered into my ear, "I don't want to do anything you don't want to do." I seized her hand with an inviting vise grip, slithered off her lap, and gently towed her up to my bedroom.

Again, a Milky Way of burning candles greeted her. She smirked, "Guess you remembered I like candles, eh?"

"And vanilla lotion and beer breath," I added.

"Yeah," she laughed, "I noticed. I didn't stand a chance when I walked in here tonight."

"Depends on what you came for, doesn't it?" I teased.

Before reaching the bed, we began kissing again. Her hands drifted under my shirt, as she massaged my neck with her mouth. Instinctively, I raised my arms, and, like a well-choreographed dance, she pulled my shirt over my head and unbuttoned her own. I was so aware, so present, completely and impulsively reacting to her touch—natural, hot, beautiful.

As if playing Follow the Leader, I reached for the clasp of her bra just after she reached for mine. Her body on top, we lay on the bed, our breasts colliding in a delicious pile of flesh. We continued to kiss deeper, harder, as her hands stroked my long blond hair. She pulled her mouth away for a moment, stared thoughtfully at me, and panted, "Your eyes are as green and intense as you promised."

I smiled and rolled out from under her. I straddled her waist and moved my hips slowly, deliberately, up and down. Leaning, I wisped my hair across her hard, blushing nipples. She shuddered and beamed with delight.

"Cathy, are you sure you've never been with a woman before?"

"Well," I offered, "never physically. But I've fantasized about it for a long time."

Reaching up, Gretchen began massaging and pinching my nipples as if she were tightening a loose bolt. I whimpered and purred—such a pleasurable pain. My rocking increased, harder, faster. Her hands slipped down my stomach and began to unzip my shorts. I gasped as her fingers lightly brushed over my clit. I felt my warm wetness waiting to be discovered by a woman. With just the command of her hands, Gretchen led me back to my coveted position as Pillow Queen.

Reassuringly, she whispered to me, "Relax, enjoy. Don't think. I expect nothing in return. I just want to please you. If you ever want me to stop, just tell me."

And with that tender directive, she stripped off my shorts and then her own. With thorough and unhurried caresses, her tongue undulated over my shoulders, elbows, and the lines of my palms. Slowly, she sucked each of my fingers and ran her hands over my quivering stomach and thighs. I writhed from her touch, but felt guilty for not returning the pleasures. As I began to move my arms, my teacher instructed "No" and used her strength to gently pin me to the bed.

"But—" I gently protested.

"Cath," she interrupted me, "my pleasure comes from pleasing you. Just focus on my touch."

Before I could respond, she slipped her hand into my cunt.

My wail of joy and surprise was matched in unison with her response of "Mmm."

As if pulling a rabbit from a hat, Gretchen withdrew her fingers and held them in the candlelight for me to see.

"Looks like you're excited. I wasn't sure," she taunted.

Grinning, she licked my wetness from each of her fingers. She must have seen me cringe because she revealed in my left

ear, "Don't worry, sweetheart, it's an acquired taste. But
once you've tried it, there's nothing that compares." Once
more, she softly kissed my cheek and worked her way down
my body with her powerful mouth. As she reached my stomach, my legs voluntarily spread. Her tongue danced over my
sensitive thighs, purposefully skipping my clit. Every sensation was sharp and stinging, intense and beautiful.

Grabbing my hands, Gretchen gave me a reassuring
squeeze as she went down on me. Her tongue massaged my
clit with catlike concentration. I wiggled, writhed, and
moaned under the control of her rhythm. No longer connected by mere wires, we became tangled fingers, sweat, and
flesh. She increased the intensity and the pulse of her tongue.
I grabbed the sheets and rocked my hips in unison with her
mouth. Faster, stronger, harder. My legs began to quiver.

"Oh, Gretchen!" I wailed.

She responded by further assaulting my clit. Bearing down
against the bed, I wrenched the sheets loose from the top corners. Fully, completely, I came in her mouth. My body was
filled with unfamiliar tingles of satisfaction.

Gretchen snuggled behind me and held me close; I began
to sob. I was embarrassed and tried to stop crying.

She caressed my hair and reassured me, "It's OK, hon.
Cry...let it all out, Cath."

She understood those tears better than I did. Release, con-
summation, realization. I was covered in sweat, sex, and
tears. A woman made love to me, and I was transformed.

Gretchen and I got together eight more times during the
next three months. Our interludes were filled with sex,
Coors, afternoon naps, take-out lo mein, and more sex.
Though we enjoyed our gluttonous trysts, we both knew our
fuckfests were not the stuff of a long-lasting relationship.

Four months after our first interlude, Gretchen accepted a
job in Alabama. Around the same time, I met an amazingly
beautiful woman named Heather in a car accident in

Philadelphia (that's a story for another day). Though Gretchen and I still write one another a few times a year, we have not talked or seen each other since the last night we shared together. But for a brief few months of my life, I too was brvncrzy.

My Bitch

Her name was Tommy. And she was a bitch. We worked together. It was one of those situations where the only contact we'd ever had was negative. Really. I never in a million years should have looked twice at her, but one day something happened, something peculiar, and I wonder even now if it was fate or destiny or some odd freakish occurrence or what, because it still doesn't make any sense.

Honestly, I didn't even think she was a dyke. Never thought about it, really. Didn't care. She was mean, and I was angry—what a combo. Who the hell needs that? As I said, we worked together. And that too was an interesting situation. It's not like she was my boss or anything, but the power differential was such that she should not have even bothered looking at me, and I certainly should not have tried speaking to her, even to just be nice.

Like all good dykes I did my time in the restaurant industry waiting tables, cooking, washing dishes, peeling potatoes, and doing anything else I could get my hands on. You name it, I did it, washed it, served it, garnished it, or in this case fucked it. I was serving the rich, snot-nosed patrons she spent her life trying to please. I hated them, they hated me, and we were all OK with that. Admittedly, I did watch her work, but I watched everyone work. That's what I do. I watch. I don't talk much, but I watch a lot. Watch and learn. I watched her day in and day out chop and create the delicious works of art that our shitty patrons couldn't or wouldn't appreciate. Every once in a while in an attempt to be engaging, I'd comment on her style or the cute pants she wore or how I noticed she had been out of town and wondered why. I never was trying to flirt or make trouble. I was just trying to be nice, something, I might add, that does not come easy to me. And she, even more bitter than I, was anything but receptive to my attempts.

When I told her I liked her pants, she said they were her least favorite, they didn't fit right. When I asked about where she went to school, she brushed me off with a one- or two-word answer. When I asked her how her vacation in Florida was, she snapped back, "I don't know. I was in Mexico." Cunt. She didn't like a goddamn thing about me. Not the way I stood, not the way I walked, not the way I interacted with our customers, not the way I dressed, not even the way I cut the fucking vegetables. She was a real charmer.

Then one day, out of the blue, she came to me and whispered into my ear, "I had a dream about you last night." What the...? Why would she dream about me? *I don't even like you* was all I could think. But that was it. Something inside me clicked, like one of the many quarters she ended up spending on phone calls to me. Something inside me jumped, hiccuped, and I was sold. It doesn't take much, I guess. Just the look of a beautiful woman, bitchy or not.

As I've said, I was easily as angry and bitter as she was. Still am. I was one of those young dykes who stomped and shuffled through life without a care for anyone around them. I rode my cheap, dented motorcycle in the snow, in the rain, in a goddamned ice storm. What the hell did I care? Life may be short, but not short enough.

But that sentence. Those few words hit me in the gut harder than the fist of any enemy ever did. I had to know what the dream was about. It plagued my mind. I was obsessed. I hated this woman. Well, maybe I didn't hate her, but I certainly hadn't given her a second thought until now. Now I couldn't get close enough to her enough times in a night. Fucking bitch, why'd she do that to me? And on top of the fact that she wouldn't tell me what the dream was about, her stupid fucking girlfriend worked with us too. Not just a girlfriend—they owned a house in the burbs and had been together nine years. Man, I was hating her more and more every day. It was almost as though she enjoyed the pain she was causing. Talk about bitter.

Finally, I had to know. "So, you gonna tell me what that dream was about?" I asked.

"No, but I'll show you."

There was no turning back from there. From that moment on, I had one goal and one goal only. I had to get her to kiss me. I'd stop at nothing. I didn't care who knew, who saw, who told anyone. All I knew was, I had to have this woman's tongue in my mouth. I came up with this plan to lure her into the basement under the guise of not being able to locate some food item. I'd back her into the walk-in and jump her. Failed. Granted, it was a stupid plan, but at least I was trying to be creative.

This stupid banter back and forth went on for some time. I, however, was not making any progress, and she was haunting my mind and my body more and more every day. I could only hope I was doing the same for her, but who knows. She never looked fazed. Just went about her merry way doing whatever it is Tommies do.

One miraculous spring evening she said to me, "Give me a ride." Yeah, baby, I'll give you a ride. But that's not what she meant. *Yeah, OK.* Why I happened to have my other helmet with me that day, I'll never know. I don't know if I was carrying it around in case of emergency or what, but I had it. Convenient. This woman had never been on a bike before, but even so she straddled that thing like she hadn't a fear in the world. I, on the other hand, wanted to throw up. She situated her tiny body behind me, and we were off. I had no idea where we were going; we just went. Every time I sped up or slowed down, her head careened into mine and cracked against the back of my helmet. I smiled. Sweet thing.

Around and around and around in concentric circles I rode, wasting time because I had her now. I wasn't letting her go, and I certainly wasn't going to let her go home to her nice little house in the burbs. No way, man. But despite what I really wanted to do, I had to let her go. We rode back to our starting point. She lifted her slightly shaky body off the seat, unbuckled her helmet, and handed it back to me. "Thanks. See you tomorrow," she said and gave me a hug. The way those arms wrapped around me, you would have thought I was the only stable entity left on Earth. You could see sparks shoot off us, ricochet off the pavement, and reflect in our eyes. Shit.

Tomorrow, then. If I thought it was bad before the ill-fated ride, it only got worse. There was no concentrating. I broke more dishes in a week than I had in the past year we had worked together. And now we were meeting on the sly. A nearby park became our solace and our stomping ground. The park was the only place we felt safe. It wasn't anywhere secret or anything, but somehow we knew we would not be found there. She would have a break from work, and I would come into town early, and we would meet there. Or we'd spend the evening working together, trying to ignore each other and meet there afterward just for the chance of one small kiss. We would have done anything for a kiss or a touch or something that would make the evil pressure in our chests go away, if only for a moment. One brief kiss or touch or look. Just something to let us both know that the other hurt just as much. Ouch. Then one afternoon after the ground had dried from the thaw, it happened. We managed to get the whole day together. In the park. It was warm and beautiful and sunny. You could smell the hormones in air. A perfect day for a fuck.

Tommy had taken to carrying a blanket in her trunk, perhaps for just such an event, perhaps not. I spread it out on the grass, and we sat—just looking at each other. I don't know who made the first move, but soon we were kissing. Passion seeped out of every pore in both of our bodies. The kisses kept coming, on our mouths, on our faces, on our necks. Sunlight heated our bodies as we heated our souls. I took off her jacket and laid it down to rest our heads. Unnecessary perhaps, but chivalry is not dead. We folded the blanket over ourselves so we were sandwiched between its layers. Her hand moved under my shirt to touch my breasts. First one, then the other. Her chef's fingers, rough from all the damage she had done to them, but still so soft, moved with precision over my body, my belly, my nipples. She focused her attention on just one breast at a time, the tips of her fingers playing me like the knives she used every day. My stomach jumped into my throat, and I didn't think I would be able to contain myself. I was convinced then and there that this simple manipulation would bring the orgasm I had spent the past weeks dreaming about. It had been a while since a woman had touched me. I uttered a moan of delight, and her hand moved from my tits to that place right below my belly button that becomes so sensitive when I'm turned on. She hovered there for a minute until I reached up and moved her hand lower onto the button fly of my jeans. Her nimble fingers easily released me and started to work their way even lower. She rested a moment with the tips of her fingers on the spot between my legs that was getting wetter and wetter every second that passed. *Please don't stop. Please.* The tightness of her hand in my jeans made the experience all that much more intense. Slowly she pushed my underwear aside and brushed one finger past my clit. I let out a moan of sensation that I have not since. It was like something out of a fantasy: a perfect day, a perfect woman, and soon a perfect orgasm. She touched me. Her fingers on my clit touched something deeper within me. "Please, baby. Please." I cried. "Don't stop." It was only seconds, I know. Only seconds passed before my feet were tingling and my legs were shaking. She knew even then exactly how to elicit from me exactly what she wanted to see and hear. Another second and it was over and I lay breathing in the smell of myself, the combined scent of cigarettes and her mouth.

I opened my eyes and looked into hers. She was grinning from ear to ear, like the fucking Cheshire Cat. "Ah, shit," I managed to utter.

We've been married four years now.

Just Like Old Friends

BY D.M. GAVIN

I had received a letter from Angela a month prior to New Year's telling me she was coming home for the holidays and wanted to spend a weekend with me. Since we'd made these annual reunions a tradition, her letter came as no surprise.

We had been friends for nearly a decade. We met when I was young and married. Angela was even younger and had just finished high school. Now she was living a state away and made treks to visit me every few months. By this time, I'd admitted to myself that I was a lesbian and had left my husband to live with a woman. It didn't take long for Angela to realize the same about herself and become involved with a woman she had met in Colorado, 2,000 miles away. In a little over a year, she dropped out of college and moved across the country to be with her lover.

I felt attracted to her the first time we met, and my feelings had grown stronger over the years. I didn't want her to leave the East Coast, but I lied to myself about why, since I was in a long-term relationship. At times I was inclined to think she felt the same way about me, but I convinced myself it was just my overactive imagination telling me again what I wanted to hear.

To complicate matters, I had begun to realize I wasn't as

happy in my relationship, which was now in its seventh year, as I should have been. Things between my girlfriend, Lyn, and me weren't as good as I wanted to believe, but I had refused to admit it to myself. Lyn had become surly and withdrawn. She had grown comfortable with our relationship and no longer tried to work to make it successful. She constantly brushed me off whenever I voiced my concerns.

Since Angela left the planning of our weekend together up to me, I reserved a suite in an elegant hotel in downtown Baltimore so the three of us could enjoy a long weekend, including New Year's Eve, together.

Lyn and I arrived first, having driven the two hours straight from work that Friday. I was excited. It took less than a half hour for us to unpack and get comfortable before heading downstairs to wait for our friend in the hotel lobby. We didn't make it. On the first stair landing, we came face to face with Angela. Our eyes met, and we both knew this visit would be different. Lyn seemed unaware of the chemistry.

I hadn't seen Angela in a year. She looked incredible. Had she always looked this beautiful? She stood before me with her dark curls framing her face, pink from the cold. Her inviting smile was aimed at me.

I tried to bury my inappropriate thoughts as the three of us headed out into the cold. We stopped at a liquor store to buy wine for our stay, and then we moved on to a gay bookstore where we browsed and laughed over a display of sex toys. Angela and I agreed instantly on which ones would be fun to try, while Lyn turned away, repulsed by any kind of sex that didn't involve a mouth or fingers.

There was an indefinable difference in the way Angela and I interacted that night. We were more intimate with each other and seemed more at ease than we ever had during our long friendship. Giggling like teenagers, we cracked jokes only the two of us thought funny. I could tell that Lyn prided herself on being the mature one as Angela and I laughed.

The more boisterous we became, the more Lyn crawled inside herself.

We headed back to our rooms, our arms laden with our purchases, and settled in for a catching-up session. While Angela and I shared a bottle of burgundy, Lyn slammed down beer after beer. Maybe she sensed what was coming and wanted to be oblivious for the occasion. Before long, Lyn was too intoxicated to remain upright and went to bed, where she passed out for the night.

Angela and I stayed in the living area, relaxing on the sofa, and resumed our discussion. The bottle of burgundy was soon emptied, and our conversation waned. Angela must have felt the electricity of the emotions flying around the room. Out of denial, or avoidance, she rose from the sofa and made a long-distance call to her ex in Colorado. My heart sank as I stretched out on the couch, wanting her to come back and devote all her attention to me. The burgundy was going to my head. During her conversation, I floated between varying levels of consciousness, some words clear, others too fuzzy to make out.

I was barely cognizant as Angela hung up the phone and came over to where I was lying. Resting her hand on my shoulder, she shook me gently and told me to get up so she could go to bed. I'm not entirely sure I knew what I was doing when I raised my hand, eyes still closed, and rested it on her side, stroking tentatively. The sound of her breathing immediately took a rougher, quicker cadence. Taking this as a sign of encouragement, I removed my hand and placed it under her shirt, rubbing the bare skin where my hand had rested seconds before. There was a sharp intake of breath on both of our parts.

"What are you doing?" she asked in a throaty whisper. Fearing rejection, I refused to answer and kept my eyes closed. She, unfortunately, took this as a sign that I was not fully conscious and that I was mistaking her for Lyn.

"Who am I?" she asked. Instead of answering, I removed my hand from her bare side and placed it behind her head, attempting to pull her toward me in a kiss. She resisted.

"Who am I?" she asked again. Finally, convinced I had been wrong about any mutual attraction, I gave up and lay still on the sofa. Angela pulled me from the sofa onto the floor, saying she needed to open it into a bed for herself. I lay on the floor in a desolate heap, convinced I had ruined my one chance.

Once the bed was open, Angela turned off the lights and climbed inside. "Get in," she whispered. I didn't have to be asked more than once. I tiredly climbed from the floor, using the streetlights streaming through the windows as a guide, then slipped in beside her. Leaning on my elbow, I looked into her face, unable to read what she was thinking, and kissed her as softly as I knew how. I was encouraged that she let me, but disheartened that she didn't kiss me back.

I lay back on the pillow and stared at the ceiling as we began to talk. I confessed that this attraction for her had been growing within me for at least the past five years and that somewhere along the line it had grown into love, a fact that surprised her. We talked some more, and after we had cleared the air about what we were feeling, and she was sure I wasn't drunkenly mistaking her for someone else, I tried again, and my insides melted as she kissed me back.

We pressed our bodies together as I kissed her, tasting the wine still on her lips and breathing in her scent. My hands touched her face, hair, and neck. I was so overcome by what I was doing, by what I had wanted to do for years but never considered a possibility, that the room began to spin, and I had to lie back again with a deep sigh. We held hands.

"I feel so guilty," I confessed. I had wanted this moment, had dreamed about it for years, and now that my wish was fulfilled, I was racked by a combination of elation and grief. "I've wanted this moment for so long, but I never thought it would come to this. And my lover of seven years is in the next room," I agonized.

Angela stroked my hair away from my face and murmured reassuringly. Suddenly, the guilt and alcohol proved too toxic a combination to bear, and I headed for the bathroom, where everything came up in a rush. I stumbled back to the sofa bed and lay weakly in Angela's arms.

"I should go to bed now. She's going to wonder where I am if she wakes up," I said, pointing to the next room. Angela sent me off with another kiss. I forced myself to sleep as excitement, mixed with guilt and wine, made my stomach flutter.

The next morning was New Year's Eve, and I experienced my very first hangover. After waking up, it took me a grand total of five seconds to remember what had happened the night before, and my stomach began flipping again. I felt as if my punishment for being unfaithful would surely be death by a severe tongue-lashing. I tried to decide whether or not I would confess to Lyn when we got home. Would she forgive even a kiss? She had told me several times over the years that only one thing would make her leave me: my cheating on her.

Lyn woke up and was more interested in watching a football game on TV than tending to my hungover body—another obvious sign of her disinterest in me. Angela woke up and joined us on the king-size bed, stroking my hair lovingly and every few minutes asking me how I was feeling. Finally, at Angela's urging, they both went downstairs to find something to ease my stomachache. After the previous night, it felt strange for them both to be alone together, but they returned within minutes with herbal tea and water, and urged me to hydrate my body. I sipped the water doubtfully, sure I would die before the day was through, but it worked wonders, and I was able to get up and dress so we could all go out for lunch.

My insides screamed the entire time. I felt reprehensible for what had happened, but it was also killing me that Angela and I couldn't get a moment alone to talk about it. She appeared so calm and normal, while I felt nothing but turmoil. *Is she sorry about last night?* I wondered miserably. Nothing in the way she looked at me was different, and I began to believe I might have imagined the entire incident.

At the restaurant we ate and carried on as if nothing had happened. My earlier paranoia that Lyn suspected something soon disappeared as the three of us talked and laughed, although I still felt an urgent need to be alone with Angela. What was she feeling about our encounter?

The opportunity came finally when Lyn offered to stand in line to pay our check and Angela went outside for a cigarette. I followed her out and stood with her in the subfreezing cold, my arms wrapped around myself—as much for support as for warmth.

"Are you all right?" I asked, unable to make eye contact. She smiled.

"I'm fine. How 'bout you?"

"I'm fine now that my stomach's settled," I answered. "What about last night? How are you feeling about what happened? Tell me what you want."

Angela took a drag from her cigarette, smiled, and responded, "More."

A slow grin captured my face, and I returned her stare. "OK. We'll need to get her drunk again. There's a liquor store across the street," I suggested, nodding in Lyn's direction as she stood inside the restaurant. My guilt disappeared and was replaced by intense deviousness.

Horribly enough, we headed to the liquor store, where we eyed the merchandise closely, suggesting to Lyn liquors with the highest concentration of alcohol. Stoli. Cuervo. Seagram's. Malibu. Crown Royal. Old Crow. I was determined to pursue a relationship with Angela. Lyn had to have known something was up since I usually discouraged her from drinking. She became obnoxious when she got drunk. Regardless, she settled on whiskey after making a fuss about drinking again after last night. We headed back to our room.

The hotel package deal included a complimentary dinner at a Polynesian restaurant. After dinner we were meeting a friend (who had just been named Mr. Mid-Atlantic Leather) at a leather bar. Fully aware of how I wanted this evening to end, I took extra care getting ready. I styled my hair and applied makeup carefully before slipping into a black crushed-velvet dress and heels.

I smiled as I thought back to earlier in the week when I had told a friend at work about the dress I had bought for New Year's. She smirked and asked if I had bought it to make an impression on "Miss Colorado," as she referred to Angela. I feigned ignorance, but my blushing cheeks gave me away. I had bought the dress with Angela in mind.

I finally began to relax when we got to the restaurant. Angela sat across from me, and Lyn sat next to me. More sure of myself now that Angela had been blunt about her feelings, I looked at her longingly across the table. She would see my looks and glance away, unable to return my gazes because she was also facing Lyn.

When Lyn got up to use the rest room, Angela and I talked openly but still shyly about the evening ahead of us. I reminded her that we had to drink enough to not cause suspicion, but not enough to damage our sobriety.

"The last thing I want is for you to be the one to pass out," I admitted.

We finished our meal, left the restaurant, and headed toward the bar. Arriving earlier than our friend Tom, we ordered drinks and took in our surroundings. After the first round of drinks, there was a commotion at the entrance as Tom and his lover walked in. They mingled with everyone in the club while Angela and I stood in a corner, looking more obvious than we should have.

Lyn spent most of her time with Tom, meeting his friends and having a good time. I think she had some suspicions about what was transpiring and tried to spend as much time away from me and Angela as she could. The men at the club certainly succeeded in keeping her mind off us, which was fine with me. I took the opportunity to occasionally whisper in Angela's ear how attractive she was and how I couldn't wait to get back to the hotel to continue what we had begun. Lyn only returned to where we stood when midnight struck. She kissed me as Angela looked on.

Ready to end the long evening, we called the hotel and asked for the limo to pick us up. The ride back was fraught with tension—on all sides. Back at our hotel suite, Angela and I were terribly obvious, encouraging Lyn to keep drinking as we nursed our own cocktails.

"Are you trying to make me pass out?" Lyn asked at one point. She finally gave in and went to bed after I promised I'd join her in a while.

When we were sure Lyn was asleep, we opened the sofa, turned the lights off, and crawled under the sheets. Our pent-up passion enveloped us as I took Angela into my arms and kissed her desperately. Our breath was ragged and hot as our mouths explored each other. I ran my hands through her hair. I kissed her mouth, her neck, eyes—any place I found exposed flesh. No longer afraid of how she might react, I ran my hands under her shirt and touched her bare skin. I raised my hand and took a breast into my palm, kneading her nipple while she moaned into my ear, sending chills through my entire body. I ran my tongue along her neck and moved up to nibble on her ear as she gasped and moved her hands under my shirt, raking her fingernails sharply along my back.

"Don't leave any marks, baby," I whispered, and she eased up.

I was afraid again. Lyn was in the next room. How soundly was she sleeping? Meanwhile, I was in bed with this person who may or may not wake the dead during sex. I had no idea what to expect.

"Can you be quiet?" I asked. Angela nodded her head and

kissed me again, harder this time. My hands trailed her sides again and moved down until they met the waistband of her panties. I tentatively moved inside and rubbed my flat palm against her stomach, feeling the warmth radiate from below, but temporarily unable to go any further.

That's it, my mind warned. *If you do anything else, you will officially cheat on Lyn, and you know what that means.*

Angela interrupted my conversation with myself by grasping my arms and whispering, "Don't tease me."

Everything but the thought of pleasing her rushed out of my mind as I moved my hand closer to her center. I reached between her open legs, amazed at the moisture that met my touch. I moved slowly at first, listening to her soft sighs as my fingers explored her, then faster as her breathing quickened. Her hips rose to meet my fingers, and her hands grasped me and pulled me closer. I held her as I stroked her and brought her closer to the climax she was moving toward. She came all too quickly and stilled my hand with her own. I held her and whispered words of affection until she caught her breath and asked to do the same to me.

Afterward we lay grinning in each other's arms. My guilt from the previous night did not return as I kissed Angela again and told her I was in love with her. She smiled.

"I love you too." I climbed from the bed and returned to the bed I—sadly—was supposed to be in.

The following day there was a noticeable change in Lyn. She was catching on to us. We made every attempt we could to get rid of her. During one of Lyn's outings, I was bending over to kiss Angela as the door began to open. I moved away quickly but not quickly enough. Lyn saw me move away from Angela's mouth and went to our room, where I found her crying. I tried to comfort her. I denied everything. I was not only a cheat; I was also a liar.

Angela and I tried to be more sensible about our feelings and agreed to attempt to control ourselves around Lyn. Our last evening together was miserable. I would be dropping Angela off at her parents' house the next day, and she would be off to Colorado within a week.

After Lyn went to bed, Angela and I walked together into the main lobby and settled into the fat cushiony sofa at the center. Completely alone, I confided my feelings again and asked if there was any way we could be together. To my utter surprise, she beamed and said she wouldn't mind moving back to the East Coast. My heart hammered at what this might mean. I was thrilled we might be together but terrified at the prospect of ending my relationship with Lyn. We held hands and talked for almost the entire night.

Toward dawn some guests came through the back door and busied themselves in the lobby. Wanting to be alone, I took Angela's hand and led her to a space behind the main stairs, pulling her into my arms. Her mouth met mine with hungry kisses. Unable to do anything more and unwilling to take a chance in our suite, I merely held her in my arms.

The following day we dropped Angela off as planned. *How can I leave her and go home with Lyn?* I thought. I had realized by this time how unhappy I was with Lyn and how wrong our relationship had become. I realized she wasn't the Princess Charming I had created. I agonized over when I should talk to her, knowing Angela and I would not see each other again for another few months.

Once apart, Angela and I spent enough time on the phone with each other to raise suspicions in not only Lyn but also Angela's parents. I convinced Angela to borrow her mother's car and drive the two hours it would take to see me. I had the entire week off from work. Lyn would be at her job. We would have the day to ourselves.

"I never got the chance to make love to you like I wanted to," I said. This reasoning was enough to convince her, and she arranged to borrow her mother's car two days later. I gave her directions to the house, and she agreed to arrive by 9 A.M.

Wednesday morning came, and Angela arrived. She would be leaving for Colorado in just a few days, but having her near eased my sadness. I put some music on the stereo, took her hand, and led her upstairs. I kissed her chilled skin, wanting to warm her inside and out with my mouth. I hurriedly removed her clothes and then my own, and pulled her forcefully into bed. Our kissed grew in intensity as our bare bodies touched for the first time.

I began making physical comparisons between Lyn and Angela. As my hands roamed her body, I thought of how different it all felt. Angela was smaller in every way: her waist, her breasts, her lips. It wasn't an unpleasant change, just different.

Holding her close, I kissed her neck. She moaned and grazed my back with her fingernails. I moved to her ears and sucked hungrily.

I wanted more, but I was suddenly shy. We had known each other for so long but never like this. I looked up at her comforting smile and moved down the length of her body, kissing her stomach and thighs along the way. Without warning, I opened her legs and took her fully into my mouth, delving into her warm taste and forcing another comparison into my brain.

She opened her legs wider and arched her back as I slipped several fingers inside her. With each moan, I thrust deeper and harder into her, until her entire body shuddered and a cry broke free from her throat. I smiled to myself as I remembered how, for years, I had known she would be like this. The smile remained as I moved up to hold her in my arms.

Before long her breathing returned to normal, and she was moving down my body, leaving scorching kisses in her wake. She teased me with her tongue as one, two, then three fingers entered me slowly. Soon we were following an identical rhythm as her fingers slid into me and my hips rose to meet her hand—first slowly, then frantically—until an orgasm tore through my body.

Instantly, I felt tears wash down my face and onto the pillow. The emotional ups and downs that had plagued me over the last week had finally surfaced. I had been trying to hide my feelings for Angela from Lyn all week. The turmoil I felt over what we were doing to Lyn, but being unable to stop myself from wanting to be with Angela, tore me apart. Besides, Angela was leaving to go back to Colorado in a little over 24 hours.

"What's wrong?" Angela asked, concern written in her eyes.

"It just hit me that you're leaving tomorrow. You're going to change your mind about being with me. I just know you will," I sobbed.

"No, I won't. I promise." She took me into her arms.

"You will," I continued, convinced this wouldn't last. I said I was sure that once she went home and told her ex about us, her ex would panic and do everything in her power to patch up their relationship.

"It won't happen. She's had the past several years to do that if she wanted." Angela held me until my tears subsided, stroking my hair away from my wet face and kissing my forehead in an attempt to comfort me.

"Don't spoil our time together worrying about that," she said. "Make love to me."

She brought her mouth to mine in a deep kiss, running her tongue along the inside of my mouth, planting an ache for her deep within me. I turned her over so that I was above her and kissed her neck before moving to her breasts. I took my time kissing and caressing each one before taking a nipple into my mouth and grazing my teeth over the swollen flesh.

I released her and turned over again, resting on my back and pulling her with me. She straddled my hips, and I moved my fingers between her legs, listening to her gasps as I entered her. She began to rock slowly, taking my fingers deep into herself with each movement. I watched her face contort in ecstasy, her head tipped back, her mouth slightly open as she rode my hand. My heart warmed, and my insides melted as she came, murmuring my name over and over.

We continued making love throughout the day, never leaving the bed. Three o'clock came all too soon, and we both knew Angela would have to leave before Lyn got home from work. We slowly dressed and hesitantly moved downstairs before embracing one last time.

"Don't worry about what will happen," Angela reassured me. "Everything will be fine. I'll call you on your birthday." And then she was off, leaving me with only memories to tide me over until we would meet again in the spring.

Unfortunately, my foresight had been well-tuned that day. Angela went back home and broke the news to her ex, who responded by begging for their reconciliation. It worked. Angela called me a week later to break the news. I was devastated...but not surprised.

I had confessed everything to Lyn the week before, only three days after the day Angela and I had spent together alone. She amazed me by forgiving me and trying to save our relationship by attempting to become a different person, one she thought would make me happy. The part of me that began the affair with Angela knew my relationship with Lyn wasn't salvageable, but I made a small attempt, even though I knew I should just end the relationship.

At the same time, Angela and I fought to save the friendship we once had. It was important to me, even through the pain, to keep the connection I had with her.

Just one month after our breakup, Angela sent me a Valentine's Day card, humbly explaining that she realized what a mistake she'd made by ending our budding relationship. My hopes skyrocketed, but my heart also sank. I was terrified of going through the gamut of emotions once again, only to be let down in the end.

It took several months to trust Angela again. I was afraid that if I resumed my relationship with her, she would hurt me once more. During those months we worked on our relationship long-distance. We talked on the phone and wrote several times a week. In July I moved out of the house I owned with Lyn and moved to Colorado to be with Angela. We've been together, happily, for more than four years now.

The Scream

BY LINDA A. BOULTER

"I'm good, really good," my new lover spoke softly and seductively as she drove toward a freshly found play area. She has a predilection for the "almost caught" kind of sex. For her, the thrill, the excitement is in the close call. This anticipation leads her to seek those spots, mostly outdoors, in semisecluded areas where she can thrill a lover. This time it was me. She is also quite charming. Combine a charming lover with an exhibitionist, and you most assuredly will be lured into her fantasies.

My sweetheart talked quietly about how much she would love to "take me" in a park. She said, "I'm quick, very quick, and very discreet. No one will know except you and me." I listened intently as she mesmerized me with silver tongue into playing a role in her fantasy.

She continued, "I promise you this will be an unforgettable experience." It sounded so tasty, as forbidden fruit always does. "Nothing else will matter except your pleasure and my passion," she crooned. Her hand kept time with her honey tones as she stroked my thigh. The motion sent shivers through my body. I surprised myself as I considered the possibilities of such an encounter. I am an introvert. The thought of being caught in such a vulnerable and private act ordinarily was not my idea of sexual play. My body, however, had different ideas. I felt myself moistening. I licked my lips as I found myself softly panting. I heard her say, "You won't regret it. I guarantee satisfaction."

Without warning, she turned into the parking lot of our local park. In the split second after she turned the signal on, I screamed. We talk about this scream now. My scream sounded both surprised and lustful. It was a "don't take me but, oh, my gawd, please do" scream. From this scream on I lost all rational consciousness. From words that spelled out how she would seduce me to actions that were leading up to the fantasy, I was thrilled. Mostly I experienced a feeling of sheer terror and anticipation. Pulling into the parking lot, she drove into the first available space. Lights out. Engine cut. When I heard the emergency brake engaged, I knew there was no stopping her. As she climbed over the brake, her knee skimmed the radio volume knob, and momentarily a song blared. I gasped. I felt the weight of her body as she lithely straddled me.

Her firm and moist lips found mine. As her tongue slipped in to explore my mouth, I felt a clunk as she disengaged my car seat and sent me sprawling backward. Her teeth found my neck, and as if I had a road map to my erogenous zones, she nibbled the nape of my neck down to my collarbone. I couldn't stop gently rocking as my hips moved up and down against her. When she eased down between my legs, I was only too happy to help remove the garments between me and pleasure. My panty hose and panties slipped off together, and I felt her warm breath blowing gently on my hair. My hands felt for her head, and, as was my habit, I started to rub her close-cropped hair. I knew from experience that I could not hurry her to the source of my pleasure. In the past she had thwarted my eager desire for instant gratification by prolonging foreplay to unbearable lengths. Tonight she nibbled my thigh, gently pausing to hover over and breathe on my labia as she moved to the other leg. The warmth of her breath very gently tickled my clit. I alternated between holding my breath in anticipation and panting in excitement. I was intimate with this stimulating torture. Sensual energy charged every pore in my body, every synapse in my brain awaited the pleasure drug that sexual release can bring.

The nibbling gently and softly turned to licking as her tongue explored the lushness of my pubic hair. Her hands gently kneaded my thighs, following up to the crevice between thigh and vulva. She found it warm and slippery. Her fingers glided up to part my lips. Her mouth found my pleasure. Small flicker licks sent shivers up my spine, and I moaned and whimpered with delight. Her tongue, flattened out, licked up my perineum, gently opening the folds of my clitoral hood to find a moistened erect pearl. Before this motion could cause me to peak, she found my clit between her lips and sucked delicately.

She told me I was pulling too hard on her ears and that she could barely hear the pants, squeals, and moans. My sounds of delight, the sensation of her ears being pulled, and the taste of my juices drove her into a feeding frenzy. The next thing I felt were two fingers slipping into my pussy—in and then out again, almost, but not quite. Her fingers curled up and caressed my G spot. As if this, the in-out motion and the ever-probing, ever-changing tongue movement weren't enough, fingers from her free hand reached up and pinched first one erect nipple and then the next. My hips, her mouth, and her fingers all kept remarkable time as I swooned into the moment. My body convulsed, and I felt a *whoosh* as warm liquid ejaculated out of my pussy. This was followed by an orgasm that I believe was the original *petit mort,* the little death. I felt like fainting and laughing and crying all at once. Even though the moment felt like an eternity, she later told me that from start to finish, the whole time we had been in the park only added up to five minutes.

As I lay sprawled in the passenger side, my feet up on the dash, a warm pool of wetness between my legs, she quickly popped up and moved back into the driver's seat. The headlights from a car pulling into the lot blinded my eyes as I opened them to see what had caused her to move so fast. She said, "I had a premonition someone would come while you were." I clutched my underwear, astounded beyond belief that she had seduced me by mere words and we were nearly caught.

Homemade Sauce

BY ANN MASTROFSKY

The memories attack at the least opportune moments: a woman reeking of her scent stumbles past me on the speeding elevated train, practically falling into my lap, embarrassing me into a sallow-faced flush; her common features suddenly appear on a complete stranger, causing me to do a double take and catch my breath when I realize it isn't her, that it couldn't possibly be her since she lives over 2,000 miles away from me, that even though it's been nearly a year since we broke up and we've had no contact since then, chances are slim she'd have relocated here just to torment me.

Our meeting was innocuous enough: a personal ad (hers), a self-consciously witty, truncated response (mine), a series of telephone calls, an airplane ticket, the creeping anxiety as the moment of connection loomed closer, leering like a molester.

Our first phone conversation ended in my first phone fuck. I took her to two glorious hours of fantasy: We fucked on the beach—in the hoariest tradition of lesbian sexual adventure—where I expertly fingered her to a rampaging orgasm after many minutes of delicious foreplay. My hand was sore and soaking from her passion, or so I told her. I imagined if we really had done all the things we breathlessly moaned about into the receiver, I'd be pretty sore indeed.

After that we talked on the phone every day. Within two weeks I was aboard an airplane, vibrator packed in my carry-on luggage, swallowing my lifelong fear of flight, and plunging into a fantasy world I knew existed but never dared grasp.

She was supposed to meet me at the baggage check. The plane was delayed by inclement weather; by the time the aircraft landed, I was berserk with anticipation. I felt like a punch-drunk prizefighter, knees shaking and palms clammy, as I staggered toward our rendezvous.

Somehow I made it to the baggage claim area without collapsing. I scanned the area, trying in vain to suppress my panic.

I recognized her immediately. She was a makeupless tomboy yet undeniably feminine, taller than her photographs suggested and cuter, with cropped hair and large, almond-shaped eyes shining with exuberance and life. She approached me, surveyed my Midwestern breasts, my strong, athletic build, my determinedly Russian features, my cropped brown hair, my green eyes, and my freckles. She smiled a wide, satisfied, shit-eating grin.

"Hi," she said.

"Hi," I stammered back.

She wrapped her arm around me and steered me to the parking lot. "It's time to get you home," she murmured suggestively, stroking my shoulder with her long, bony finger. Into the summer heat we went. Her ancient car, so decrepit it seemed to actually sprout moss, was blisteringly hot. The vinyl seats were like frying pans. Gallantly, she unlocked the passenger door for me and opened it. I threw my bag onto the floorboard and climbed in.

She opened her own door, slid behind the wheel, and inserted the key into the ignition. But she didn't crank it. Instead she turned sideways and looked at me, tenderly, hungrily. Between my legs, a familiar dose of electricity emanated and traveled up the length of my spine. She moved closer to me, rested her head on my shoulder, and sighed softly. "I had such a hard day," she whispered. Instinctively, I stroked this stranger's face, savoring the closeness. Her hands wandered over my middle, caressed the expanse of my stomach underneath my oversize cotton T-shirt.

She continued to explore my belly, remarking from time to time on the smoothness of my skin. "You're such a butch girl," she cooed, "but you're so soft and gentle. What's up with that?" I could only gurgle incoherently in response, the heat of the day and the heat of my body rendering me useless.

When her fingers found the thin stripe of pubic hair leading from my navel to my cunt, she moaned, then removed her hand from my body and sat upright. "I've got to get you home," she exhaled breathlessly. Eyes glazed with sex, she leaned over and kissed me. Our first kiss was very different from the many others we would enjoy for the duration of our affair; it had a perfunctory air and didn't linger, though there was that promise, that certainty of passion to come.

We held hands during the ride home. She lived in a pleasant, four-room apartment that had once been the lower floor of a single-family home. She parked her car in the long, sloping driveway and carried my bag up her wooden stairs and into the apartment. Her large white dog greeted us with expectant whimpers and great tail wags. We both hugged the dog; he seemed to like me.

"So," she said, stretching. I smiled and patted the couch. "Come here," I said softly. She obeyed, sitting on my lap. I stroked her back, her shoulders, her long, thin arms as she relaxed into me, each of us finding the other's touch and scent exhilarating. Slowly and deeply, we kissed, our tongues wrapping around themselves, our hands grasping and kneading, reveling in each other's taste and response.

Then she stood up, removed her shirt, and led me to one of her two bedrooms. She motioned to the floor, then to the single bed lying in wait for us, which she brought out for the occasion. She smiled, and I knew from the glint in her eye exactly what heights of pleasure would follow. During our marathon sessions of phone sex, the literal and figurative climax of our lovemaking had been prolonged with intense talk of fist fucking. When I had whispered to her every detail of my entire hand, thumb turned inward and fingertips slightly bent, slowly penetrating and then deeply fucking her cunt, she went wild. Within minutes, we had worked ourselves into a frenzied and uncontrolled orgasm, leaving the telephone dangling helplessly by the bedside.

I removed my own shirt and moved closer to her. I felt my breathing in my chest and my head. Her cheeks were flushed, and we were both already drenched with sweat. "Let's shower first," I suggested. She agreed. Together, we walked arm in arm to the bathroom.

The water felt like a baptism. She washed my feet, my legs, my asshole, my cunt, my breasts. I washed her hair, her navel, her underarms, her back. As she turned around to shut off the water, I knelt behind her and washed her asshole. At my touch, she sighed with pleasure, bucked, and pushed her ass toward me. I set the washcloth down and grabbed her slender thighs with my hands. I'd never rimmed anyone before; I'd never particularly wanted to. But this woman took me to heights of passion no one had ever approached. I tongue her asshole, tentatively at first, then with growing passion.

It tasted sweet and slightly bitter, redolent with the odor of her body. She groaned in ecstasy at the surprise. I quickly reached around her front and began to stroke her clit with my index finger, pushing her ass harder onto my face with every stroke. I steadily worked her asshole with my tongue, twirling her clit in tiny circles with my finger, softly at first, then with more and more pressure as she moved her hips with the rhythm of my thrusts.

I took my other hand and played with my own clit as juices flowed from her cunt onto my fingers.

"Stop it, stop it," she heaved. "You're going to make me come too fast."

We kissed passionately, toweled off, and padded nude to the spare bedroom. We lay on the bed and embraced.

"Goddamn you," she whispered as she pressed her body into mine. "You're so impatient." I reached down and touched her cunt. She was wetter than any woman I'd ever been with. "See what you do to me, you cute dyke?" she asked.

She kissed me, took my hand and pressed it over her cunt, squeezing my palm with her thighs. Then she took her own hand and stroked my clit. I'm a notoriously fast comer, and I was so turned on from eating her ass that the staccato thrusts from her knuckle sent me rocking and screaming into orgasm before I could even begin to think of holding out, holding back. She watched me come, proud of her prowess, licking my neck, my ears, my face. I clutched her long, skinny arm, the one that had made me feel so good, and stroked it lovingly, thankfully. I rested for a few minutes, chest heaving. Then I raised myself up on one arm and smiled at her. She smiled back.

"Are you ready, baby?" I asked. "Are you ready to be split open?"

Her brown eyes melted with desire. She lay back, spreading her legs far apart, waiting to receive me. Beginning with my tongue, I licked her body from head to toe, sucking, rolling, and flattening her nipples with my lips, lightly dragging my teeth over the underside of her breasts, her navel, her sides, and paying special attention to her cunt. I teased her clit and the folds concealing her vagina for several of the longest minutes she had ever known. When I was satisfied she was ready, I lowered my lips to hers, kissed her, and cupped my palm under her vagina, my index finger poised at its apex. Within seconds, she instinctively rocked her hips to receive me, and her cunt absorbed my finger as if it were part of her own body. Slowly, agonizingly, I began to slip my finger in and out of her cunt, feeling her move with me, refusing to quicken my pace, wanting to drive her insane with lust, watching her beautiful face contort in response to me. My own cunt ached from excitement.

"How many, baby?" she panted.

"Just one," I whispered in her ear, licking it.

"I want more. Give me more," she breathed.

In the same manner, I gently inserted two more fingers inside her. Now the first three fingers of my hand were fucking her cunt with renewed intensity. Her vagina was a warm, wet glove that cinched itself around me, becoming a single entity with me.

"Give me all of you," she cried suddenly. "I want all of you, baby!" She raised herself to her haunches. I added my pinkie finger first, wriggling and snaking it inside her, careful not to move too quickly. She was sweating, eyes clenched shut, mouth open wide to reveal her teeth, her tongue, the roof of her mouth. When four of my fingers were safely and comfortably inside, I pressed my thumb close to my palm and slowly began to thrust. She sighed loudly, arched her back, and spread her legs as far apart as she could. Oceans of wetness poured from her cunt as she welcomed me into the deepest caverns of her body. "God, baby, feels so good," she screamed. Both of us were molten with sweat and sex, and as I pressed my fist as deeply inside her as I could, I reached around with my opposite hand and began to lightly stroke her clit. At that she screamed again and let herself go, coming and coming ferociously.

After we lay recovering for a while, I withdrew my fist from her limp, spent body. I went to the bathroom, cleaned myself up, and wet a washcloth with cold water. I returned to the bedroom with the washcloth, where my lover lay spread-eagle on her bed, body still trembling in the aftermath. Gently, I wiped her down. She murmured her appreciation, rested her head in my lap, and contentedly purred as I washed her. Later, after a midnight snack and tending to the dog, we snuggled together in the master bedroom before drifting off to sleep.

I didn't know then, at the beginning when everything was glorious and so much remained unspoken, how much there was to learn about the stranger whose bed I had set alight that steamy summer evening. During the three months of our torrid affair, I would discover there was somebody else already in the picture and that there would be more; that she was not monogamous, though I was; that she was not looking for love, though I was. In the end, my heart would be broken and nearly destroyed by the brown-eyed girl with the longest fingers I'd ever seen. But for those three months, I enjoyed deeper passion than I had ever known.

I haven't touched a woman since. My heart insists I get to know someone better next time around. When I do find myself in bed next to a beautiful woman, my mind will undoubtedly drift, if only for a second, to the sound of jet engines taking me to a small town thousands of miles from my home.

Please Wear Romantic Attire

I checked the address on the Valentine's Day party invitation one last time before I folded the red card and crammed it into my pocket, no doubt breaking or at least bruising some of the tiny pink hearts that decorated it.

"We hardly know these people," said Pip, and it was true. We'd met them just last summer on Martha's Vineyard, at the home of the only rich person we knew. "They're probably rich too," Pip said, her eyebrows settling into an arrow of consternation. Her eyebrows are expressive; indeed, she is the only person I know who can elevate them independently, in a manner she copied from James Bond in his Sean Connery incarnation, having practiced in front of a mirror because she thought it was sexy. I felt it looked far sexier on her than it ever could on James Bond, but then I liked most of the expressions that passed across her somewhat piratical face, with its beaky nose and oceanic blue eyes. Right now, she was worried about her attire, whether it qualified as romantic, whether she would be underdressed. "I can't bear to think what they'll make of *you*," she said.

At least my underpants qualified as romantic. They were a brief snatch of black lace, cut just below the start of my pubic hair and crested with a pearl. Almost everything else was black leather. My trousers were tight, though not uncomfortable, curving around my buttocks and firmly holding my crotch. Pip had bought me the cowboy boots for my birthday, and the left one flaunted a set of silver chains. My tiny Native American vest exposed my back, arms, shoulders, and the tops and sides of my breasts, which were forced up and into a cleavage. My shirt was black cotton, with Victorian leg-of-mutton sleeves and a demure row of buttons up the front. The neck plunged dramatically, exposing the tops of my breasts, clutched in a glimpse of taut black leather.

The jewelry I chose was all silver, a thick dog chain and a slender one for contrast, a heavy earring in my left ear, and on the right middle finger a broad ring depicting two dolphins entwined in an embrace.

Just before we left, I pulled on my jacket. It was Pip's first Christmas present to me and my most treasured possession. All the leather we have since added to my collection has been modeled on the jacket's soft, thick, jet-black shine. It cuts away to the waist but curves around my breasts and shoulders. It has short zips down the back and at the cuffs. I have only to put on this jacket to rise to the challenge of looks and glances that black leather attracts. People react in various ways when I wear black leather. In bars some women ask to touch it. Some women turn the other way. Some assume a flirtatious air of mock submission, and others add an almost imperceptible edge to their manner.

The party was indeed wealthy, professional, and delicate. The couple who hosted it were as nervous and attentive as any other aspiring suburban pair. I was amazed to find they not only had a champagne cooler but also servants who removed glasses as soon as they were put down and who discreetly replenished the plates of creamy little desserts as fast as they were consumed. The only thing that gave it away as a lesbian event was the absence of men.

As I munched happily through flaky confections that col-

lapsed and oozed in my mouth, and engaged in polite conversation with the socially easy, I assessed appearances. Our
hostesses were elegant: Louise in a loosely cut jacket and skirt
and Pat in a crisp white blouse, severe black skirt, and red
rose. There were other variations on the theme of "Romantic
Attire," from matching T-shirts (I'M CHARLENE'S GIRL/I'M
SALLY'S GIRL) to shirts with red hearts.

"Don't leave me," said Pip. "I'm having a shy attack."

"And what do *you* do?" said a tall woman in a flowing
purple dress. A large necklace made of gold coins clanked
against her bony clavicle. She held her wineglass at a perilous
angle, as if she were too tired to hold it straight.

"I'm a commercial window cleaner," I said. "How
about you?"

She threw her arm back in an expansive gesture, slopping
Californian zinfandel onto the shag carpet. "How lovely!"
she said. "I love that women are in all the trades." She bent
toward me, "I expect you hang from those tall buildings.
Aren't you terrified? I can't even clean my second-floor windows. Maybe I should hire you!" She tossed back her head
in a sort of neigh, as if the idea of hiring a big old dyke like
me to wash her windows would be an act of most delicious
rebellion.

I hate this whole predictable routine, partly because it's pa-
tronizing and partly because it makes me feel that hanging
from buildings is the only thing that would make my work
romantic or interesting. "No, I don't hang from buildings," I
said, and then, somewhat cavalierly, "and I don't want to
clean your windows either."

She brought her artistic gyrations to a halt. "Why not?"

"Because you'll get upset when I put my bucket on your
Shiraz rug," I told her. "And you'll wait until I've gotten
all the way back down the ladder to tell me there's a tiny
little spot in the corner of a third-floor window. I know
your type." I smiled at her to take the sting out of the joke,

and she smiled right back and took hold of my arm.

"You must be quite strong," she said, and gave my biceps a squeeze.

"Oh, yes, she is," said Pip, and I noticed her eyebrows were expressing a certain exasperation, her buccaneer's eyes a somewhat steely indignation. "Why don't you take off your shirt and show the nice lady?"

I have learned from experience that the only way to retain any dignity when Pip makes these suggestions is to act promptly.

As I undid the short row of buttons at the front and slipped off the cotton shirt, I was unaware of the crowded room behind me until an arm crawled playfully around my leg. I turned to meet a concerted and admiring stare. The combination of my well-defined arm and shoulder muscles, my tight black leather, alcohol, and the spirit of Saint Valentine produced a palpable wave of sexual energy in the room. As I turned away, rather confusedly, the bony woman stroked my arm gently.

"Nice deltoids," she murmured.

Out of the corner of my eye I saw Pip's sardonic smile. We left shortly afterward, and when we got home I went into the bedroom and pulled off my boots. Next I peeled off my trousers, folded them, and set them carefully beside the boots. As I considered taking off my black lace panties and the vest, Pip looked around the door.

"Leave that on until I get back from the bathroom," she said casually.

When Pip came back, she began to play with me gently, stroking the black leather vest, pulling the fringes, and examining the way my breasts bulged against the top. She rolled me onto my stomach and untied the strap that held the vest together. It came away in her hands, and she stroked me with it so I could smell the leather. I tried to kiss her, but she pushed me firmly back onto the bed, untied the two chains around my throat, and ran the cold metal slowly across my belly. Then Pip turned her attention to my nipples.

She took my right nipple firmly between her fingers and twisted it until it swelled and stiffened. She coiled the heavy chain in a spiral around my breast, pulling it tightly so that it sank into the softness. Then Pip squeezed breast and chain together with both hands, leaving the nipple straining to be touched. She leaned down and put her tongue to it, then raised her head to look at my reaction.

"That's so good," I said. "I want you to do it harder."

Pip gave my breast a rough squeeze and examined the way it made my aching nipple stand up even farther before she took it between her lips. Her other hand strayed to my left breast, then grabbed it. She fumbled until she found that nipple too, and trapped it, squeezing and twisting breast and nipple together. Meanwhile, Pip's teeth had replaced her lips at the first nipple, nibbling and teasing it. I opened my legs wide, rolling my hips and hoping she would touch me, but she only smiled and picked up the heavy dog chain with her left hand. Her right hand began to rub the hairs at the top of my pubis. As Pip looked into my eyes, she slid her fingers down the outside of my soaked panties and brought them to my face for me to smell. She pulled my panties off and pushed my legs apart again, with a hand on each knee. Casually, she licked her lips.

Parting my wet and sticky hairs, Pip flicked her tongue over my clitoris. I jerked and shuddered as she slowly pulled the chain up and across the slit of my vulva...hot, wet tongue and chilled, sharp chain together.

"So, you like this, do you?"

"Yes, yes, oh, God..."

I was at the point of orgasm when suddenly Pip was on top of me. Her hands clutched my buttocks as she rode me, giving me just enough to keep me groaning and gasping.

I felt the heat of her against my leg. As Pip and I both came near to fusion we slowed and stopped. I rolled off her T-shirt, stroked and fondled a hanging breast in each hand, licked and sucked the tightness of her nipples, forcing her to press her inflamed sex against me again. After a few minutes, Pip took my wrists and forced them above my head. Picking up the leather vest, she blindfolded me and went to work on my nipples again, wrapping the chain around each of them in turn, twisting it to the point where pain and pleasure mingle. Forcing and squeezing my breasts together so that my nipples nearly touched, Pip passed quickly from one to the other, biting and sucking, holding both breasts in one hand in order to fuck me with the vibrator. She let me feel its snub nose seeking entrance before she sank it deep into me, plunging it again and again, all the while kneading and teasing my tits hard, and harder. I felt Pip's lips at my neck, and moved in a way I knew excited her, until she took hold of me with her teeth, growling softly with pleasure.

Finally, she left the vibrator inside me and kissed me, filling my willing mouth with her salty tongue, reminding me that while others might look, I want only her to take me like this.

Lifting the blindfold and slipping out the vibrator, I rolled Pip onto her back, and took position above her, my knees on either side of her head, my hands fumbling with her panties, all pretense of elegance gone. I moistened her swollen clitoris by smearing it with the flood I found between the folds of her labia. I rolled it gently between my thumb and finger, and started up the same rhythm on the breast and nipple I held in the other hand. From her position below me, Pip entered me again, a mute appeal for the same attention on my part. When I lost count of the fingers she was pumping into my dripping wet slit with the same insistent beat I was using on her clitoris, I rolled Pip around until we were side by side, and slid down to make the most of her hot, wet cunt, inhaling her, teasing my fingers at the edge of her vagina until she forced herself over and around me. I rewarded her with the hard insistent pressure of my tongue and the sly relentless movement of my fingers, bringing her to the edge, then slowing just enough to keep her hanging there, gasping for air, pinned to my touch.

I slid my fingers out carefully and used them to rub her clitoris in a firm circular motion, moving my mouth to hers, and my other hand to her breast, holding her on the very brink of orgasm. I slid my body onto hers and clutched her shoulders to drive my hips into her, feeling her shudder, hearing her moan softly again and again as I was driven by the same wild unstoppable joy as she was, and knew that in five, six, seven strokes more we would both explode. I drew Pip to me, wrapping my arms around her, and as our mouths fastened together blindly we were rocked by the same blast. We clutched each other as if to take protection from its force, as if we expected clouds of dust, debris, pieces of masonry.

A while later, we reoriented ourselves in the bed, plumped the pillows, set the alarm ("My God, it's 2 A.M.!"). Pip fished her pajamas out from under the pillow. I struggled into my oversize T-shirt, which pronounced me a member of the teddy club.

"Romantic attire," I murmured softly as we snuggled together in the wet patch, but she was already asleep.

Close Shave

My workout had been demanding that day, and the steam
bath afterward felt particularly good. Lying naked on my
towel in the steam room was always pleasurable, and I'm
proud to show off my body to everyone. I have worked hard
to stay in good shape, not an easy task at 42, but the results
of my weight training and aerobics are readily apparent.

Since I usually had the steam room to myself, I was at first
disappointed when the door opened. But when I glanced up
to see who had entered the room, I recognized the cute red-
head from the weight room. As she removed her towel, her
beautiful breasts swung free as she leaned over to spread her
towel on the tier opposite me. She shot me a big smile and
said, "How nice to have company in here." I turned on my
side to talk with her, giving her a full view of my 36D breasts
and well-trimmed pussy.

Although I had never had a liaison with a woman before,
I had fantasized about it dozens of times and had recently become increasingly attracted to women, particularly large-
breasted, slim-hipped women like myself. And there were
constant thoughts of sucking on another woman's breasts,
touching our nipples together, caressing and fingering all the
places I loved to be touched myself.

"This is a great health club," she said. "Sure wish we had one like it in Rochester. By the way, I'm Rachel."

"Nice to meet you, Rachel. I'm Kathy. What brings you to Washington?"

"I'm in town for a three-day conference and staying at the Marriott across the street. Do you live here?"

"Yes, I have for many years," I said. "What kind of conference are you here for?"

As we continued to chat, I learned that Rachel is a CPA, and her conference was an update on the latest tax changes. We hit it off immediately, and as we spoke, her eyes occasionally focused on my nipples, which had become erect. I discreetly admired her body as well; her shaved pussy really turned me on.

"You know, I haven't really met anyone since I arrived here. Would you like to have dinner with me? It's always so lonely when you travel," Rachel smiled.

I do my share of business travel as a computer consultant and certainly know about loneliness on the road, but detected she might be looking for more than a dinner companion. "I would love that, Rachel. I don't have anything planned tonight."

"Great. Since you know your way around here far better than I, would you mind coming by my hotel for a cocktail before we go out? I'm in room 504."

"Sounds good to me. See you around 7 o'clock?"

"I'll be ready," she smiled again.

Rachel and I left the steam room together, not bothering to wrap our towels around us, and I couldn't help staring at her nice ass as she walked toward the showers. My pussy was already dripping wet when I got in the shower, and I was eager for the next two hours to pass. Although she had not said anything suggestive, the vibes were definitely making me tingle.

Once I got home, I selected a sexy cream silk blouse and

opted not to wear a bra. In spite of my age, my tits have not sagged, and they look great under a silky blouse. I paired this with a knee-length black skirt with a high slit on the side, and wore only a pair of lacy thong panties. I thought of not wearing any at all, but I was worried about a big wet spot forming on the back my skirt during the drive to her hotel. A pair of black low-heeled pumps completed my outfit. My body stays tanned year round, thanks to twice-monthly trips to a tanning salon in the colder months, so I rarely wear nylons.

I knocked on Rachel's door promptly at 7 o'clock, and she looked radiant in a peach silk sweater and matching silk miniskirt showing off her long slender legs. "Wow, you look beautiful," I exclaimed.

"You mean I look different with my clothes on?" she laughed as she handed me a glass of wine.

I must have blushed because she laughed again and said, "I know what you mean. Isn't it a shame we have to cover these beautiful bodies with clothes?"

I agreed and told her I thought she had an incredible body, and especially liked her shaved pussy. "That's something I've just done recently," Rachel admitted, "and I'm still getting used to it. Do you really like it?"

"Oh, I think it's very sexy. But how often do you have to shave?" I asked.

"At least every other day. Have you ever done it?"

"No, but I've thought of doing it many times. I was afraid I'd cut myself, though."

"I have an idea. Why not let me help you do it—right now?" she asked.

The idea of Rachel shaving my pussy made me so wet, I thought I was dripping on her floor. "Oh, no, I couldn't ask you to do that. I—" I started to protest, but she quickly piped in. "It's settled," she said. "Let me just order room service while we finish our wine, and we'll just make an evening of it here. OK?"

There was no way to refuse an offer like that, and we sat on the sofa in her sitting room and waited for dinner to arrive.

We both opted for a light meal and enjoyed pleasant conversation and a lot of laughs while eating. Finally, Rachel said, "OK, are you ready?"

She must have sensed my nervousness at the prospect of another woman touching my most intimate areas, and said, "I'd like to ask you a personal question, if you don't mind. Have you ever been intimate with a woman before?"

"I guess you can tell I'm pretty nervous, huh? No, I haven't, but I've certainly fantasized about it enough!" I laughed.

Rachel gently took my hands in hers and told me, "Just relax. I promise we won't do anything you don't want to. Now, how about changing out of those lovely clothes while I get ready to shave that pussy?"

Rachel decided to do it on the sofa, and spread several towels out after retrieving a bowl of hot water from the kitchenette. She watched me closely as I removed my blouse and skirt, and asked if she could pull off my thong panties. "You do have a beautiful body, Kathy. I'm going to take off my things too, so I don't get any water stains on this." With that, she slid out of her sweater and miniskirt. She also wasn't wearing any panties, and her shaved pussy looked plump and sweet. My nipples were already like pebbles, and I felt myself getting wet.

"I'm going to kneel here on the floor while I do this for the best view while I shave you," Rachel said. "Pull one leg back and keep the other leg down here. Wow, what a beautiful pussy you have."

With that, Rachel proceeded to shave me, gently and slowly. She warmed the lather in her hands before massaging it into my pussy hair with her slim, long fingers. As I sat with my legs spread wide and my pussy only inches from her face, I couldn't help daydreaming what it would be like for her to kiss my pussy lips and twirl her tongue around my clit. She started at the outer edges of my bush, the razor tugging gently against the hair and leaving a clean path behind. Every time she applied the lotion she rubbed it gently through my hair to be sure the skin beneath was lubricated.

As Rachel shaved closer and closer to my smooth inner labia, her touch sent shivers through me as her fingers touched and pulled my pussy lips this way and that. Occasionally her fingers reached inside my lips, touching my clit, as she held the skin taut for the razor. My fantasies were becoming more and more explicit as she continued to gently pat the warm shaving cream behind my pussy hole to ensure a clean path there as well. Rachel put her soft warm hands on my inner thighs to spread them farther apart as she put the finishing touches on my clean-shaven pubic mound. By the time she finished and used a moist towel to clean up any remaining shaving lotion, I was hotter than a firecracker and nearly panting.

"There," she said, "just like a newborn baby girl." And then she slowly pulled my pussy lips apart and with one finger stroked my engorged clit. "You are so wonderfully wet, and I can tell how much you enjoyed being shaved. Why not lie back on the sofa and let me admire your beautiful body for a while?"

I couldn't have stopped her if I had wanted to. As she ran her soft, warm hands all over my body, I quivered with excitement. She squeezed my tits and nipples, gently licking and sucking them. Her soft lips on my nipples lit a fire in my pussy, and I started wriggling around on the sofa. She slowly moved her mane of red hair down my torso, beneath my navel, ending with her tongue in my newly shaven pussy. She flicked her tongue around my clit and in and out of my pussy, then inserted two fingers deep inside. It took less than a minute for me to explode in the most incredible orgasm I had ever had.

Rachel smiled at me and said, "I hope this first experience was good for you, Kathy. I love licking your pussy."

"I want to know what that feels like. Would you let me do it to you?" I asked.

Rachel suggested we move to the king-size bed, and pulled down the covers to reveal fresh sheets. As she lay on the bed, I admired her voluptuous tits with my hands and mouth, amazed at how wonderful it felt to caress another woman. Like a kid with a new toy, I explored her entire body with my hands and tongue, marveling at the softness. Under her neck, down her sides, down her long legs...when I got to her sweet pussy mound, I opened her lips with my fingers and licked her sweet juices. It felt so soft and smooth, and I was so carried away with the new sensations that it surprised me when her hips started bucking up and down. I was making her come! I continued probing my tongue in and out of her pussy until she begged me to stop.

As I moved up the bed to lie beside her, Rachel reached out and hugged me. Our tits squeezed together, and once again electric shocks ran through me. We kissed for a while and finally fell asleep in each other's arms, exhausted. We made love again and again while Rachel was in town, and we have plans to meet in Rochester in a few months.

Waiting for Real Love

BY JANE WOLSEY

I had my first sexual encounter on my 31st birthday. A long time to wait, by today's standards, but when no one asks to go to bed with you, you learn to be patient and satisfy yourself. Unlike a lot of women, though, I waited for love, real love. I wanted to be crazy in love with the first person I ever slept with, and not just do it to get it over with as my friends and sisters did. How could I know my first love would be my boss's wife?

Her name is Geri, and thankfully, she feels as strongly about me as I do her. A lithe, beautiful, older woman with dancing blue eyes, she was 48 when we first made love but was often mistaken for 32 because she takes such good care of herself. With her red hair, slim build, and the softest skin that all women should envy and imitate on this planet, it didn't take long for me to fall head over heels in love with her less than a year after we met.

We began our relationship as client and hairstylist. I had just moved from another county and needed a new stylist, and who better than my boss's wife? I was happy to give her the business in her new occupation. Gradually we moved into a real friendship. Hanging out together, going to museums, plays, and movies soon became the norm, and her husband didn't see anything wrong with it. In fact, he encouraged it, as I liked to do so many things with her that he didn't enjoy. He didn't know making love would be one of them.

Eventually Geri and I became close friends, and she stopped taking my money for haircuts. We'd barter sometimes—a movie or dinner for a trim. It seemed fair and innocuous, and I was happy with the arrangement. One night, when she complained of a sore shoulder, I offered her a back rub in exchange for my monthly trim. Geri agreed readily. In the privacy of her home salon, I would feel this love for the first time.

After the cut I sat her in the chair and began to work on her shoulders. That's when I got to touch her silken skin. As I kneaded it and worked my magic on her soreness, I found myself getting very excited. I wanted to kiss her neck so badly, I could hardly concentrate on anything else. My body felt on fire, and I was blushing uncontrollably. We conversed about mundane issues, and I was glad Geri couldn't see my face in the mirror. Her head suddenly bobbed up and down.

"I'm not hurting you, am I?" I asked.

"No. Oh, that feels so wonderful. Are you sure you haven't missed your calling as a masseuse?"

"Maybe I have," I replied. I could think of little else to say; the thought of her bare skin against mine filled my head. By the time I finished, I was shaking all over. I tried to cover it up and prayed she wouldn't notice. Geri was, of course, totally unaware of my feelings for her. Or so I thought.

We continued to grow closer and closer. I kept my feelings to myself, but came out to my one gay friend, Joey, who was extremely supportive while warning me about what I was getting myself into.

"It's never easy being in love with a straight, married woman," he told me over and over. But his words didn't stop my feelings. I was happier, though, for I at least had come out, in word if not in deed. I had said those three little words that would change my life forever: "I am gay." I only wished it hadn't taken me until I was 30 to figure it out.

Five months later a miracle occurred. Geri and I had spent the day at a fashion show, a harmless event attended by many people, including her husband. Later, as I was home alone watching TV, she called me and, out of the blue, said those fateful words: "Jane, I'm falling in love with you."

When I finally got my heart down from the ceiling, I didn't know what to say, so I replied excitedly, "The feeling is mutual."

"Is it?" she asked.

"Yes, of course. Oh, Geri, I can't believe you feel this way. I've felt the same about you since before spring."

"What are we going to do?" I heard the concern in her voice.

"I don't know, but I must see you soon. I need to talk to you about this face-to-face."

Geri and I made a date to see each other on Sunday two days later. I wish I could remember more of what we said on the phone, but those words at the start of the conversation never stopped buzzing in my ears: *I'm falling in love with you.*

I mean, I had never heard those words spoken to me before. I reveled in the knowledge that someone other my family and friends loved me for me—and wanted my body badly, as I would soon find out. Just imagine the elation, the unbelievable emotion swimming through my body and mind as I tensely waited to see what would happen next.

I was both excited and terrified. As a teenager I never even had a steady boyfriend. Would I make an ass of myself courting her? What were the right things to say and do? I couldn't act more experienced than I was—she already knew I was a virgin. And how would I face my boss every day, feeling the way I did? I finally decided that since Geri was more experienced, I'd take my lead from her and keep my cool at work as best I could. It wasn't easy, but I managed.

We began this new stage in our relationship by talking

many hours about ourselves and what we wanted. It was obvious she was unsatisfied in the bed department in her marriage, and I wanted to rectify that. Our talks soon turned into necking on my couch. Necking turned into heavier petting with our tops coming off in a matter of weeks, and our eyes, tongues and fingers exploring more each time. One time Geri and I went at it pretty heavy in her hot tub; it was the first time I took her breasts in my mouth and heard her gasp with pleasure. That was sheer joy. But we needed to wait until we could be alone overnight before we could sleep together. Fortunately, that day would come on my birthday in February.

Geri's husband, a golf fanatic, was going on a trip to Florida to play golf with several buddies and would be gone for five nights. Five nights! I couldn't believe it. I would have her to myself for five glorious nights. Finally, she would teach me everything about sex, and we would teach each other the wonders of our bodies together in bed. I don't know who was more excited, she or I. Geri had never slept with a woman either, but I tell you, knowing about his trip almost four months in advance made it the hardest Christmas and New Year's ever. I don't know how I survived the anticipation until February without going crazy.

The day finally arrived. I packed my overnight bag to take to her house, and we began with a nice birthday dinner at the Outback Steakhouse. OK, the steak on my plate wasn't exactly the meat I wanted to eat right then and there, but watching Geri watching me, knowing what would come later when we got back home, made it worth the wait. We flirted, rubbed against each other under the table and did all manners of things to get ourselves hot and ready for our first time.

When we got back home, I opened her gifts to me: a book, a framed quotation, and a lovely vanity chair she had hand-painted. I delighted in each one. Geri knew what I really wanted for my birthday, though, and I was more than ready to receive it and her. Soon after, we made the bed in the loft.

The full moon bathed the loft in a clear, pure, gray-blue light from the ceiling windows. We could see everything. The setting couldn't have been more perfect.

We kissed for a long time, endlessly it seemed, with deep, soft, wet kisses that left me breathless. Geri remarked, "God, you kiss so well. I can't believe you've never kissed like this before."

"With you as my teacher, it doesn't take a lot of instruction, trust me."

As we kissed, Geri slowly undressed me and I her. I was stupid to wear panties underneath my pajamas, but she soon had me free of them.

"Beautiful," was all she said when she gazed upon my 38DD breasts in the moonlight. She sucked my breasts and brought my nipples to firmness in no time.

"Do you really like them?" I asked. I had always been a bit shy about how large I was.

"They're like alabaster, Jane. So pretty. So soft." She made me feel like the sexiest creature alive, each touch bringing goose bumps to my flesh as she caressed my breasts affectionately.

She lay on top of me, kissing me deeply. I thought my head would explode. Nothing had ever felt so right. Our flesh seemed to melt into each other, and then I knew for sure my life would revolve around being able to feel this way again and again with her.

I touched her below and gasped. "God, you're soaked," I said. The one thing that to this day constantly amazes and thrills me is how incredibly wet Geri can get. Her wetness was so warm, so soft. I explored with my fingers to find her below the comforting veil. Her breath shortens when I touch her each time, but I can't help admiring her wetness. I could drown in it.

All night long we explored each other with our tongues and hands. After what seemed an eternity, Geri slid her hand down my stomach, stopping at my soft pubic hair, and whispered, "May I?"

"You don't need my permission, love. Please," I answered. She smiled and withdrew her hand, and started kissing down my body; I ached for her to reach my clitoris. Soon she had me begging with her teasing licks and kisses, and I knew there was no going back. My body would be as committed to her as my heart. And I was happy she offered to go first, not really confident I knew what the hell I was doing.

Geri went down on me and licked my pussy. As she repeatedly stroked her tongue along my labia, over my clitoris, and back down again, my body quaked with pleasure. My hips bucked, and my breathing quickened with each glorious caress of her talented tongue. My hands didn't know what to do with themselves; sometimes I would touch her hair, sometimes I grabbed the sheets. Afterward, I couldn't catch my breath for ten minutes. I didn't come, but God, the sensations! I didn't have to. I was on a high that took so long to come down from that I think she actually got worried.

"Are you all right?" Geri asked, a hint of concern in her voice.

Between breaths I got out, "Yes, but I feel like I ran a marathon or something." She laughed, which made me laugh. Sex was supposed to be fun, right? We laughed a great deal that night, making new noises, playing with our bodies, talking nonsense about sex. We continued our intense lovemaking for hours, mostly kissing and touching, until we finally collapsed from exhaustion in each other's arms. Our first night brought no orgasms to either of us but gave instead complete trust and love.

Geri and I dozed off in each other's arms. This was another feeling I had never experienced and would find tremendously peaceful: having the person you love asleep in your arms. No words can describe how this feels to someone who's slept alone as long as I have. The only word that comes close is *perfection*.

Just before falling asleep in her arms, I decided that with the morning sun it would be my turn to get her juices going. I wanted to hear Geri come in my arms and see her body experience pure joy. We awoke with the light streaming in above and started kissing again. I moved her onto her back and began rubbing her clitoris with my left hand. Her eyes closed, and her mouth went slack as the sensations began to course through her body. She moved only slightly, letting me do all the work, but I was more than ready to oblige her. Faster and faster I moved my hand, whispering in her ear, "Come for me, baby. I want to hear you. You want it. You want it all. Don't let it go."

"Oh, oh, that feels so good," Geri cooed. "Don't stop, whatever you do." I knew she was close as her back began to arch.

"Oh, yes. O-o-oh," she cried as she shook uncontrollably. Her whole body bucked back and forth as I held her tightly in my arms and continued working on her engorged clitoris. "That's it, baby. God, that's incredible. Keep it going. Don't stop yet." Geri continued that way for several minutes while I smiled down on her warm, quivering body. I had given my first orgasm.

Never had I felt such joy, such passion, in my life. Bringing her to orgasm was as exciting to me as having one myself, maybe even more satisfying. Hearing her pant and moan up a storm proved endlessly titillating and spurred my desire all over again to hear her come once more. On our second night, I decided I would try it with my tongue.

She didn't move right away. I whispered my love for her in her ear, holding her close, letting her know I was happy to pleasure her. Geri said she felt rejuvenated, and I felt every emotion, sensation, and experience related to sex you could possibly find a word for in the dictionary. I was truly overwhelmed, and, thank God, felt shameless. I felt no guilt for having committed adultery, no guilt for betraying my boss. To this day I still feel no guilt, no shame, for loving this incredible

woman who gave me myself at a time when I was seriously
questioning who I was and what I wanted to be in this world.

Geri opened many doors for me that day and continues to
do so even now. We are not together, but we are still the best
of friends, and I look for every opportunity to show her my
love in bed. It isn't easy, but she's more than worth the wait.
My promise to her that night is the same I make today: If she
were mine I would never hurt her, never leave her or give her
a reason to leave me, and I would make it my mission in life
to give her joy every day.

Maybe one day she'll be mine, but probably not. But since
no one else is knocking on my door to steal me away, even if
they could, I willingly play the waiting game. After 31 years,
I think I'm an expert by now.

Lily Tomlin for My Birthday

BY BLEAU DIAMOND

Birthdays can be eventful or stressful. Most people evaluate their lives sometime around New Year's, but since my birthday is two weeks after New Year's, I like to do the assessment then. The year was 1988, and I found myself coming up short: I hadn't accomplished some of the goals I had set for myself, and I hadn't readjusted them when I saw they were unattainable.

I needed hope. No, I needed more than hope—something to believe in and carry me through. *The Search for Signs of Intelligent Life in the Universe,* starring Lily Tomlin, was playing at the Curran Theater in San Francisco. It was the weekend of my birthday. I had no lover, no girlfriend to share that moment with, so I wanted to go out of town to ease my loneliness. Traveling alone was engaging because of the sense of adventure I had harnessed from my days of being a Girl Scout. I decided to go to San Francisco to see Lily Tomlin. I wanted to meet her. I wanted Lily for my birthday.

My flight to San Francisco was quick. After settling in at a bed-and-breakfast in the Haight District, I headed downtown.

When I arrived at the theater, I followed the alley to the backstage door. *Should I open it and go in?* I thought. *What if they throw me out?* As I opened the heavy steel door, a woman in a sleek black tuxedo appeared. She was an attractive, medium-built woman with short, curly brown hair.

"Can I help you?" her friendly voice asked.

"Yes, I'm here from Phoenix. It's my birthday, and I would like to meet Lily."

She smiled, "I'm from Phoenix too. Wait a minute and let me see what I can do." She shut the door, and my impatience surfaced. I wondered if she would come back.

The door reopened, and she said, "Lily's getting ready for the show. Why don't you come back afterward, and I'll introduce you to her."

"Really?" I wondered if she was putting me on.

"Yes, really. But you'll have to hurry back after the show. It gets crowded fast."

"Thanks," I said. "I appreciate your help." And just as she was shutting the door, I called out, "What's your name?"

"Pamela. I'm her stage manager." And the door closed.

I sat in my balcony seat and watched the show through binoculars. I thought about Lily's gift to entertain. I thought about how my life might have been different if I weren't so shy. But mostly, I felt anxious about meeting Lily. As I watched her performance, anticipation drove me crazy.

After the show, I raced down the stairs, out the front, and toward the back door. As a crowd of women gathered, I felt discouraged, thinking I wouldn't get to meet her. But as soon as I saw her stage manager, I shouted, "Pamela! Pamela!" She saw me and pulled me ahead of the crowd and into the back room where people were socializing.

"Where's Lily?" I asked, trying not to appear impatient. I had heard of other celebrities who don't like to meet their fans after shows, and thought she might have already left the building.

"She's probably changing out of her costume," she said.

I noticed Lily's name on one of the closed doors. As it began to open, Lily appeared, almost magically. Had she read my mind? Lily walked out to her stage manager, and we were formally introduced. She shook my hand and said, "Happy Birthday." Pamela must have told her about me. I felt as if I were in one of those shows where the magician knows the audience, as if Lily had memorized everything Pamela had told her about me. She knew I had come to San Francisco just to see her show and to meet her. I felt her energy, pure and kind, unconditional.

"I'm so nervous. I'm shaking and have goose bumps," I told her.

"Goose bumps are a good thing. It means you're alive," she said, trying to calm me. "Did you come to San Francisco by yourself?"

"Yes, I did."

"Well, good for you!" she declared. And for a moment I felt a union of our ambitious spirits, hers to perform and mine to seek adventure.

"Did you enjoy yourself?" Lily asked.

"Yes, you were great."

"Good. Thanks for coming to my show," she said with a grin that brightened the room.

She signed a copy of her book for me and wrote "Happy Birthday. goose bumps!" She was charming and personable, and made my birthday special. She even posed with me for a few pictures.

I thanked both Pamela and Lily, and off Lily went to meet her other "guests," as she referred to them.

Afterward I caught a taxi and went straight to bed with Lily on my mind. I had the most amazing dream about her, which I recorded in my journal:

Last night I dreamed of her again. Probably the first time she was aggressive with me, the first time she craved me, wanted to taste me, and did taste me. The first time she came up to kiss my lips after tasting me, my wetness all over her swollen tongue and thick red lips, my wetness now deep inside her. Creating more than a memory. Creating me inside her—forever. My wetness that I am now tasting on her lips and her tongue, my smell on her breath, my smell on her chin, my smell on her nose, her nose that she used to bury in me, to reach my insides, to reach inside with her tongue and feel me, her tongue that expanded and stretched inside me as my juices fell onto her tongue, and I could feel her swallow my juice as her neck came up against my bottom and my thighs. I heard her sucking on my clit and her brief hesitation with the motion of her tongue as she swallowed my juices inside her, and all along, I barely wanted to sigh or scream with delight because I was so enjoying listening to her as she was exploring me for the first time, as she was exploring me at last. After all this time, she was mine. And as she came up to kiss me, after I had orgasmed and pulled her so tight into my clit that I felt her breath panicking to breathe, I released her and let my juices flow down my leg and onto the white cotton sheets. My juices blended in like clear water lying like a bead upon a waxy surface, my come on her chin and mouth, and as she came up to kiss me, she said, "You taste so good. I want to taste you like this every morning." And, of course, I smiled. Brightly.

I awoke from the dream wet, and so I decided to go sightseeing and then somewhere to cool off. I went to Fisherman's Wharf and wrote in my journal. Later that afternoon, I caught a taxi to Osento, a women's bathhouse. I had read about it and found the idea intriguing: *women, naked women!* Phoenix didn't have a place where naked women lay around on towels, and I wanted to know what it felt like to be exposed. Would I feel self-conscious, compare my breasts, inspect the amount of hair between my legs and theirs? What would it feel like to be unclothed in front of strangers?

A short, stocky, muscular woman behind the desk greeted

me, introduced herself as Sandy, and after determining I was a novice, said she would give me the standard tour.

"The standard tour. What's that?" I asked.

"Oh, you'll see. But before we leave this area, you must remove your shoes."

"Why?" I questioned. But she never answered. She merely folded her arms and waited for my compliance.

I liked her aggressive tone; her being in control allowed me to relax into my role as newcomer. Not knowing what to expect, I began to feel stimulated. As I removed my shoes and made the first step toward disrobing, a part of me felt liberated. The other part of me was filled with anxiety—the same feeling I had watching Lily perform the night before.

I threw my shoes to the side in a pile with a dozen other pairs. My palms began to sweat. I was about to enter my first bathhouse. Alone. No lover to stand next to and hide my form into. I felt exposed. Would the other women know I was scared? Funny how clothes can accentuate our personalities, and the absence of clothing can strip us of our confidence.

Walking down the hall, I noticed the silhouette of a naked woman leaving through the back door. As the door opened, the light revealed her figure: tall and lean. Her glistening brown hair flowed to her shoulder blades.

"Who's she?" I inquired, hoping the tour would end before the woman left.

"She's a regular," Sandy scowled.

"What's her name?"

"Why don't you ask her yourself? We had to throw her out once for having sex in the quiet room. None of that is allowed here. No touching. Anyway, she threatened to sue us, so we had to let her back in. Best to stay away from her."

Hmm, just my type, I thought, *wild, indecent, naughty.*

We headed outside, and when Sandy pointed to the dry sauna next to the wet splash, I tried to look in the small window in the middle of the door, but the glass was dense with mist. Images, not faces, were all I could see.

Sandy opened the sauna door. My heart skipped a beat. Oh! It was the woman I saw earlier. The door swung shut before I could get more than a return glance.

I focused my attention on the wet splash Sandy insisted I use. It looked like a huge white porcelain bathtub and was kept at around 40 degrees.

"The wet splash stimulates lactic muscle build-up. You have any of that?" Sandy asked.

"I don't know," I answered carefully, not wanting to commit to anything. It was January in San Francisco, and I had worn a shirt, sweater, and jacket to Osento. Fog was coming in as gently as the sun was moving behind the clouds, so I was the least likely candidate for the wet splash. Besides, I couldn't concentrate since I was preoccupied with the naked woman in the sauna.

After viewing the meditation quiet room, I thanked Sandy for the tour and headed to get undressed. I held up a towel to cover my body while I walked to the unoccupied shower. Alone, I felt relieved. *Maybe this was a mistake. Maybe I should just go home,* I said to myself. Then I reminded myself why I was there: to see and mingle with naked women.

I decided to find the woman who had invoked my restlessness. I entered the sauna, so nervous that my hand slipped off the doorknob when I tried to close it behind me. *Smooth,* I thought as I grabbed the doorknob and pulled the door closed. Three women were in the sauna, and there she was, leaning up against the back, with her foot on the only seat available.

"There's room," she said with an air of authority, as she moved her foot.

"Thanks." I approached the bench and flashed her a smile. The other women got up and left since I had let so much heat out of the room.

"Don't mind them," she said.

Every inch of her was wet. Had she waited for me? Put herself in jeopardy for me? Risked heat exhaustion?

I sat across from her, a stranger, staring at her breasts. I liked their natural shape. Her nipples were as small as peanuts and as hard; her breasts were round, full, plump. I focused on the color contrast of the tan line and the milky white round part of her breasts. I wanted to touch them. She had protected them from the sun, but would she protect them from me?

I was so entranced by her naked body that I didn't see her staring at me with her piercing dark brown eyes. She sat and waited for me, and my eyes couldn't bear to hold her stare for more than a moment before I felt dazed by her soul's shouting words of seduction into me.

My right leg needed to stretch out, so I propped it between her legs, unaware I was giving her a view of my hidden areas.

I closed my eyes, and then my other senses became electrified. Her layers of cologne permeated the steam in the sauna. I smelled the cologne she had worn the night before into the bars to seduce women. I opened my eyes and looked into hers, this time without turning away because of the intensity. Yes, I could smell women on her. She smirked, as sweat poured off her skin, releasing more cologne and delicious odors.

I couldn't stand the silence any longer.

"You look like you could be Lily Tomlin's sister," I uttered, struggling to catch my breath.

"I get that all the time," she said, and I sensed her borderline confidence and cockiness about her appearance. "Did you go to her show?"

"Yes. I flew in from Phoenix yesterday, and met her last night."

"You met her?" She raised her eyebrows.

"It was my birthday, and that was my birthday wish. Before the show, I met her stage manager, Pamela, and then after the show, I was invited backstage."

"Wow, that's great. Lucky you."

"Did you go to the show?" I asked.

"Yes, as a matter of fact, I did. I went opening night, and everyone thought I was Lily and wanted my autograph. Well, happy birthday! Did you get what you wanted?"

"Not quite," I answered.

"Let me guess. You wanted Lily to take you home."

"No," I said, but I was lying. Sure, I wanted to know what it felt like to be with someone classy and famous. Doesn't everyone?

She reached down and pulled my leg up closer between her legs and started to rub it.

"Soft," she said. I smiled. "Let me see your palm." I leaned forward and held out my left hand.

"Does it matter which?" I asked.

"No. Close your eyes."

I hesitated. It was easier to close them before she had touched me. Now I needed all my senses just to keep abreast of her advances.

"Trust me," she whispered. I closed my eyes and felt the wooden floor wobble. *What now?* I thought. She took my hand and placed it in hers. "You can open your eyes now."

She had simply held my hand. Nothing else. I had gotten myself worked up for nothing. She let go of my hand, and I relaxed into the curve of the sauna. She was testing me, but why? *Oh, what is she doing to me? She is so beautiful. A woman of substance, a woman of mystery.*

After a seductive staring match, she leaned forward and touched my breasts. "They're beautiful," she said as she pressed her fingers around my nipples. I gasped and didn't move. I was stunned. *Is this what they do in San Francisco?* A bold feeling swept through me, provoked by her unexpected touch. I leaned forward to touch her breasts. The sweat from her nipples melted into my hands.

"I want to kiss you," she said in a commanding tone.

I didn't respond. Frozen. Stillness except for the drip of sweat pouring off our bodies. Silence except for the noise of the sauna rocks and the gentle wind outside pressing against the wooden door.

She leaned forward and began kissing me gently on the lips and the side of my face.

She whispered in my ear, "I want you."

I tried to breathe, but the sauna heat intensified her passionate kisses, and I had to pull away or risk passing out.

"What's wrong?" she asked. "Why did you pull away?"

"I don't even know your name."

"Lexi. My name is Lexi. And what is your name?"

"They call me Bleau."

"Nice to meet you," she said shaking my hand.

We talked about the show and ourselves, but the conversation was never intimate. There were no details. I don't even know if Lexi was her real name. I stared at her features, which reminded me so much of Lily's. I realized I had allowed a stranger to touch me intimately and that the touch had triggered no emotional feelings. This was anonymous sex, just like the boys do. This was exciting bathhouse anonymous sex, and I wanted more.

All of a sudden, Lexi jumped up and said, "I'll be right back."

I walked to the window, wiped the steam off, and watched her climb into the wet splash. As she came up, her nipples hit the cold, and water froze on her breasts. It looked as if icicles were dangling from them. *Delicious,* I thought.

Lexi headed toward the sauna, and I returned to my seat, pretending not to notice when she came back. Her sudden departure had left an uneasiness in the air. I thought she might have been reconsidering our kiss. After all, she was rather reserved personally, if not sexually. She was a genuine paradox.

"I love women, don't you?" Lexi declared.

I wanted to get to know her, how she thought. You can tell a lot about people when they are dressed and have their things about them. But when they're naked, you don't have a clue about their socioeconomic level, their class, their style. Nothing. *By all means, let her talk,* I thought.

"Tell me what you love about them," I said.

"Oh, I love to sit with a woman and stare at her until I know she's getting wet. And then let her saturate her jeans waiting for me to touch her. And when I do touch her, I like to go slow, tease her, let the clit slowly build up, until it wants it—you know, until the clit is begging to be licked. Then I like to slowly lick her, push my tongue deep inside, and lick her until she comes."

"It's quite an art for you, isn't it?" I couldn't help saying. I had nothing to compete with what she'd said. What could I say, "Yes, I'd love for you to lick me"?

I continued, "Do you introduce yourself to every woman who turns you on?"

"No, but when I see a woman alone, who has traveled quite a distance to fulfill a fantasy, I get interested in helping her fulfill that fantasy."

"You do?"

"Yes, I'd love to spend the evening exploring you. Would you like that?"

It was now my turn to ignore her question.

"So, can you sleep with someone you aren't in love with?" I asked.

"Of course. I don't confuse sex and love because I don't say things that aren't true just to get sex. If I wanted to sleep with you, I would tell you. It's rather simple. But lesbians like to complicate it. We tell our friends that we slept with someone, and they expect us to be moving in together. I don't feel guilt when I'm honest."

Something about our conversation made me uncomfortable, and I placed my towel over my body.

"Don't cover up. I want to look at you," she said. She used her feet to pull at the towel, leaving me on display, doing to me what I had wanted to do to other women. This wasn't what I had planned. The other women were supposed to be candy to *my* eyes. I hadn't visualized my being candy to any-one else.

As Lexi talked, her eyes roamed freely. How did she invent that luscious stare? How did she come to seduce me with one look? And that lip licking she did throughout our talk—was she moistening her lips because they were dry or was she pre-tending to lick my taste off her lips? Was my taste on her lips driving her crazy?

"Come sit next to me," she said.

I nodded shyly and moved next to her, our skin now touching. I wanted her to lay me down and press herself into me. I wanted to feel her body cover mine in a rapture of one-ness. She was a perfect fit with my body, and I imagined how her breasts would feel as they pressed into my nipples. I won-dered how much of her pussy juice would flow out and into me as she pressed her toned body into mine.

We went back to kissing, and she let her fingers expose and plunge into my wetness. I was so busy feeling an orgasm rush to the surface that I didn't hear the door open and two women come in.

Laughing, Lexi and I immediately departed the sauna. She seemed too brazen to let them affect her, but I was rat-tled. Here we were sitting in this oval-shaped sauna on a bench, next to each other, her finger inside me, fucking me, and these women walk in. We left the smell of sex and the trickle of pussy juice on the bench. I wondered how long the smell would linger in the sauna and how soon we could finish what she'd started. I felt undone.

We went inside and into the crowed Jacuzzi, which was filled with eight other women. My frustration rose when I noted we had an audience and that we wouldn't be able to continue where we'd left off.

By now I was feeling liberated enough to lie around naked.

I got out and lay on the cold tile surrounding the Jacuzzi, the coldness pressing into my bare butt. Lexi stood inside the Jacuzzi and used a plastic cup to pour the hot water over my body, lingering at my pussy as she poured, spreading my legs apart. As the water hit my clit, which begged me to let it have a miniorgasm, all I could do was bite my lip and hold on.

"Are you staying in the Castro?" Lexi asked.

"No, in the Haight. By Golden Gate Park."

"Let's get out of here." The words I had been waiting for.

I was ready from the moment I'd seen her silhouette. No, I was ready since I'd awakened from my wet dream. No, I was ready once I'd decided to go on this adventure. I started to feel anxious, excited, nervous, and all that culminated into an erotic aura. Yes, I was ready for anything.

Still wet from the Jacuzzi, we raced into her Honda, and she drove us to where I was staying. She didn't offer to take me to her place. I knew why. This was anonymous sex. There was no finding each other after this. No phone calls. No letters and no surprise visits.

I was stimulated, my clit bulging in my jeans, waiting for her and feeling I was going to explode as we drove through the city. My room seemed so far. *Why don't we just pull over?* I thought. *I mean, if she touched me like that in the bathhouse, maybe that's the way it is in San Francisco.* I watched her shift gears, up and down, down and up, a prelude to a sexual dance, watching her fingers, watching their discreet movement become a sexual dance, observing her fingers tightly grip the ball of the gearshift, stroke the gearshift. I savored the knowledge that those same fingers were going to fuck me.

We arrived at my hotel, and as we entered the room, Lexi wasted no time. She removed her rings, one by one, from her long, angular fingers. She carefully set her diamonds on the dresser. Her hair, though it appeared the sauna had deflated any natural curl, still looked superb.

She lay on the bed and said, "Come on over here and lie next to me." I lay with her and closed my eyes. I let her undress me, pulling off my layers of clothing. "This isn't Wisconsin!" she laughed as she pulled off my T-shirt.

"But it is cold to a Phoenician," I protested.

Lexi smiled and let her brown hair fall into her eyes. I reached up to push away the strands of hair that hid her magnetic face. Her skin was so close to her bones, not one inch of sagging, even at her age. She was about 20 years older than me, and her beauty was irresistible.

I let her take me into her arms, the smell of the Jacuzzi and sauna on her skin. I felt as if I were in a dream, lying with a woman's woman, someone who could and did have any woman she desired. She kissed me gently on the lips, pulling me in closer. She explored my boundaries, placing kisses down my neck, on my breasts, down my stomach, down one leg, and inside my thigh, gently separating my hair and seeing my clit rise to greet her lips, like an ice cream cone that's gone soft and is waiting to be licked.

With most women, you go slow, "going down" reserved for more advanced dates. But this was it. There was no tomorrow. I felt my internal boundaries buckle and give way to her insistent tongue. I unleashed my passion.

Her tongue was so similar to the one I'd experienced in my dream. Her tongue, so wet, diving in deep. As she came up to kiss me, I realized I was either dreaming again or that I'd had a premonition of this moment. How could my dream have foretold this?

Her eyes begged me to let go, and I did. My voice carried my orgasm into the pillow, and I didn't say the courteous "I love you," or the obligatory, "I am in love with you." No, I simply said, "Thank you."

Lexi dressed and left quickly. I watched her walk away, down the cold street, and get into her car. The headlights popped on and a sliver of light reached up and into my eyes, illuminating my truth and new possession: hope.

Lexi was willing to let me believe that for one brief moment I was with a celebrity: someone I would never be able to have coffee with, someone I would never be able to walk into a bedroom with without falling down from fright, pure and simple fear.

It was one of the best birthdays ever! Goose bumps!

Heidi

BY H.L. SHAW

It was the first time her boyfriend had left her alone for the weekend.

She was a freshman, I a junior. I knew her through her boyfriend, who was my age, and through the theater department, in which we were both involved. She was from a podunk town in southern Indiana, where she had been county queen the year before. She was gorgeous, tall, and slender, with clear blue eyes and a straight sheaf of pale gold hair that fell to her waist. She had a corn-fed quality about her, and she had, indeed, grown up on a farm.

We knew each other moderately well, though we were not close friends. During the winter-term show we both learned to knit and spent long hours knitting in the sound booth together. She finished a slight, lumpy blue scarf while I, to this day, have about one foot of knitted maroon still hanging from my needles.

The weekend in question was in late March, and it was the first warmish day we'd had since last fall. There was still a brisk feel to the air, and at night the chill seemed too damp, but the days were reasonably sunny and brought us out of our seasonal depression left over from the Midwestern winter.

A mutual friend was throwing a dorm party that weekend. I have one picture of her from that party: She's standing in her blue jeans and denim jacket with her back to the camera, and you can just see the profile of her pert little nose. I don't remember exactly when during the party this was taken, but it must have been early on, as she later took her jacket off, and we certainly weren't taking any pictures as we hurried out the door together.

Ah, but I'm getting ahead of myself.

As was usual for these sorts of parties, we were drunk. It's unfortunate, as it blurs the memory terribly, but it's true. I was sitting across from her on the floor, happily fuzzy and social. We were leaning in and whispering to each other, and the intimacy of talking quietly to her in the midst of that loud, confused drunken party was exhilarating.

Still, I was slightly taken aback when she told me she had a confession to make.

"I want to kiss you."

We'd been talking about how much we liked each other and how we certainly should hang out more, as we thought we'd be great friends. All this proved to be true, and still is to this day. Yet at that party, I had something more intimate to confront.

"Really?" I thought about it only a moment. "I'd like that."

A moment later, we were whispering even closer together. I felt the heat of her breath on my cheek, the warm air sliding down my neck, as she whispered, "You're so cool, so beautiful...yes, you are."

"Oh, God, no, you're the beauty, Heidi."

As I said, we were both drunk, so I don't remember how we decided this, but soon we were leaving together, arms linked, heading toward the dorm lounge. We both lived across campus and weren't ready to make that cold walk back. We descended the stairs to the basement TV lounge.

Now, I had kissed a woman before, once, during an innocent seduction my freshman year. My friend Mila and I had lured a male friend of ours into her bed, and we had lain on either side of him, stroking and caressing each other. We had leaned over him to kiss several times, but somehow his presence made it less sexual. It had been thrilling, but I knew nothing would come of it.

Kissing Heidi was completely different. For one thing, by the time we got into the lounge and locked the door, I was so hot from her heated whispers that I forgot to be nervous. We sat on the couch, grabbed each other, and kissed like teenagers. It was new, and she was so fresh, so soft. We broke the kiss, and I told her this. It seemed to excite her even more.

Having no experience with women's sensuality outside my own, I was pleasantly surprised at how easily she was aroused. Soon I had my hands on her breasts, amazed at their heaviness in my grasp. Her small fingers worked their way over my nipples, turning me on more than any boy ever had. I kept my left hand on her breast, gripping her under her ear with my right, and sucked on her small, sweet lips.

We made out on the couch until we couldn't stand it anymore. We didn't dare remove any clothing, as someone was bound to disturb us before too long. We'd left the party together in a casual way, but we'd be missed after too long. We decided to make a final exit, wearing our coats. Besides, Heidi thrilled me with the teaser: "My roommate is gone for the weekend."

The walk through campus remains shaky in my memory. I remember our holding on to each other, stumbling drunk and giddy. I remember thinking fuzzily about where we were going and what we intended to do once we got there, knowing I should be shocked, scared, or at least amazed, but approaching it nonchalantly in my intoxicated state.

Her room was on the third floor of an all-girl dormitory. We entered, and she started fiddling with the room, throwing dirty clothes off her single bed and quickly straightening up. I was somewhat surprised and a bit embarrassed that she cared so much about what I thought. I spent the time looking at her snapshots; there she was, as a beauty queen, as a high school cheerleader, looking fresh-faced and clean-cut smiling next to her farm-boy boyfriends. Her high school experience obviously had been much different from mine, yet I knew she and I had plenty in common; she had never snubbed me or acted in the superior way cheerleaders at my old high school had.

"Cheerleader, huh?" I commented.

"Yeah. Please don't hold it against me."

I smiled, "Hold what against you?" and gathered my courage (but flipped off the lights) and pushed her down on the bed.

She sighed eagerly, reaching to pull me on top of her. The next thing I knew, I was on top of her, kissing and rutting, grinding my crotch against hers. I knelt up like I'd done with so many boys and pulled off my shirt, then hers. She twisted under me as I circled her slim waist with my hands. Her hips flared out in a gentle curve, and I dipped my pinkies under the waistband of her jeans before moving my hands to the underside of her breasts.

Her breasts were larger and softer than mine. Her pale white flesh glowed softly in the dark room, and I lowered my lips to the darker skin of her nipples. Her skin seemed too soft, almost saggy, as I sucked her in. I ran my tongue along the underside of her breast, then tried a flicker around the outside edge of her nipple. She cried out and pushed her chest firmly against my mouth. I took that as a hint and sucked as much of her breast as possible into my mouth. Then I moved to the other.

She grew impatient, I think, as I was too timid to move away from the relatively safe area of the breasts. She flipped me over and straddled me. I found myself using my favorite line from a previous boyfriend, "You look so beautiful...like a smooth, pale marble statue come to life." She moaned as I reached up to touch her breasts, then pushed my hands away as she leaned down and drew my nipples into her mouth.

She was technically rougher than any guy I'd been with, but the way she sucked caused me none of the pain I would have expected. She sucked with her mouth wider, pulling on more of the surface area surrounding the nipple. She swirled her tongue around the lightly erect nipple, causing me to gasp at every pass. Then she licked down the underside, kissing and sucking diagonally across my abdomen to my belly button. She gave my navel a deep, soul-searching French kiss that distracted me entirely. The next thing I knew, she was leaning back and yanking my jeans down my thighs. Before even putting her hands there, she pressed her hot mouth against the soaked panel of cotton between my legs. I cried out and arched my back, excited by the thrill of doing something I had always considered "forbidden."

She licked with her tongue along the edge of my panties, then under the edge. Soon she had my panties pulled between my folds while she licked my outer lips. I groaned and thrashed in frustration; the panties were covering all the "crucial" parts, and I ached to feel her small tongue against my clitoris. She nibbled my inner thigh, then looked at me with a devilish grin while she hooked her index finger under the gathered material and drew it aside, exposing my expectant organs. Starting from the skin under my vagina, she placed her tongue firmly on my flesh and drew up, licking open my folds, then hooking her tongue wickedly under the hood of my clit. I know I yelled something at this, but I held as still as possible, not wanting to thrash myself away from her sweet little mouth. She began sucking, nibbling every so often at my lips, and dipping her finger into my hole. I know I came more than once. But I began to feel I was being too greedy; letting her work me over like this was an indulgence, and it was time to indulge her.

Once I had flipped her over, I started on her breasts again, nervous as all hell to take her pants off, even though she'd just done the same for me. Then she truly shocked me:

"Tie me up."

"What?"

"Hold me down, tie me up...oh, God, please...tie me down."

So I found a winter scarf and a pair of tights, and tied her wrists to the bed. I'd fantasized about bondage plenty, but had never managed to bring this up with any of my lovers. Here I was, tying down the first woman I'd ever been with...during my first time!

But I found it easier to take her pants off once she was secured. Perhaps it was because she was unable to show me what she wanted done, so I had to do it on my own. I felt it silly to tie her down only to suck her breasts again, so I slowly undid her fly and eased her jeans off her fucking perfect hips and down her shapely legs. I found myself down at her feet, and I scooped up one impossibly white foot and French-kissed the arch. She groaned, and I drew my mouth along her calf, licking the back muscle and sucking on the underside of her knee. I knew I was avoiding the issue, but the way she bucked and moaned made me realize my nervousness had caused me to stumble onto something. I took my time, worshiping and washing the lower half of her delicious body with my tongue.

When I finally made my way up to her mound, I withdrew my tongue and used my entire face to nuzzle her there. Then I took a deep breath, inhaling her aroma. She was slick with a thin, salty wetness that had a slightly sharp smell. I dipped one finger in her and licked it clean. The flavor lingered on my tongue, changing the longer it stayed there, until I understood why people used words like "honey pot" and "nectar." I felt as if I were tasting the essence of life between her legs. I lowered my face and began to feast.

I'd never before experienced another woman's arousal so intimately. I was shocked and pleasantly surprised at how easy it was to make her come. She made the coolest sounds, so much better than any porno and certainly much sweeter and more genuine than any man I'd been with. It occurred to me that she could be faking it, but I didn't think so. She writhed under my attentions, crying out my name a few times and shuddering whenever another orgasm hit her.

The neat thing about women, I noticed, is there's no definite end to sex. I could have stayed between her legs until the sun came up, though the position was cramping my neck a bit. I thought I might have been blundering around down there, but she was so responsive, it didn't seem I could do anything wrong. Eventually I untied her, and we continued our make-out, holding each other and kissing deeply. I fell a little in love with her during those deep, soulful kisses. I kept thinking, "She's so soft...so soft."

I didn't spend the night. Her twin bed was too narrow, and I didn't think I could face her first thing in the morning. Besides, she had been loud, and I'm sure her neighbors had wondered what boy she had brought home while her boyfriend was out of town. The small Baptist school we attended couldn't handle my emergence from her room.

The next morning my mother drove Heidi, me, and a male friend of ours to the mall to go shopping. It was nerve-wracking waiting to have a moment alone with Heidi to discuss the previous night. Finally, our friend disappeared into a music store, and we looked at each other over a kiosk.

"So...are you going to tell Keith?"

"I talked to him this morning. I told him you and I just kissed."

I nodded. That's all she would tell him, then.

"Was he jealous?"

"He was surprised. I think it doesn't matter much, though, since you're a woman."

I was a little disappointed by her tone. I was obviously not considered a threat to their relationship, certainly not to him, and not to her either. All morning, as we had pretended to browse the stores, I kept thinking about her and what we had done. I couldn't keep myself from wondering what it would be like to actually *date* Heidi; I kept imagining myself as her girlfriend. Sure, there were things about her that would annoy me. In fact, I consoled myself by thinking how much it wouldn't have worked because of how high-maintenance she is. But I was still somewhat disappointed I wouldn't get the chance to find out.

Heidi and I continued our friendship in a less sexual way, though we ended up close friends. I would occasionally add spice to her and Keith's sex life by joining them in bed. This always made me a little sad, as these sessions would inevitably end with me watching them fuck, usually in my bed since I had a single room.

Did we tell anyone? Oh, we each told a few people. We had a mutual friend, Adam, in whom we both confided. Adam considered himself bisexual, and he was the only other person we knew at school who identified as such.

I avoided telling Heidi how I felt a little in love with her; I mentioned once in passing that I had wondered if she and I were going to start dating. She laughed it off, though I know she understood my underlying seriousness.

A few years later we moved out of the dorms and into an apartment together as roommates. We had a long, long talk about what had happened. By that time, my crush on her was replaced by familiarity, and neither of us was threatened by unbalanced feelings; we were now just very good friends.

There was a time, when she was between boyfriends, when she treated me as if I were her significant other. More than once I found myself telling her in irritation, "Heidi, I'm not Keith. I won't fall for that trick because I've used it myself." Still, we were never sexual again without a male involved.

A few months later she and Adam started dating, and now, a few years after that, they're talking about getting engaged. Some of my happiest moments were hanging out with her and Adam in her apartment. I'd chat with them as they lay in bed while I flossed my teeth. Often I'd jump into bed with them, to snuggle or tickle or just to talk. There was an easy, nonsexual intimacy among the three of us; a bond against the judgment we would face outside our home in the small Midwestern town.

I moved out West a year ago, and I've blossomed in a more accepting environment. I pride myself on my sex-positive outlook and can openly discuss my lifestyle with friends and coworkers alike. But I'll never forget those intimate moments with Heidi that showed me there's more than one way to love your friends.

Luna and Me in Hawaii

BY LILITH LYNN ROGERS

Part I

Luna and I had been in Hawaii for just over a week. It was our first big trip together since we'd become lovers eight months before, and I was excited.

We had decided to come to Hawaii back in October when my landlord unceremoniously tossed me out of the cheap, sweet little house I'd lived in for three years. He'd unexpectedly announced it had been sold. It really bummed me out.

"I need something to look forward to," I told Luna. "Let's spend January at your cabin on the Big Island. We'll get out of Northern California in the worst month of the year, and you can show me all your favorite places from when you lived there."

"I'd love to do that, sweetie," she replied with her usual enthusiasm. "Let's go!"

Hawaii was as wonderful as Luna had promised. From the first night we'd arrived and spent the night in Luna's friend Julie's beautiful screened-in bedroom with tropical fruits and flowers all around us, our lovemaking—which was almost always great—was spectacular. We both seemed inspired to new heights of inventiveness and orgasm by a power outside ourselves.

Maybe it was the sweet, soft air, the brilliant colors—lush green tropical growth, blue, blue ocean and sky, black, black lava. Maybe it was all those soft and juicy tropical fruits—papayas, mangos, guavas, bananas, and lilikois. Maybe it was the undulating rhythms of the mellow Hawaiian music that always played in the background. Probably it was just us—alone together and away from the distractions of our busy lives in California. Whatever it was, it was magic. We were on fire for each other, and every time we made love the flames rose higher.

Now we were driving up the Kona Coast in a funky little car Luna had rented from Jackie, one of her old buddies. Except for sometimes having to start it by laying a butter knife across a couple of screws, it was an OK car.

Luna looked absolutely fabulous. She'd gotten nice and tan after a week on the beach. Blowing out the car window, her wild, curly, dark mane was curlier and wilder than ever from all the humid salt air. Her eyes shone with delight. She wore a new lei of yellow and pink plumeria blossoms I'd just bought for her at a roadside stand. She laughed delightfully as the juice of the strawberry papaya she was eating spilled down her chin and almost formed a puddle in the lap of her bright red sarong she'd mysteriously managed to tie behind her neck and drape over her whole body.

"Better pull up your sarong a little and let that juice spill on your belly, honey," I advised. "You don't want to stain such pretty cloth." I was driving with one hand on the wheel and one on her bare shoulder, one eye on the road and one on her.

"OK," she laughed and opened her sarong all the way to her breasts. "Is that better?"

"Umm, much better," I said approvingly. (She's always so wonderfully bold and unpredictable.) I moved my hand from her shoulder to her poochy brown belly. "I'll just rub the juices in for you. Papaya juice is good for your skin, you know."

"Oh, yes, I know." She kept laughing and put her hand on top of mine. "Here, let me help you with that."

Well, I couldn't help moving my hand down her belly and into that place between her legs I find so intriguing. "Honey," I whispered, "I think some of that papaya juice has seeped down here too. It's all wet."

"Oh," she moaned softly under my touch, "you'd better rub it in. I hear it's good lubrication for old yonis like mine."

"Sweetie, I sure haven't noticed your precious old yoni needing any extra lubrication, but your every wish is my command. Or should I say your every command is my wish? Anyway, how's this?" And I started to rub a little harder.

Needless to say, it was getting pretty hard to keep driving, and my steering was becoming fairly erratic. Thank Goddess there's not much traffic on the Big Island because it wasn't easy to keep even one eye on the road or hand on the wheel.

"Maybe I'd better pull over, Luna, so I can do a more thorough lube job," I teased.

"Great idea, honey," she murmured.

Fortunately, I spotted a nice little clearing surrounded by trees just off the road and eased our car right on in there, turned off the motor, and shifted my complete attention to my "work."

"Is there any more of that papaya left, honey? I think I feel a little spot in here that's not quite as wet as the rest."

"Umm, ooh, what?" She was pretty far gone now. "Here, take it."

I took a small piece of that slippery, soft, orange fruit and pressed it into her warm, wet cunt with my palm. Bent down in her lap, I started licking it back out with my long, well-trained tongue.

"Ooh, Lilith baby, that feels good," she purred as she pressed my face deeper into her. "I just love the way you do that!"

"Umm, umm...this has got to be the best papaya I've ever tasted," I murmured into her pussy as I licked and licked.

Suddenly, she was really wet and juicy, and she was coming so big. She pulled my head from her lap and leaned back against the seat to catch her breath.

"Thanks for cleaning up that papaya juice for me," she laughed. "We wouldn't want to return Jackie's car all messed up."

"My pleasure." I ran my tongue around my lips and licked the combination of juices. "Call on me any time you need help with a little job like that. Guess we should keep on going now. We want to get to the campsite before it gets too late, right?"

"Right as usual, sweetie. You want to keep driving?"

"Sure. I like driving in Hawaii. Somehow, it's much more fun than it is back home."

"Really? I wonder why?" And she rearranged her red sarong so only one breast was showing. "Maybe I better cut back on your enjoyment just a little so we'll get there before dark."

Amazingly enough, the car started without the aid of the butter knife, and we cruised on up the road toward Kona.

Part II

After driving along the windy road a little while, we stopped for a yummy lunch of mixed veggies and tofu on the porch of the Aloha Theater in Kainaliu and picked up a few more strawberry papayas at the fruit stand next door.

"Can't ever tell when you might need a bit more lubrication, can ya, honey?" I joked.

"Or you either, bubala," Luna replied. "But woman does not live by papaya alone, my love," she added and bought us a big loaf of homemade bread—baking is a special art on the Big Island—some local avocados the size of small footballs, a couple of lovely red mangos, and other goodies. "This ought to get us through the night."

"I don't know. Seems like all our appetites have increased here," I laughed and patted my growing belly.

It was late afternoon as we passed through the tourist mess of Keilua-Kona. Luna was driving now, teasing me about my being too butch to wear a sarong in public, making it too hard for her to reach me through my pants.

"That's OK, sweetie. You can catch me up later when there's not so much traffic," I said.

Since Luna had lived on the Big Island for several years sometime back, she knew all the best places to go, and now she took us right through the busy business district of Kona and out to Old Airport Beach, where the Hawaiian locals and haole hippies hung out. This city park used to be the old airport, and we drove down the former runway to get to the beach. Luna parked at the far end of the runway, past the picnic tables and the bathrooms. We grabbed our camping gear and started walking around the far edge of the bay where we could just barely see a nice private spot with our names on it.

Halfway around the bay, we came upon a cute, young hippie woman sitting near the path. Glancing her way, I noticed she was smoking a big doobie. She grinned at us and said, "Aloha, ladies. Care for a toke?"

"I'd love one," Luna replied. "*Mahalo*." She took a big drag, then passed the joint to me. I inhaled deeply and coughed a bit. I'm not much of a *pakalolo* smoker—only on special occasions. But I felt this was already shaping up to be a special occasion and, anyway, in Hawaii you go with the flow. It was definitely what Luna would call *da kine* stuff. Just one puff totally mellowed me out.

"*Mahalo nui loa*," I said and handed the joint back to our new friend. When I looked out at the world before me, I noticed the sea was looking much bluer than it had a moment before. The sky too. "Awesome," I commented as we continued down the path.

We set up our little bed in a small sandy spot among the lava not far from the water's edge. Since it was a bay, there wouldn't be much tide to worry about, and since it was Kona side, it wasn't likely to rain. We went for a short dip in what Luna explained was the "Queen's Bath," a protected pool of water surrounded by big lava rocks. The water was warm and caressing. "A perfect spot for the queen of my heart," I said as I floated her gently in my arms.

As the sun set, we sat at the edge of the world, feeding each other bits of delicious avocado and bread, kissing and laughing, singing little sunset songs as more and more spectacular shades of orange, yellow and red infused the sky. "Wow, they don't make up those postcards, after all!" I exclaimed. "This is incredible."

A fairly good-sized yacht had washed up on the shore around the far edge of the cove from us. The waves were slowly beating it into driftwood, casting a sad yet romantic spell over the scene. "I'm glad that wasn't our ship coming in, honey," I sighed and pulled Luna close.

"Oh, Goddess. Look over there, babe. The moon is rising behind the mountain. It must be full tonight. Are we lucky ducks or what?" Luna said. "I don't care if our ship ever comes in, as long as we have this much fun waiting for it. Let's get to bed, honey. I think I hear a mango calling me."

We slipped into our soft, cozy bed all alone under the big Hawaiian sky. As the full moon rose, she cast a shadow of the mountain over the calm bay in front of us. "What's the name of the moon goddess in Hawaii?" I asked.

"Hina. She's one of Pele's sisters."

"Hina. Luna, that's you, my beautiful moon goddess." I pulled her to me and started kissing her all over. "Oh, baby, you turn me on so much. I can't believe how sexy this whole island is! And especially here."

"I know," she replied, pulling herself back a little. "I'm inspired to try more and more new tricks on you. And I still have to eat my mango. Let's see how this one tastes."

Quick as a wink, Luna split the skin off one of our red

mangos and slipped the sweet orange fruit into my mouth. Before I could bite into it, though, she slipped it out again and kissed me. "Umm. Yummy," she murmured.

Then she rubbed the mango over my breasts and around my belly, then slowly and tantalizingly slipped it in and out of the lips of my cunt. "Oh, Luna, honey. Oh, that feels divine," I crooned.

She started licking me all over in the places where she'd just rubbed me down with the mango and mumbled about how good it tasted. She licked all over my neck and around my titties, over my belly and around my thighs. The whole time she licked, she pressed that mango in and out of my cunt, first slowly, then faster and faster and farther and farther into my big wet cunt.

"Oh, Hina, Hina," I called, holding her wild, curly hair tight and gasping for breath as my orgasm built and built and built. "Oh, honey, take me over the edge. Come into me more. Please take me. I can't stand it anymore." And Luna pressed the mango all the way into me as she licked and licked my clit, and I came so big. "Oh, Hina, oh, Goddess, thank you."

I pulled Luna up to lay in my arms just as the big ol' moon cleared the mountain and filled the whole sky around us with her silver light. "Oh, honey, I think our ship has definitely come in. Don't you?"

"I do indeed," she whispered. She felt soft and lovely in my arms.

"Say, I could go for a bite of that mango now," I said after a while. "Where is it?"

"I don't know. I lost track of it in the excitement. Is it next to you?"

I felt around. "Nope, not there."

"Well, then, it must still be in you."

I squirmed around a little and felt it inside me. "Jeez, can you take that thing out of me?"

"I'll try, honey." She stuck her fingers inside me and said, sounding worried, "It's too slippery for me to grab. What'll we do now? You don't want me to take you to the hospital, do you?"

"No way," I laughed nervously. "Can you imagine how those guys would look at us? Let me try something."

I climbed out of bed and sat up on my haunches in the bright moonlight, pressed on my belly, and bore down hard like I did when I had my babies. That mango squirted right out.

"I don't feel so hungry anymore," I said and tossed the mango out to sea.

Luna laughed and pulled me back down to our bed. "Next time Hina comes to visit, I'm gonna tell her to be a little more restrained."

"Just a little more," I agreed, "but not too much. I do like her wild."

And somehow we fell asleep with that big full moon shining over us as we dreamed the most delicious wet mango dreams all night long.

Ruby

BY ROBIN ST. JOHN

She sends an E-mail message telling me she and Danni are planning their marriage and telling me other stuff too. I am in a hurry, and I read it quickly. My initial reaction is boredom. Long weeks have passed since she's written anything interesting, anything that stirs my blood. Later I remember her message, I think about it, and I say to myself—but as if she could hear me, as if we were sitting across from each other at my kitchen table, drinking coffee—*For Christ's sake, Ruby. How can you be so stupid?* Finally, days later, I send her a message, short and to the point. It says simply: *Ruby, when are you going to stop saying no?*

Ruby walks such a fine line; it's a wonder she can keep her balance, especially in those spiky-heeled shoes she wears, a holdover from her marriage to a shoe fetishist. She got in the habit of dressing her feet to please him and never dropped it, even though they have been divorced for years. I remember her telling me (while her knees rubbed against mine under the table and we shared a piece of banana cream pie) how he had loved for her to walk on his chest wearing nothing but spike heels, how he had insisted she arrange her 100 pairs of shoes methodically in the closet. I shake my head, thinking, *Ruby, how could you say yes to that and keep on saying no to the things that move you, make you wild?*

Danni is madly, maniacally jealous. She is so jealous that Ruby has to write to me on the sly, and only once in the past five years have we talked on the phone. How it used to excite me to hear her voice, measured, careful, but with an underlying huskiness that seemed to betray something else, something unexpressed but looking for a way to get out. I saw that in her, that thing, and tried to coax her to let it free, but she always came back to that fine line, that narrow space they inhabited, where Danni had her pinned to the wall like a butterfly on a board, her beautiful wings spread and spectacular but useless.

I don't imagine I might make her happy. It isn't that. I just wonder at her willingness to settle for so little, her willingness to be locked there, fluttering like a caged thing dreaming of the outdoors. We went on a walk once: a fine, clear cold spring day, along the creek bed where the snow-cold water trickled around the rocks. We stepped across on stones, laughing, trying to keep from slipping. She wore a black raincoat, fashionable and impractical boots; I had on jeans, a sweatshirt, pragmatic sneakers. The sun mingled with the frosty air and graced our faces; we sat on a picnic bench, and there I pulled her to me, kissed her for the first time, shocked at the warmth of her skin, her lips.

We talked on the phone, imagined dancing, wrote long letters full of barely disguised desire, laying our hearts and bodies on the pages in metaphor, optical illusions of the third eye. We joked about reading between the lines. Life between the lines. When do you get to that moment when you look at the words and just say, "This is what it says"? No ambiguity. No chance of misinterpretation, of misconstruction, of miscalculation of intent.

Ruby, I remember you from a distance, gliding across the floor in the lobby of the theater where the ballet had just finished: all in black, elegant, heeled boots to the knees, your auburn hair flowing around your face, your shoulders. All you needed was a pointed black hat to make me believe you were a witch. I remember you reaching for my hand as we ran laughing across the street to get out of the rain, ducking into a bookstore, a café, a candle shop. I remember the way your chin came just to my shoulder, the feel of the bird-fine bones of your hand in mine, your pale thin lips poised in that inscrutable line of denial, that unmistakable hieroglyph of "no."

We sat then, finally, on the sofa in my friend's apartment, borrowed for a long lunch, because we had nowhere else to go. You wore red lipstick and a checkered blue sleeveless shirt, and you looked at me impassively as I unbuttoned it, pulled it away to reveal your breasts, smaller than mine, your teardrop nipples. I reached to take one into my mouth, and you watched, saying no with your mind while your body clamored yes, a teardrop hardening like hot ice under my tongue, you clearly resisting the urge to put your fingers in my hair.

I unzipped your white slacks, lifted the edge of your blue silk panties with my fingers, slid my hand over the soft rough hair hidden underneath. I parted you, found you wet; I withdrew, licked your juice from my fingers, kissing you, forcing you to taste yourself on my lips like wine after sipping.

"You're wet," I said, and you smiled your enigmatic smile, your eyes and mouth speaking different languages. You opened my jeans, made a brief exploration of your own. "Hmm," you said. "A similar phenomenon."

"Let me love you," I whispered in your ear, my lips close against that delicate place where damp tendrils of your hair curled in defiant contradiction to your determined rigidity. "Let me make love to you."

You shifted restlessly, zipped, buttoned, straightened, wiped the fine dew of sweat from the small of my back with your hand, and said, "No. I can't."

"Why?"

"Because," you whispered. "I want to remember wanting you."

Ruby. Ruby. Will the memory of food fill the belly? Will the memory of water soothe the dry and clamoring throat? Ruby, ask yourself.

Who's That Girl?

BY MIA DOMINGUEZ

Rather than spend another typical restless Friday night alone, I decided to check out the neighborhood bar. Oz isn't a pickup place, just a cool little hangout to get a good, strong drink served by a wickedly hot cocktail waitress, catch up with everyone, and sing a song on the karaoke stage if you feel so inclined.

I walked inside and ordered my usual Midori sour while scanning the bar for an empty seat. Friday evenings are unusually crowded since there are so many businesses in the area. Groups of coworkers come to relax and let their hair down after a stressful week. This is where the karaoke machine becomes a hilarious form of entertainment. It's a rite of passage for the shyest of any bunch—the one who's had one too many—to get up on stage. There the shy ones embarrass themselves to such an extent, they may decide never to show up for work again.

I took a seat at the bar and waved hello to Ernie, my favorite bartender.

"*Hola,* Mia. Next one's on me, baby."

"*Gracias,* Ernie. Better start on it now. I'm ready."

"Looking for someone tonight?"

"No. Why would you ask that?"

"You're never here by yourself," Ernie stated in his heavy Spanish accent. "The only people who show up alone are people looking for someone or waiting for someone."

"Sorry, Ernie. Neither is true in my case. Just bored."

I turned to the stage, and a woman sitting at a table next to it caught my eye. She was with a group of four other girls, and was definitely the most attractive. Dark blond, wild curls framed her fair-skinned face. A natural beauty, she wore little makeup, and her big green eyes were lined with dark, long lashes. Her lips were full and glossy.

She stood out in that crowd of boisterous girls since she was the only one not shouting obscenities at the gentleman belting out Sinatra's "New York, New York" on stage.

"Ernie, who's that woman?" I asked.

"You like her, huh? She's not a regular. I don't know."

How could Ernie acquaint himself with every woman in the bar except the one I'd wanted to meet?

There were numerous ways I could meet this woman who was possessing my thoughts that evening. Admittedly, I get a little tongue-tied when talking to a woman I find that attractive, so simply walking up to her and introducing myself was out of the question.

Sure, I could follow her to the ladies' room. We'd engage in idle chitchat while washing and drying our hands and fixing our hair before going back to our tables to sit alone. A good plan, but how was I supposed to keep her in the ladies' room long enough to convince her to come home with me?

Suddenly I realized she might not be interested at all. I've been known to convert a woman's sexuality once or twice in my life, but those women were at least curious for my touch. If this woman didn't wonder at least a little, what kind of chance would I have? After ordering another drink, I decided not to spend the night worrying. If I was going to meet her, it would happen without reducing myself to stalker tactics.

I turned my bar stool to face the woman singing. She was

strikingly familiar, but I couldn't place why. For a moment, I thought perhaps she and I had shared a night together. She was pretty, with a cute figure, big tits, and a Betty Boop face. I definitely would have spent the night with her. But I don't usually forget the women I sleep with.

The singing woman was devastatingly gorgeous, but my thoughts were completely engrossed by the woman at the table across from me. She looked in my direction a couple of times, but perhaps it was the heat of my stare she felt, rather than interest for me.

Once the woman on stage was done with her rendition of Linda Ronstadt's "Blue Bayou," the women at the table began clapping and cheering. She walked over and sat down with them. She was one of them, one of the four women who accompanied the woman I wanted. Now all I had to do was figure out who she was, so I could ask her for an introduction.

The singing woman stood up from her chair and walked toward me. All at once I became terribly nervous and excited. She must have known who I was!

"Mia! Oh, my God! How are you?"

It finally hit me. We had gone to high school together. We were best friends almost 15 years ago, but everything came back to me as if it were yesterday.

"Bebe! I'm doing great! How are you? It's been forever."

"You know, I hate to say it, but I'm on my way out. My husband is waiting for me at home, and I'm already an hour late." She reached for a napkin and jotted down her telephone number. "Call me tomorrow."

I jumped off my bar stool. "At least let me walk you to your car."

Bebe and I left the bar arm in arm, hugging and reminiscing about the trouble we'd gotten into as rebellious teens.

"I'm sorry you have to leave so soon. I was going to ask you a favor."

As I started to ask, she interrupted.

"Lea!" Bebe yelled. "I"m over here!" It was her. She walked toward Bebe and me, smiling and greeting me.

"Hi. Saw you inside. My name's Lea. What's yours?"

"Lea, this is my old friend from high school, Mia." She reached for my hand, and I extended mine to meet hers for a soft, lingering handshake. Bebe and I talked about old times for a moment, then I turned to Lea.

"So how's your hubby going to feel because you're not home yet?"

"Oh, I don't have one of those," she answered.

"Why not?"

"I just haven't met the right one yet."

"The right one?" I asked, hoping she'd contribute a bit more information.

"I'm really picky and have yet to live out all my fantasies." We smiled at one another devilishly.

"Sorry, girls. We really gotta go now," Bebe interjected. "I gotta drop Lea off and then drive all the way home, so we have to run."

A disappointed expression emerged across Lea's face, so I tossed my idea out, to see if she would take the bait.

"Bebe, why don't you go ahead home? I don't think we want to get you into any more trouble than you're in. I'll take Lea home—if she doesn't mind."

"Is that OK with you? The two of you hardly know each other," Bebe questioned.

"It's fine with me," Lea assured Bebe. "Mia and I can get acquainted, and maybe when you're allowed out again, we can all get together for a drink. I love making new friends."

"Me too." Smiling at Lea, I added, "I'd love to make a new friend tonight."

We said our good-byes and sent Bebe on her way. Lea and I stood close to each other, so close that our breasts brushed against one another. It was electrifying.

"Would you like another drink?" I asked.

"Actually, a drink sounds great, but I don't feel like going back in there."

"Do you want to go somewhere else?"

"I'd love a nice glass of merlot, and I've got a couple bottles at home. I'd like for you to join me, as long as you don't have anywhere to be."

Her invitation overwhelmed me, but I tried not to let on. "Sounds great. Let me open the door for you." I let her into the passenger seat of my car, and soon we were on our way. Lea lived about ten minutes away from the bar in a quaint, Victorian neighborhood. We got out of the car and walked up to her house.

Her home was lovely and feminine with a haunting floral fragrance. Jasmine in the entranceway. Roses in the sitting room. The decor was cozy and comforting, with overstuffed furniture and elegant French artwork adorning the walls.

"Mia, have a seat and get comfy. I'm going to change clothes, then I'll be back. If you'd like, you can uncork the wine and let it breathe for a moment."

It was a cold night, and Lea had an inviting marble fireplace, so I took it upon myself to build a fire in front of the soft chenille throw I had spread across the floor. I grabbed two glasses from the kitchen, uncorked the merlot, and brought them to the floor with me.

"Oh, thank you, Mia. I'm so glad we're on the same page."

"Great minds think alike, I suppose. Come sit here in front of the fire with me."

Lea, who had changed from her conservative beige pantsuit into a gold-and-black satin kimono and black, high-heeled maribou slippers, instantly erased any doubt about her intentions.

We drank the fruity merlot while becoming intoxicatingly familiar with one another.

"Can I ask you a question, Mia?"

"Sure, ask away."

"Do you have a lot of experience with women?"

"I would say so. I'm a lesbian. What about you? Are you bisexual or simply curious?"

"I wouldn't call myself curious. I'm serious. But I have no experience with women at all...with the exception of the women in my fantasies."

I let out a bit of nervous laughter. Lea leaned into me and continued, "Tonight I would have met you whether you knew Bebe or not. I saw you the minute you walked in. You're not a difficult woman to ignore, so beautiful and sexy. I became entranced watching you get up and sit back down on your bar stool. Your dress rode up, and I wanted to see what you had on underneath. The men sitting behind me were commenting as you walked by, noting how your tits bounced when you walked and saying you couldn't possibly be wearing a bra because your nipples were so hard, practically cutting their way out of that dress. The way they talked about you made my mouth water. You do have some luscious tits, you know."

"Why, thank you. I'm flattered by your testimonial," I smiled. "Would you still like to know what's underneath my dress?"

"Oh, yes, Mia. I've wanted to know all night. Please show me everything."

I sat up on my knees and pulled my formfitting black jersey dress off my voluptuous body. The men were right. I wasn't wearing a bra, only a black lace thong, black stockings, and black leather boots. Lea stared as I pulled her hands up to my tits and guided them across my firm flesh and hard, excited nipples. She sat up on her knees and brought her mouth up to my porcelain breast, brushing over my warm skin with her soft tongue.

I loosened the sash from her kimono, sweeping it from her shoulders and allowing it to fall to the floor. She wore nothing underneath. Her body was shapely and taut: full, firm tits, a nice round ass, and a well-trimmed pussy like my own.

She permitted my desperate hands to travel across her warm velvet skin, making me wetter with every passion-filled second. I laid her down on the soft throw and crawled on top of her. My flesh transformed to fire as she pressed every part of her body against every part of mine.

Lea put her mouth to mine, kissing me deeply and passionately, beckoning my tongue to dance with hers in long, engaging kisses. She thrust her pussy into mine. Slow, tender thrusts became faster and harder, rhythmic. She was hot and wet, yearning for me to send her into an orgasmic state, and I obliged her every command.

My mouth slid down her body, stopping to taste her sweet, smooth flesh, then slipped farther down to drink her dulcet, warm nectar. I spread her lips apart and began to playfully tease her clit with my tongue. Lea held my hair tightly between her fingers, forcing my head between her trembling legs. I drank her in as if she were the only drop of water in a vast dessert, bringing her to climax several times, one after another, each one stronger than the last. Lea continued to thrust her pussy into my mouth before her orgasm came to a thundering crescendo.

Lea begged for me to stop, but I could not allow her to go. While nibbling on her thighs, she became crazed once again. I touched her smooth pink flesh, moistened by her fits of passion. I had the pleasure of pleasuring Lea with an ecstasy she had never before experienced. Her moans and lusty whining left me longing to explore her sensuality even further.

I prodded her pussy with two of my fingers, delving deeper and deeper into her satin flesh, as she let out sweet sighs of contentment. Blowing into my ear, sending tremendous chills up and down my spine, she whispered to me, "It's my turn now."

As much as she wanted to taste me, I didn't want to stop playing with her. We engaged in the most incredible 69 I've ever had the privilege to partake of. Her body was novice to other women, but she became the most skilled apprentice in the few hours we shared together.

Lea quickly made my list of the quality few who have led me to lose my inhibitions. Her touch was tender yet firm. Lea's pursuit of my eroticism was undying, and so flattering, because she was so gorgeous.

The feel of her tongue inside me was all the encouragement I needed to come for her repeatedly. I longed to play out her fantasy until she was thoroughly gratified and expertly educated. Needing to feel her deep inside, I lay on top of her, keeping her between my legs, cradling her ass in my hands to bring her nearer. We kissed and brought our bodies closer and closer with slow and steady thrusts.

Lea began to orgasm, grinding herself into me increasingly harder. Our hot, throbbing pussies fused into one another. Lea began biting my nipples, making me scream and beg for more. Our passion produced a dizzying heat.

We experienced one another for hours until the night moon was exchanged for the morning sun. We lay on the floor, spent. The fire was spent, too, along with the merlot. It was three in the afternoon when we finally awakened. Scatterbrained and hurried, I scrambled for my dress and panties.

"Do you think we can see one another again?" I asked.

"Sure, why don't you call me."

I sensed the hesitation in her answer. Her satisfaction last night wasn't in question. Lea had been all mine for the evening and fully pleasured by my expertise. She desired to experience me, and I allowed her an opportunity to explore her sexuality with depth and fervor. The mystery was over, and that had to be OK for me.

"You know, I enjoyed our evening together, and if it was only for one night, I understand. Curiosity is a wonderful thing, and it's OK if you don't want this to go any further. I'll give you my number, and if you'd like to see me again, give me a call."

"Thank you, Mia. I will call you."

Lea never called, and I never ran into her again. She was only one of many women for whom I would pleasurably provide their first woman-to-woman experience. For some, like Lea, it was the excitement of the moment. Being taken by another woman is an extraordinary erotic journey. Some are forever changed, and some only wish to visit. In any case, it is always a wonderful memory.

A Natural

BY AMY E. ANDREWS

The taxi pulled up to the apartment of my drunken date, who was more than a little annoyed I wasn't getting out with her. She tearfully slammed the door, and I shifted my full attention to the cabbie, who had no interest in driving me across town. I pleaded and negotiated, promising him $10, $15, then $25 to get me to Gwen's. Shaking his head and muttering under his breath, he jerked the cab into drive and headed down 17th Street.

"Where to, exactly?" he asked.

With both trembling hands, I held the tersely scrawled note she had slipped into my blazer pocket two hours earlier. It read: *Gwen, 701 South Carolina Avenue. Hope to see you tonight.* I handed the note to the driver.

Traffic was thick that New Year's Eve of '93, and the drive seemed long. My head leaned and bounced against the cold window of the cab as the city rushed by in a dreamy blur. I had met Gwen for the first time at Remington's a month ago. I was taken with her immediately, captivated by her seductive drawl, the subtle swing in her walk. My ears strained to overhear her conversations across the room, which were mostly about her sex life with her ex, Rhonda. She spoke of blindfolds, ice cubes, dildos, butt plugs, belts, and handcuffs in a melodic, drawn-out Southern manner. "I'll try anything one time," I heard her say. Intimidated and intrigued, terrified and transfixed, I labored to listen across the pool table, her words etching themselves indelibly on my brain.

Tonight we had spoken at length for the first time. I mostly listened, soaking her up, basking in the heat of her delicious attention. She talked about her tough breakup with Rhonda and how she just wanted to have fun for a while. I told her I was also having fun dating casually, not interested in being in an exclusive relationship with anyone. I placed a spontaneous finger inside the dimple on each of her cheeks and smiled into her face. She kissed the tip of my nose, then said, "You already have a date tonight," and briskly walked away.

The cab pulled into the unplowed alley between 7th and South Carolina and braked abruptly, snow crunching underneath the thick tread of the tires. I placed the agreed-on $25 in the driver's gloved hand, knowing and not caring that I had no money left to get home. I climbed out of the cab on woozy, rubbery legs.

Gwen was standing inside the iron-gated door of her English basement digs, her beautiful face framed by the wrought iron. A sweet stab of excitement rushed through my body, slowing to spread itself gently over my cunt.

"I'm glad you came," she said with a glassy-eyed, squinty grin, fingers fumbling with the keys in the gate's lock. Her tousled, blondish hair looked wet, and her breath stank of liquor.

She pulled me inside and relocked the iron gate behind me. I stood in the foyer and bent to untie my shoes, feeling a rush of panic. *I can't believe I'm here with this woman I barely know,* I thought. *I'm so wet I could come without being touched.* My clit throbbed in anticipation of my first night with a woman.

"Will you take your clothes off for me? Your body is so beautiful." I barely heard her words, hearing instead the

rhythmic cadence of her sensual Southern drawl. I still hadn't
said a word. A wave of heat washed over my face in embarrassment. "Take them off here. I'll get us a drink. What do
you want? We can meet in the bedroom. Will you be ready
for me?" She touched my arm and winked, then turned and
headed toward the kitchen without waiting for my reply.

I was alone in the marble-floored foyer, but I felt as if I
were being watched. My trembling hands rested on the silver
buckle of my black leather belt, making me speculate about
her sex life with her ex. I wondered how exactly they had
used their belts. I pulled it from its loops and lay it gingerly
at my feet on the marble floor. Beads of sweat began to form
on my upper lip and forehead.

I pulled off my turtleneck, then peeled off my slacks and
socks and tossed them into a corner of the sunken living room.
I fingered the elastic band of my crotch-soaked Jockeys and
slowly slid them over my hips and down my thighs. I stepped
out of them slowly, one leg, then the other, and brought them
up to my mouth and nose. Eyes closed, I breathed deeply of
my own powerful essence, my senses heightened beyond belief. I resisted the urge to throw myself onto the floor and
plunge my own fingers deep into my swollen pussy. *No, I've
had enough of that,* I thought. I was ready for the real thing.
I walked resolutely toward Gwen's bedroom.

The beat of the club music that blared through the apartment resonated up from the hardwood floor through my
body and bounced out like a sonic sounding device, testing
my depths. Spikes of icy-hot longing rushed under my skin,
through the richness of the blood that surged rapidly through
my veins.

I wondered how long she'd make me wait. I imagined myself an impatient child, desperately in need of Gwen's disci-
pline. I was sweating and flushed with furious desire. I found
her king-size bed and eased myself under its ironically sweet,
flowered comforter.

Gwen walked into the bedroom holding a bottle of champagne and an opener. She sat on the edge of the bed and said, "Have you ever made love with a woman?" I pulled the comforter up a bit higher. This felt awkward, and I didn't answer. "Are you nervous?" she asked. I managed a shy smile.

She set the bottle and opener on the night table and crawled into bed with me, fully clothed. I reflexively recoiled from the chilly hand she slid over my naked belly. "I have a beautiful woman in my bed," she said. Gwen's green eyes held mine intently, challenging me, inviting me to release the shame that imprisoned me for years. I leaned over, touched her face, and kissed her lips.

Then my body took charge, remembering its powerful desire, and my anxiety dissipated. I unzipped her pants under the covers while she removed her own blouse. I kissed her warm wet mouth, her earlobes, her eyelids. I devoured her, placed my tongue in the folds of her skin and ate. I licked the salt from a sweaty night of bright lights and dancing off her lithe, taut body. I drank the musky desire that mixed with liquor and rose from her pores. Gwen arched her back, inviting me to suck her hard raisin nipples, and moaned under my touch, my teeth, my tongue. I slid my hand down her belly to her thighs, over her ass, and back around, finally, to her hungry cunt. Her pelvis arched to meet my touch, legs spread wide, delicate neck rising from the pillow in an elegant swan-like curve.

I slid my fingers inside her, first one, then another, letting her desire guide me, letting her pussy massage them in a rhythmic dance of its own, until she shuddered and cried out, her cunt gripping and releasing my fingers in a furious climax.

Feeling a rare loss of inhibition, I bit hard on my lower lip to keep from shouting either "I love you" or "Fuck me," neither of which seemed appropriate.

It was all over in less than an hour. "You were so good," Gwen said, with a drowsy sidelong glance. "A natural." She pulled me onto my side, wrapped her arm around my middle, and folded her knees into the backs of mine. Spooning, she called it. I fell asleep long after Gwen, staring at our lumpy silhouette on the wall projected by the crisp, wintry moonlight of a brand new year. I didn't dare move, lest I disturb the erotic dance of the fine hairs on the nape of my neck, set in motion by Gwen's soft, steady breath.

We had sex for two months. I wanted to tell her I loved her. I wanted to say it every minute of our affair. But Gwen was determined not to let this go anywhere. She had "rules," which she laid down as readily as she spread her legs for me, over and over. We were not to eat meals together or go anywhere as a couple. We were not dating. We were fucking. And the fucking soured over time as my heart shriveled from the lack.

Finally able to hear friends who insisted I deserved better, I ended our bittersweet affair. I ran into her a week later and went home with her again. She tied my wrists with my black leather belt and fucked me for the last time.

A month later she moved back South. I haven't seen or heard from her since, but she's with me, lover after lover, telling me to relax, that I'm a natural.

Ya Gotta Start Somewhere

BY J.L. BELROSE

She's prompt—actually, three minutes early—and announces herself with two distinct raps on my apartment door. Not loud. If I hadn't been hovering in the kitchen, listening, waiting, I wouldn't have heard them. I want to sprint to the bathroom and gargle, but I can't keep her waiting. I rub damp palms down my jeans and open the door.

She isn't what I expect. Not tall and dark. Her earth-colored hair is fastened back with an elastic band. Her features, in a rather broad face, are regular but not outstanding, with no trace of makeup. Not even lip gloss. She's short too. Maybe 5 foot 3 or so. And no sleek black leather. All denim. Altogether, she isn't the elegant, imposing figure I'd conjured in my mind. But...she does have attitude. I'll give her that. She's sloped against the wall beside my door, her thumb hooked into the strap of a blue canvas duffel bag slung over her shoulder. "Hi," I say, conscious I've been staring at her too long without speaking. She doesn't answer. I pull the door open, as wide as a jumbled pile of shoes and boots and an empty beer carton will allow, and stand well back, giving her space to make an entrance.

She strolls into my living room and dumps her bag onto my couch. Her presence reverberates off the walls in the tiny room. "So..." she says and slides flat hands into her jeans so her thumbs hook outside the pockets. I notice her gold thumb ring.

"So?" I answer.

"Do you have the money?"

Her voice is grittier than sandpaper, and the skin down my back reacts as though it's been scratched. There's an involuntary reaction between my legs too. I dig into my pocket and pull out the two fifties I have carefully folded and stashed. I extend them toward her, praying my hand won't tremble. She says thanks without expression and scrunches the money into her back pocket.

"So," she says, "may I have a coffee?"

Coffee? I want to ask whether the time will come out of the hour I've just paid for, but I don't. I say, "In here?" thinking she'll settle into my couch and have me serve her.

"The kitchen's fine," she shrugs.

She lays claim to one of the chrome chairs beside the table and hunkers down loose and easy, one arm hung over the back of the chair, her other arm laid out along the table's edge. I'm plugging the kettle in when she states, "I don't do blood or scat. I'll do piss, but I'm not keen on it."

I try to think how to answer. Should I say "That's cool" or what? I take the coffee out of the fridge where I keep it, and my brain feels frozen too, like it's been in with the ice cubes. I can't think. She prompts, "What about you?" and I realize I'm supposed to reciprocate with similar information, such as limits and needs.

"Ah, no. I don't do that heavy stuff at all. I'm...sort of conservative."

My hand tremors as I measure the coffee into the Bodum. I'm acutely aware how closely and silently she's observing me. "Look," I say, forcing myself to breathe. "I might as well be honest. I'm not experienced at all. I thought Gracie made that clear when she set this up."

"No, she didn't. Well, not exactly. She said she thought you were stone."

I decide to kill Gracie. Gracie, who is supposed to be my best friend. Gracie, who assured me she knew a professional who's really, really sweet with novices. Gracie, who said nothing, absolutely nothing, could go wrong.

Embarrassment rises up my body like mercury in a thermometer. This pro is close to figuring out I'm the nearest thing to a virgin she's ever met. Then I'm going to have to explain to her why I thought...why Gracie thought...I should...

"So, do you have any fantasies?"

"No, not really," I answer honestly, wondering how to invent some real fast.

"None at all?" she asks, the rasp of incredulity not quite concealed.

"Not really," I say again, keeping myself turned away from her, so she can't see the blush I feel creeping up my neck. I direct all my attention to the boiling water I pour into the Bodum.

She extracts a pack of cigarettes from an inside pocket. She puts one to her lips and lets it hang. I want to tell her I'd prefer she didn't smoke in my home. But if I try to speak, my voice will curl back into my throat and choke me. I'm relieved when it seems she isn't going to light up anyway...until I realize she's probably waiting for me to produce the light. I've already been dreading pouring the coffee, envisioning my hands shaking, spilling, clumsy. I know my chances of holding a match steady to the end of her cigarette are way less than zero.

I abandon the coffee making, go to the far end of the table and slump into the chair, my hands pushed between my knees. I'm disappointed almost to tears that our "date" hasn't worked out. But it hasn't, and now all I want is for her to leave. I don't even care about the money. She can keep it.

But first, it seems, we have to drink the damn coffee. She's gotten up, opened my cupboard, and chosen two mugs, and she pours it. She stops. I figure she's going to ask for cream or something. Instead, she turns around, leans back against the counter, and says, "So...would you like to watch?" A smile curves her thin lips, and her eyes fix on mine, as she moves her hand to her crotch. She reaches between her legs, then pulls her hand slowly forward over her cunt, and stands there holding herself.

I stop breathing.

"OK," I say, totally forgetting I'd been seconds away from asking her to leave.

"OK," she mimics. "Just OK? I think you should say 'Yes, please.' "

I don't remind her I am, after all, the one who's paying. Things have turned around somehow. It seems more like she's doing me a favor for which I should be grateful. I decide to play along. "Yes," I say. "Yes, please."

"You may sit and watch, but I don't want you to get off your chair, and I don't want you to touch me." Her voice scrapes deliciously down my back. "Do you understand? Do you agree?"

"Yes," I say.

"I think you should say 'Yes, thank you,'" she corrects.

She taunts me with her eyes, teases me with her puckering lips, as she moves her hands up under her jacket, onto her breasts. She is attractive. I don't know why I didn't see it earlier. Her face is expressive, alive. "Yes," she says, grinning. "You're interested now, aren't you?"

I smile back but can't speak.

She shrugs out of her jacket and places it over the back of her chair. She lifts one side of her T-shirt, exposing a breast. It hangs soft, flat. The nipple is small and inverted. She licks the forefinger of her other hand and circles the nipple, stiffening it into one of the longest knobs I've ever seen. I realize I'm working my thumbs against my fingers and sucking my lip. I swallow as I think about taking the knob into my mouth, licking it.

"Are you going to behave yourself? she asks.

I hadn't moved. I'd wanted to, but I hadn't. I agreed not to touch her, and I won't. I'm slightly insulted she would question my integrity, but then I see humor crinkle her eyes. "Perhaps," she says, "You should be restrained. What do you think? Do you need your hands tied behind your back? Or can I trust you to behave?"

I know I have a choice, but the more I think about being tied up, the more appealing the idea becomes. I know I can trust her. Gracie has said so. And I feel it too. She has pulled her T-shirt down, has stepped back, and, hands behind her, is leaning against my counter again. She waits patiently for my answer. I make a decision. "Yes," I say. "I want to be tied up."

"Yes, please," she corrects.

She goes into the living room, and I hear a zipper, which I assume is on the duffel bag. She returns with a soft white rope, which she uncoils in front of me, letting me see it, letting me think about it. "Put your hands back, please. Cross your wrists." I do as she directs. She circles behind me and wraps my wrists, passing the rope between my arms and knotting it. Then she stands back and regards her work. She seems satisfied with what she's done.

"Do you mind if I change the music?" she asks.

The music? I smother my exasperation. First coffee. Then music. What the hell am I paying her for? Why can't she just get on with the job? Maybe the tape I have on is close to finished, or maybe it has already repeated a few times. I don't know, and I don't care. The last thing on my mind is music. But, of course, I don't say so.

From where I sit, I can look at an angle through to the living room and see her going through my tapes, taking her time about what she wants. I try not to fidget. But out of curiosity, I cautiously test the rope. She glances occasionally in my direction, so I move as little as possible. I don't want her to see what I'm doing as I check for slack in the rope binding my wrists and try to find the knot. I find it. Easily. Even though she had seemed so skilled, I realize I'm not too securely bound. I'm sure I could free myself if I tried.

"Can I turn this light off?" she asks as she saunters into the kitchen. "There'll be enough light from the living room and hall, don't you think?"

She's right. The indirect light is softening, soothing. She pulls her T-shirt over her head, removes her boots, jeans, and panties, and displays herself in front of me, moving to the rhythm of Queen Latifah's "Hard Times." I instantly forgive her for everything and anything, and swear never to complain again no matter how long she makes me wait. Her cunt is smooth and flat, the darker inner lips barely protruding. A small gold ring gleams on her clit. She straddles my knee, swaying to the music, her cunt only inches from my face. If I stuck out my tongue I could lick her. I feel my throat dry as I swallow.

She raises her leg, plants her foot on the edge of my chair, and steadies herself with a hand on my shoulder. With her other hand she strokes the inside of her thigh, gradually higher until she's fondling her labia. Then she slips in her fingers. Two fingers. Then three. In and out. In and out. So close to my face her arm almost grazes my cheek. In and out. In and out. I hear the sweet, wet noise she's making and see her soft flesh stretch back and forth with her massaging fingers. I can smell her and almost taste her. I look into her face. She stares unblushingly into my eyes as her hand maintains its even rhythm.

She lifts her fingers to her mouth. Involuntarily, my mouth opens. "No," she says, and licks her hand, sucks her fingertips. "You don't get to taste. You just get to watch. You agreed."

I've learned a lesson. I'll think much more carefully in the future about what I promise. I squirm in my chair. I consider tugging at the rope.

She asks, "Would you like to watch me play with my cock?"

I go still. "Yes, I whisper.

"Yes, please," she corrects, the volume up on "please" as if she has a student who's deaf, as well as difficult.

As soon as she's in the living room getting her dil, I squeeze my legs together and rock on my chair, trying to rub against myself enough to ease the gnaw in my clit. But she's back too soon, with that wide smile of hers, waving her dil in the air, flaunting it in my face. She tickles its head with the tip of her tongue, as her eyes watch me. She holds it between her teeth as she tears open the small square foil pack, and flirts with me, outrageously, as she rolls the condom down the shaft. She's having fun. And I'm catching the joy. I'm giggling back.

She positions herself over my legs again, and I watch her separate her labia with her fingers and push the thick shaft into her well-lubed hole. She begins to rock and moan, her eyes almost closed, and I see the muscles of her abdomen contract as she works the dildo deeper and deeper into herself. I see the unwillingness of her cunt to release the shaft as it withdraws, and the clenching eagerness as she thrusts it back in. I hear her breathing turn jagged in her throat. I want to reach out and cradle her breasts with my hands, and seize her hips and bring her to me, pulling her into my face, onto my tongue. I want to. I want it so badly it hurts. I look to her face for permission.

A groan escapes her slackened mouth. With a hand on my shoulder for support, she goes still. She clenches the dildo once, twice, and again. Then, after a moment, she eases it out, pushes away from me and places the dil on the table. She circles around me, gives the rope one little tug, and it falls away.

I bring my arms forward, surprised at the stiffness across my shoulders. She coils the rope and places it on the table. I should say something, like "Thanks," but I don't. Again, I'm shy and awkward, tongue-tied. She lifts her jacket off her chair and drags it on. "So..." she says, as she leans back against the counter, "Now it's your turn."

It takes me a minute to register what she's said and what she means. I can't look her in the eyes. I shake my head. "I don't think I can do that," I say, addressing her feet.

"You've never gotten off in front of anyone before?"

"Not unless they were sleeping."

"That doesn't count," she replies.

I know it doesn't.

"So..." she says. "OK, what would you like to do?"

I shrug. I've never been able to talk about what I want.

"Well," she says, in a testing way, "Your time's almost up anyway."

"Yah, I was thinking it probably was."

"So, we're OK then?"

"Yes," I say, "we're OK."

I watch her as she dresses. She doesn't hurry. Neither one of us says anything. There's nothing much to say. She unbags her cock and tosses the rubber into the plastic shopping bag that's hanging on a drawer knob near the sink. I get up from my chair, but I stay back, not wanting to crowd her. Then, as she's leaving the kitchen, she digs into her back pocket and pulls out one of my fifties. She comes back and places it, crumpled, on my counter. "Here," she says, "There's a discount for first-timers."

I say, "Thanks," but I have some trouble about getting a refund. It's like I've let her down. Or let myself down. And the fact that she really is nice, and I like her, doesn't make me feel any better. I don't want her compassion. I wish I could tell her how I feel, but I can't. I don't know what to say. It's like I'm inside a huge granite monolith, and I go round and round exploring the cold smooth walls, but there's never a way out. Not even a crack.

I leave the money lying on the counter and stand near the door where I can watch her, as she takes a white towel from her bag, neatly wraps her dil, and packs it and the rope away.

As I wait, my mind leaps ahead to the condom I'm going to retrieve from the clean plastic bag I'd just hung near the sink before she arrived. I'll get myself off, as soon as she's gone, with the scent of her in my nostrils, on my hands. The taste of her on my tongue. And I've already decided there'll be another time. And it'll be different. I'll be prepared. I'll know what I want and be ready to ask for it.

I open the door for her as she approaches, with her bag hung over her shoulder. She stops in the doorway, looks me in the eyes, and winks. "You know," she says, "there's a discount for regular customers too."

Before I can answer, she's swaggering down the hall. She's almost at the elevator before she lifts her hand in a backward wave. Without glancing round she says, "So call me, OK?"

I almost say "OK," but I catch and correct myself. "Yes, thank you," I say, even though she probably doesn't hear me.

Deep Song

BY B.J. KRAY

They say a mother's love is the best kind of love. But what would I know, never having been mothered or been a mother myself? At 18 I came close: The test was positive. That's the term they used; it wasn't positive for me at all. It was a call from the doctor to commute my death sentence; I hung on the line waiting…waiting. No such luck. I was pregnant. So why is a mother's love the best? Why is it the sweetest, the most heartbreaking and profound? I don't know, never having experienced it.

I can only guess; maybe it's the tearing through. I did that. The nine months in the womb, I only did seven. The cord that fastens emotions like a bowstring, mother to child—tight yet sloppy. The primordial fluid, blood, and tears spilled out onto the operating room floor, on the latex gloves, the white smock, the mother's belly, my mother's belly. As she bled— all over me—her flesh ripped apart by my falling, falling down the cunt shaft into this crude world.

Now, as I write, my father is dying. The cancer has spread uncontrollably through his lungs, to his ribs, and the fluid in his spinal cord is flowing in the wrong direction. The morphine has to be given by Syrettes three times a day, and patches are attached to his back loaded with the stuff. The nurse comes every day, and every second day she changes the patch. I am envious of this part, the junk. I have never done junk. The patches seem like such a pleasant way to ingest the drug.

I have read about junk in William Burroughs's essay on the Algebra of Need. A mask evil wears is the face of total need. I felt this need. I won't try to water it down, make it more socially acceptable, more chic, or correct. It was simple, my need, my desire for a feminine love.

Her hair was black like Poe's raven, thick and coarse. It was long and beautiful, and when the breeze came across her veranda, this black wave of hair stirred and had motion like a jazz note. Like Billie Holiday's singing, that's how she made me feel. Deep Song—listen to it! Her skin was predictably soft. Eyes were blue, *bleu*. Her lips were velvety and thick. They kissed as though it was her first time with a woman. Me too. We were full of pent-up passion. She made me let go in her arms. To whisper enchanting lies, to forget my suffering. I said I love you. It just rushed out like a dog fenced up in a yard who suddenly sees the gate open; those words busted out of my mouth. She answered I love you too, and the words fell like silk over my body and melted in the warm Louisiana air.

Breathing, a cigarette, a shot of vodka. Many shots of vodka. The bed was Victorian. For us there was the kitchen, the floor, the living room, but I remember best the mahogany wood of the bed. It's clear, as if I am there now. Her breath and tongue moving across my body, into my open thighs, delicately resting on my clit. Her nails were closely cropped, her fingers long and thick for a woman. She was a sculptor. She worked with her hands. I wore a brown silk skirt and a cheap department store garter, which she promptly ripped off me.

It's my 25th birthday. I think about William Burroughs, his search for the ultimate high in Bogota, the Algebra of

Need and its extension beyond junk and love. The mother, the cunt, the taste of her mouth when it was wet with me. Her lips, her fingering. My father has morphine injected. He can't walk anymore. Somehow I go on. Somehow we all go on.

Contributors

AMY E. ANDREWS, a lesbian-feminist writer and activist, lives and works in Washington, D.C. This is her first published story.

J.L. BELROSE is a reclusive artist living near Blue Mountain in Ontario. Her work has appeared in the *Queer View Mirror* anthology, *Lezzie Smut, Siren, Quota,* and *The Church-Wellesley Review,* and she's in the rewrite stage of her first novel. She shares her home with a kick-ass Muse and a pit bull named Onyx. They sleep late every morning.

LINDA A. BOULTER would like to dedicate her story, "The Scream," to her lover, holy companion, and partner, Deb. "We live and love in Victoria, B.C., with five children between us. I'm a writer of all sorts, writing everything from advertising copy to erotica," Linda says.

CATHLEEN BUSHA, born in Lancaster, Pa., in 1971, played basketball in college, taught eighth grade English for four years, and began working on a master's of counseling in Philadelphia. After a four-month cross-country camping trip with her partner, she has settled down in Tucson. She spends her time counseling at a domestic violence shelter, mixing mochas at a lesbian coffee shop, hiking among the saguaros, photographing sunsets, and, of course, checking her E-mail.

BLEAU DIAMOND was born in England and now lives in Scotts-
dale, Ariz. She divides her free time between writing erotic
poetry and stories, and hiking in the mountains surrounding
Phoenix. Her short stories appear in the Alyson anthologies
Awakening the Virgin and *Early Embraces II*.

MIA DOMINGUEZ is a 33-year-old single parent who lives in
Long Beach, Calif., with her 12-year-old son and three-year-
old calico cat. She is working on a nonfiction book about
meeting women through personal ads and hopes to see it
published one day.

FEMJOCKSA, a 40-year-old woman, originally from South
Africa, has never been published before. Drawn to Bud-
dhism, she is searching for balance inclusive of the spiritual
and the sexual, intimacy and solitude as well as a cure for
lesbian bed death.

D.M. GAVIN lives in the Washington, D.C., metropolitan area
with her partner of four years and her two teenage children.
She works in the nonprofit sector as a graphic designer and
writes in her spare time.

BRENDA HANSON is unsure of her whereabouts. Wherever she
is, she's there with the love of her life and their five cats. She
does whatever it takes to pay the bills. Her work has appeared on cocktail napkins all over town.

ANGELA HARVEY, a graduate of the University of Wisconsin–
Madison, is a Los Angeles–based writer and editor who buys
at least two lottery tickets a week and dreams of being a con-
testant on *Hollywood Squares*.

LOU HILL is a retired military officer who lives in southeast-
ern Michigan with her partner, their son, and a houseful of

animals. She writes novels and short stories, several of which have appeared in anthologies.

ABBE IRELAND says, "Big changes this year going from two part-time jobs to one full-time to support my writing habit. Any day now, I'll be able to quit my day job altogether. Besides writing, I'm also a rabid women's sports fan. It's a thrill to finally see women being allowed to really play—and I *swear* that's all there is to it."

B.J. KRAY has been a member of Andre Dubu's Thursday night writing group for two years. During her time in the group she has written a novella, *Vodka Nectars,* and 16 short stories, of which "Deep Song" is the first part of a trilogy. B.J. has also maintained a longtime literary mentor relationship with the beat poet Diane Di Prima.

ISABELLE LAZAR, a New Yorker, relocated to the fertile ground of West Hollywood, Calif., where she's found others of her persuasion. Though still sampling the various flavors of the cornucopia of women around her, she would, nevertheless, like to thank Dr. Taylor for her kind, patient, though unwitting, suggestion; it changed her life.

ROSALIND CHRISTINE LLOYD writes the travel column for *Venus Magazine.* Her work has also appeared in *On Our Backs* as well as gay and lesbian publications in New York and Atlanta. In her other life she coordinates events for a nonprofit women's organization. A native New Yorker and a Harlem resident, she lives with her extraordinarily beautiful life partner, Pleshette, and her unruly feline, Shuga.

SANDRA E. LUNDY is a writer and attorney living in Boston. Her poetry has appeared in *Poetry Motel/Wallpaper Series, Amethyst, Bay Windows, Sojourner, Dyke'atude, Violence*

Against Women, Common Lives/Lesbian Lives, Under A Gull's Wing (anthology), *The Artful Mind,* and elsewhere. She has published short stories and essays in *Hurricane Alice, Common Lives/Lesbian Lives, Out in the Workplace, Body Politic, The Silverleaf Anthology of Lesbian Humor,* and other journals and anthologies. With Beth Leventhal, she edited *Same-Sex Domestic Violence: Strategies for Change* (Sage, 1999).

ANN MASTROFSKY has lain with several women since writing this story. She is working on her first collection of short stories and can often be found hawking merchandise on eBay.com.

REGAN MCCLURE lives in Toronto and is working on a novel. She enjoys throwing javelin and riding her bicycle. She hopes her writing will complicate the way people view the world.

KATHY NORTON, a 42-year-old native Washingtonian, works for a leading insurance firm as an actuary. She enjoys living in Washington, with all it has to offer, though she travels a great deal to all corners of the world.

TASHA PERNA, 34, is an athletic vegetarian living in upstate New York. She has always dreamed of being a writer and feels there's a poetry to life when we open ourselves to it. She enjoys walking in the woods with her dog and has whiled away many summer afternoons sailing.

CAITLYN MARIE POLAND, born in Liverpool, England, has a degree in sociology-psychology. A social worker, she enjoys playing guitar and writing songs. Her work also appears in *Lip Service: Alluring New Lesbian Erotica* (Alyson, 1999).

KARIN POMERANTZ is a writer and self-publisher living just

outside Boston. She has spent most of her life trying to figure out what happiness is and how to obtain it. In her many quests, she has discovered that love and pain are equally beautiful; she has explored a wide array of sexual desires and positions; and she has realized that if you open your eyes and pay attention you can figure out and do anything.

KRISTEN E. PORTER is a femme-top lipstick boy who lives in Dykeland (the Jamaica Plain section of Boston). She was a presenter at the 1999 Outwrite Conference and is the coeditor of *Philogyny,* a Boston-based 'zine for women "who fuck, suck, stick, lick, and love other women." This is her first published work. She makes her living sticking needles in people.

CLAIRE ROBSON, a British-born writer who lives in New Hampshire, teaches writing workshops and founded *WOW!!* (Women of Words), a writers group noted for its diversity of age and background. She has published her work in numerous anthologies and journals, and has read at colleges and bookstores throughout New England. When not writing, Claire manages Beantown Shiners, her Boston-based window cleaning company, and works as a court-appointed special advocate for abused and neglected children.

LILITH LYNN ROGERS has been writing for a while now—almost as long as she's been loving women. More of her passionate prose is available in the recently published *Persimmons and Other Lesbian Erotica* from Earthy Mama Press. Lilith and her partner, Luna, live in Northern California but visit Hawaii as often as possible.

ROBIN ST. JOHN lives and writes in Sacramento. In her spare time she works as a paralegal and also delivers newspapers because she likes looking at the stars and loves the exercise. She is also the mother of two teenagers and surrogate mother to one cat. Robin has published several short fiction pieces and is working on a novel.

H.L. SHAW is a poetry editor and how-to columnist for the online erotic E-zine www.CleanSheets.com. A transplanted Midwesterner now living in the Bay Area, she's been writing erotic poetry and reading it to semishocked café audiences for years. She was a featured local poet in the 1994 Lollapalooza Poetry tent in Indy, but her recent credits include an erotic reading at the 1999 My Sucky Valentine benefit for the San Francisco Sex Information Hotline. Her ongoing goals include writing and publishing fiction, maintaining her online journal, making her own clothes, and keeping her garden weeded.

RAVEN SPRING was born in New York City and resides in Seattle. She is a published author with an MA in counseling psychology who loves animals and the great outdoors.

LINDSAY TAYLOR, originally from Connecticut, received her BS in mass communications, magna cum laude, from Boston University in 1985, and has resided in the San Francisco Bay Area ever since. Her work has appeared in anthologies such as *Heatwave: Women in Love and Lust* (Alyson, 1995) and *Electric: Best Lesbian Erotic Fiction* (Alyson, 1999). She gives readings at bookstores throughout the Bay Area.

AMY WANDERS is a 24-year-old soon-to-be mother in Olympia, Wash. Having just graduated from Evergreen State College, she is moving back to Portland, Ore., to pursue a graduate degree.

JANE WOLSEY, a 33-year-old fund-raiser, lives in Maryland with her calico cat, Lucy. She spends her free time traveling, reading, and writing lesbian fiction. She hopes one day to write a lesbian novel and have her first screenplay reach the right person's hands in Hollywood.

ZONNA is 38, bisexual, and living in New York. Insignificant details, such as the lack of a publishing deal, have never stopped her from expressing herself any way she can. When she's not writing (lesbian vampire stories, erotica, novels, and dyke dramas), she performs as an out musician, as she has for the past nine years, and is involved in a sensitivity training program aimed at educators and youth groups. Her first published piece recently appeared in *Philogyny,* a Boston-based 'zine.